South San Francisco Public Library
3 9048 10048219 3

W9-AHG-029

KILLING TITAN

Also by GREG BEAR

Hegira
Beyond Heaven's River
Psychlone
Strength of Stones
The Wind from a Burning Woman (collection)
Corona
Songs of Earth and Power
Blood Music
Eon
The Forge of God
Tangents (collection)
Sleepside Story
Queen of Angels
Eternity
Anvil of Stars
Bear's Fantasies (collection)
Heads
Moving Mars
New Legends (anthology)
Dinosaur Summer
Foundation and Chaos
Slant
Darwin's Radio
Collected Stories of Greg Bear
Vitals
Darwin's Children
Dead Lines
Quantico
City at the End of Time
Mariposa
Hull Zero Three
Halo Forerunner Trilogy
War Dogs
Killing Titan

KILLING TITAN

GREG BEAR

www.orbitbooks.net

The characters and events in this book are fictitious. Any similarity to real persons, living or dead, is coincidental and not intended by the author.

Orbit
Hachette Book Group
1290 Avenue of the Americas
New York, NY 10104
www.orbitbooks.net

Printed in the United States of America

First Edition: October 2015

RRD-C

10 9 8 7 6 5 4 3 2 1

Orbit is an imprint of Hachette Book Group.
The Orbit name and logo are trademarks of Little, Brown Book Group Limited.

Library of Congress Cataloging-in-Publication Data

Bear, Greg, 1951-
Killing Titan / Greg Bear.
pages ; cm
ISBN 978-0-316-22400-0 (hardcover)—ISBN 978-0-316-22399-7 (ebook)—ISBN 978-1-4789-6017-1 (audio bk. (downloadable))—ISBN 978-1-4789-3639-8 (audio bk. cd)
I. Title.
PS3552.E157K55 2015
813'.54—dc23

2015020920

To Patrick M. Garrett, Captain, USN, (Ret.)—our favorite Commodore.

And to his uncles:

George C. Garrett, Motor Machinist Mate Second Class. Submarine USS Wahoo, *bombed and sunk in the La Perouse Strait north of Japan, OCT 1943.*

John S. Garrett, Seaman First Class. Destroyer USS Caldwell, *damaged by a bomb off the island of Samar, Philippines, DEC 1944.*

And a tip of the hat to Nigel Kneale.

KILLING TITAN

PART ONE

ICE MOON TEA

The hardest part of war is waiting. The boredom can drive you nuts. You start doing things like playing football with ordnance—I've seen it, lived it. Lots of casualties happen right in camp when there's no real fighting. Days and weeks and even months filled with nothing, then more nothing—the mad ol' ape inside starts to leer and gibber and prance—some of the best of us show signs of going trigger—

Then, WHAM! We're called up. We cross the vac. We drop. It gets real. All the shit happens at once, in a bloody, grinding flash—and if you live through it, if you survive with enough soul left to even care, you spend the rest of your fucked-up life wondering whether you should have done it different, done it better, or not at all.

All for glory and the Corps.

The Battle of Mars is over. I hear we won. Maybe so. But when I left, seventeen months ago, we had just had our asses handed to us by the Antags.

Some new and unexpected elements had been added to the

usual drop, scrap, and stain: a tall young dust widow named Teal, a fanatical clutch of settlers who called themselves Voors, and a crack Special Ops team whose orders included zeroing fellow Skyrines. And as backdrop to our finest mad scenes: a chunk of ancient moon called the Drifter, maybe the most important rock on the Red. Not our usual encounter.

When a lucky few of us made it back, we weren't celebrated. We were hunted down and locked away.

MADIGAN MADRIGAL

Since returning to Earth, I've spent most of my time in an isolation ward at Madigan Hospital, north of Skybase Lewis-McChord, sealed like a bug in a jar while the docs wait for me to sprout wings or grow horns or whatever the fine green powder that coated the insides of the Drifter wants me to do. DJ—Corporal Dan Johnson—called the powder Ice Moon Tea. Is he here at Madigan? I know he came back. So did Joe—Lieutenant Colonel (brevet) Joseph Sanchez. Joe told us all to lie low and stay away from the doctors and not cause a fuss. I suppose I screwed that up, too.

I sent out my first packet just two weeks after I arrived at Madigan. My first and so far only report—along with a coin that I found in the pocket of some old overalls I wore in the Drifter. I have no idea whether all that got back to Joe.

There's a lone fruit fly in the room with me. I've left it a piece of Washington State apple on the gray desk that serves as my writing table. He's my buddy. Maybe he dreams about being human.

I dream about being a bug.

Ninety-seven days. That's how long I've been here, with the docs filing past my window and telling me it won't be long before the Wait Staff comes to see me, and maybe I'll get to tell my story directly to the Gurus, really, and that will be a *good* thing; don't worry. Be happy. I've been debriefed and inquested and examined and cross-examined, from behind thick glass—squinted at from high and low by disembodied heads until they've blurred into one giant, whirly-eyed wizard.

One head rises above the whirl, however: high, smooth brow, impeccable English with a South Asian lilt, Pakistani or Indian, doctor or scientist, not sure which; soft, calm voice. Precise. Reassuring. Civilian clothes. Never reveals his name, position, or rank. He's talked to me, with me, five or six times, always with a gentle smile and sympathetic eyes.

My personal favorite. He's the first I'll strangle with my bare hands when I get the chance.

ONE FINE DAY IN THE BUGHOUSE

"How are you today, Sergeant Venn?"

"Still waiting."

"I understand you've been brushing up on your Chinese. And your Hindi and Farsi."

"Urdu, too. Also."

"Very good. Your skill with languages is impressive. Better than it used to be."

"More time."

"I envy that."

"No you don't."

Without skipping a beat, he continues, "I am indifferent at Farsi myself. If you will allow me, I'd like to ask how you are feeling, what sorts of dream you have had since returning to Earth?"

"Weird dreams. I've explained."

"Yes, mostly—I have my notes. But I'd like to hear it again, in case we've overlooked something important."

"Come in here with me, sir, and I'll give you the details up close."

"I note your frustration, Sergeant Venn. Perhaps soon."

"You still think I'm contaminated."

"We have yet to determine anything of the sort. Still, you have described coming into contact with nonterrestrial organisms, including Antagonists. All by itself, direct combat with our enemy mandates a period of quarantine—usually, a few weeks in Cosmoline tells the tale.

"But I am most curious about this powder you describe, which you touched, smeared on your skin, inhaled—inside the Drifter. You say it was produced by a crystal pillar that rose within a mined-out cavity that the Muskies, the human settlers, called the Void, or the Church. You tell our doctors that the powder gives you vivid dreams, dreams of living in another time, another place. Curious and interesting. Do you believe these dreams are historical, referring to real events—or delusional?"

Like that. I'm in the hands of experts.

Fuck me.

THEY'VE GIVEN ME a paper tablet and a notebook and pen. No computer. No way to reach the outside world or do any research worth a damn, though they bring me books from the base library or a thrift store, old language textbooks and tattered paperbacks from the last century. I'm reading Elmore Leonard and Louis L'Amour and Jim Thompson, plus a few old novels. I've asked for Philip K. Dick. I've asked for Kafka. I've asked for T. E. Lawrence. No joy.

I'm writing again, but it's not like I own my life or this

story. Maybe the docs will come back with answers I can use. Right. Until then, here's what I think I know, on my own terms: the brew I've slowly distilled from my last deployment on Mars—a sour liquor of intoxicating fact mixed with muddy water.

But here goes.

A LOCAL'S GUIDE TO THE RED

A generation before the Battle of Mars began, settlers from Earth, Muskies, discovered a huge, mostly buried chunk of ancient rock. They called it the Drifter. They did what Martian prospectors do: scoped it out, found it interesting, and started to dig.

The Drifter turned out to be a piece of ice-covered moon that fell on Mars billions of years ago. Along with deep aquifers washing around its plunging roots and abundant reserves of pure metal—nickel-iron, iridium, platinum, gold—the Muskies discovered something else, something that changed their game completely: a fractured, battered tower of crystal hundreds of meters tall, from that distant age when the old moon supported an ocean beneath its thick ice shell. A sloshing, inner sea filled with life. That pillar seems to have been part of the archives of an ancient civilization that came to an end when the moon—with all its ice, ocean, and metal-rich center—was tugged from its far orbit, fell downsun toward Mars, and broke apart in the red planet's tidal forces. I can see it, almost, that amazing disaster. The huge fragments shaped a dusty, ice-fogged plume, then impacted around the planet like a short, loose whip—drilling through crust, mantle, even pushing down close to the molten core. The collisions happened in mere minutes but released tremendous energies, dividing the northern and southern hemispheres, sending shockwaves echoing, stirring up immense volcanoes—and adding trillions of tons of water to a formerly dry world.

The fragments of old moon brought something else to Mars. Life. And here's a whizbang conclusion to *really* dream about in the dark watches of the night—

The blowback from those collisions could have fallen deeper into the solar system and seeded *another* world, brought another dead planet to life:

Earth.

ANOTHER FINE DAY IN THE BUGHOUSE

Tell me once more, please, about the Drifter, Sergeant."

"I've told all I know."

"But *I* want to hear it again. Tell me about what the settlers found inside the Drifter, and what they did with it—and what *you* did with it when you got there."

"We didn't do much of anything with it. We were busy trying to stay alive."

"You didn't arrange to bring back samples?"

"Fuck no."

"Please. We're on Earth now. What about your fellow Skyrines? Did they bring back materials?"

"Not that I know about. I've said this over and over..."

"Please be patient. We're being patient with you."

All behind the glass.

BUNDLES OF TROUBLE

Through their chosen human interpreters, the Gurus made it clear to the people of Earth what would happen if we let our mutual enemy, the Antags, have their way with the solar system. The Gurus told us it had happened many times before, and that the ultimate result would be the conversion of every planet, every moon, every asteroid, into raw materials out of which Antag engineers would assemble a kind of gigantic clockwork for harnessing the sun's energy, and then would convert the sun itself—said energy to be shipped thousands of light years, through means not revealed, to power other star systems and to further promote the conquest of other planets around other suns....

Boosting their geometrically accelerating plans for conquest of the galaxy.

Bottom line, if we do not hold them on Mars, they will drop toward the Earth and our system will quickly become a weird clockwork of rotating wire, armillary rings, vast complex mirrors redirecting the sun's light and heat into absorption dishes wider than Jupiter... which will then beam it someplace else through I don't know what method, maybe an opening in the fabric of space-time, maybe just shooting it at light speed to someplace special—

Could be the Gurus don't want to explain further for fear of scaring us silly. If you know you can't win, you don't fight, you give up, right? We have to be able to believe that victory is possible, with a little help now and then from the Gurus. Real super-science stuff, like spent matter drives and suppressors and disruptors—even the Cosmoline in which Skyrines are packed while flying transvac, so beloved by the Corps. Most Skyrines accept this hook, line, and radar dish because it's kind of exciting. Makes us part of a big picture, fighters in a just and necessary war.

But after a few days on the Red, and especially when our drop is fucked, questions can arise among even our densest warriors, given time to think things through. I'd like to meet an Antag someday away from a battle, on equal, unarmed terms, buy him a Romulan ale, and ask him or her, or it, friendly-like, what the fuck do they tell *you* to keep you climbing into your ships and shuttling down to Mars or Titan?

Because up until just recently, when we crawled into our space frames and made the long journey for this campaign, we were *winning*.

We were sure of that.

Now...

I'm out of the whole fucking mess. Locked in my room, going nuttier than I remember being before—and nutty on two worlds, because my *other* self, the self that returns when I'm asleep and keeps trying to remember that old ice moon, keeps trying to bring back a lifetime billions of years gone—that carapace-coated asshole is every bit as bored and crazy as me, with even more reason.

To add convincing detail, the bug in my dreams, he or it, comes in two parts—an ornately figured parasitic passenger riding a great big, ugly sonofabitch, hanging on just behind a triad of compound eyes. I don't know which one does the steering. Maybe they trade off.

At any rate, just when I think I understand those amazing memories and thoughts and opinions—just when I want to tell other people the truth about that other, ancient world—

It all lifts up, turns sideways, shoots away.

Whoosh.

DAY 98

I ask for—and to my surprise receive—books on planetary science. No Internet. Just books, and while books are good—some are great—I've got big questions about what's really out there that the old books don't answer.

If what's in my head is real, then what kind of real is it? Dead and long past, or present and threatening? Am I communicating with actual intelligences, somehow still alive, still active, after billions of years? Not easy questions, and no easy answers.

My questions began about the time I returned from the Red to Skybase Lewis-McCord and hitched a ride with a colonel's secretary, and she told me there was fighting on Titan, way out around Saturn—that she had lost a son out there—

And I felt the truth of it.

For weeks now, I've been curious about old moons. Especially the big moon families that circle the outer gas giants. The Saturn system is the most spectacular, but to me, all the old moons seem important if I'm going to solve the puzzles that keep me awake all night. I don't know where I am. I mean, I know I'm back on Earth…

But I don't know *who* I am.

Who is back on Earth? Just me?

There must be enough value to somebody that the wizards behind the glass pass me old textbooks and feed this particular curiosity. But they don't seem willing to teach me more about physics. Still, it's good to get a change in my reading—away from literature and back to science. Whether I'm curious, or my inner Bug is curious, is a question to which I have no present answer. But I want to find out.

So I'm reading up on old moons. The books, being printed and bound and from the base library, are out of date. I can fill in some of the details by listening to Bug. Bug doesn't know anything about Titan, specifically, but it has a broader understanding of ice moons than the textbooks. I presume the inquisitors will eventually ask about my reading, what it means to me, what I'm learning, and what I'm adding all by myself. But they haven't. Not yet. My first clue that the forces behind my detention could be in deep disarray.

They still aren't asking the right questions.

DAY 100

Here's how I hope it will go when they decide to spring me. Some of the docs will realize I pose no danger. They will ask permission to enter the suite. I will say yes. What choice? Anything to get shit to happen. The suite is clean but every Skyrine knows how to make weapons out of common items and I've had lots of time to think. My plan will move to the next stage. Two of the docs will enter wearing puffy yellow MOPP suits. A Marine MP will accompany them, also in yellow, packing enough hurt to discourage bad attitude. They will suggest I stay back, tell me to sit in my best chair, then ask the same questions they've asked over and over. One will take pictures of the other—with me in the background. For this first intrusion into the bughouse, they will not stay long, but by God, they will put themselves closer to the war, to those far-off battles, to imminent peril—to *me*. That will accelerate their climb in the ranks.

I'll be so cool that frost will whiten my brow. I'll smile and nod and thank them for all they've done. Then I'll brain at least one of the bastards before they realize I've gone total trigger.

DAY 102

As if things haven't been weird enough:

Last night, Captain Daniella Coyle came to visit. She just popped up in my head. Coyle died on Mars, deep inside the Drifter—in the Church. Apparently she doesn't know that. She tried to speak to me. At least I *think* she did. What I picked up was like looking at an empty word balloon. She hasn't come back since. But I think she will. Captain Coyle was nothing if not determined.

DAY 120

I've exhausted most of the textbooks. Jim Thompson starts giving me the willies. So much thud-thud stupidity leading to so many dead-end alleys of despair. Reminds me too much of my own life before I enlisted and even for a while after. I switch paperbacks and read *Robinson Crusoe*, an old, safe book that arrived in my pass-through box as a split-spine Signet Classic.

As usual, while I read, I eat dinner off the steel tray—and come upon this:

> Let no man despise the secret hints and notices of danger which sometimes are given him when he may think there is no possibility of its being real. That such hints and notices are given us I believe few that have made any observation of things can deny; that they are certain discoveries of an invisible world, and a converse of spirits, we cannot doubt; and if

the tendency of them seems to be to warn us of danger, why should we not suppose they are from some friendly agent (whether supreme, or inferior and subordinate, is not in the question) and that they are given for our good?

IT'S A LIFE

Half-asleep, wrapped in my bedsheets, I feel a not-so-gentle prod deep inside my head, as if someone or something is rummaging in my attic and opening old trunks. I'm too tired and discouraged to fight it. Memories come back in waves. Memories that sometimes explain nothing—like random bits of beach wrack washing up on my convoluted shores. Memories that ride high in emotions, too.

Let's look at you and Joe.

Joe Sanchez and I had a long, winding history on our way to becoming Skyrines. To me, it seems he was always there—has always been there. But of course, there have been gaps. Some long ones—like before our first drop on Mars. I didn't see him for over a year, during the last phase of training. I thought maybe he had been selected out for special training, but when he reappeared, all was fine; he said he'd been hanging out with a lady in Virginia, while taking some OCS courses at VMI. I have rarely if ever questioned Joe's word.

And of course that last drop on Mars. He had gone ahead; we had reunited at the Drifter. No explanation there, except that our units had been reassigned at the last minute.

But there were also clear, marked-out moments that seemed like beginnings. I think on one now, lying back in bed with my eyes closed; I can almost see the lowering sun, the line of clouds hugging the western horizon.

The trestle.

The time Joe and I nearly got ourselves killed.

I suppose every Skyrine, every fighter for a nation, a polity, a socially segregated club, starts off believing in the purity and magnificence of trial and adventure. As a child, I sought adventure wherever I could find it—sometimes getting myself into real scrapes with danger and with the law. I was harum-scarum, reckless, but I was also pretty smart and so I seldom got into a fix I could not, all on my own, get myself out of. But on three occasions, before I reached the age of sixteen, I came close to getting myself killed.

Once, I was following a train track in Southern California, not far from where Pendleton still trains and houses young Skyrines. I was with Joe. I was usually with Joe when we weren't off trying to pick up girls, which we did separately.

Back then Joe Sanchez was a brown-haired Huck Finn kind of guy, a year older than me, as smart as I thought I was, and even more resourceful. We had known each other for two years, we were happy, we were seeking adventure.

Young men who think they're smart tend not to make straight, linear plans, but to engage in ingeniously crooked schemes and maneuvers, just to try things out. Just to test the world. That's their job. Our job.

Our crooked plan was to walk along the tracks and jump

out of the way as trains came howling around the far headlands, through a cut in the Del Mar hills—passing behind Torrey Pines State Beach. We paid attention and walked the tracks and jumped out of the way as the engines and bright cars streaked past, though a few engineers were provoked to let loose with that impressive horn and glare at us as they flashed by in their long steel monsters.

But then we came to a bridge over the tidal inlet, a creosote pile kind of thing that might have been fifty or even seventy years old, just tracks, no cars, no clear path for a pair of reckless kids bent on a crooked lark.

We were halfway across that bridge, looking down through the ties at shallow turquoise and gray water lapping against the piles, enjoying the ocean breeze as seagulls wheeled and screeched. Joe was grinning like a bandit, walking ahead of me, teeth on fire in the lowering sun, glancing back and raising his arms as if he were a tightrope walker—brown hair rippling, brown arms reaching—when about two miles back we heard a train blat out like an angry dinosaur.

The engineer had glimmed across the low tidal inlet flats and with his sharp eyes discerned two scrawny figures in the middle of the bridge, with about a hundred and fifty feet left to finish gingerly walking, tie by tie, balancing, trying not to step through the spaces between—and the engineer had no doubt, given the train's speed and our steady, careful pace, that we had to speed it up, had to run along the ties like circus performers or cartoon characters...

And then he knew what we knew.

We still wouldn't make it. The train would be upon us before we could finish the crossing, and the water was at least thirty feet below, with a two-foot shoal over sand and gravel and eelgrass to break our fall or our necks.

So we did what we had to do. We laughed like loons. The fear was amazing. We ran, no, we *danced* along the ties. We ran and stumbled and recovered and ran. We slipped—Joe dropped his leg between two ties—I came down off a rail, one foot in the air, and somehow, we both scrambled up, unhurt, to keep running, all the time crowing and shouting and screaming—Move, fucker! Speed it up! Speed speed *speed*!

I managed to mostly balance on the left rail, stepping foot over foot, the toes of my shoes catching my pant cuffs, like my own legs would kill me if they could—

And my friend cried out, his voice breaking shrill, "It's right *behind us*! Fuck fuck *fuck*!"

I did not look back. I knew what I had to do—this was adventure, scary but chock-full of living, the height of everything I'd experienced until now—it was *us* versus *the monster*, and the engineer was leaning on his awful horn and the air filled with the most intense, gut-vibrating noise I had ever experienced.

I knew that I had to jump and break my legs.

Or die.

Joe screamed again, looked back at me with the face of a maniac, and dove off the tracks. His legs splayed as he flew a yard out from the bridge and then straight down, arms wheeling. I lost sight of him when I jumped, but I didn't fall—I clung to the left rail with my fingers, feeling the polished, sunwarm steel sear my fingers, hot as a steam iron, while I nearly bit through my cheek—legs and feet dangling, maybe a second before the train's thousand tons of pressure pulped my hand and I fell anyway—

And my toes came down firm on a board. A crosstie. I could not see it but it was there—I could feel it. I let go of the steel rail and hugged a thick black piling, smelling the pungent tarry heat of creosote, just as the train roared over at forty or fifty miles per hour, wheels a few inches from my face, my feet trying to keep their purchase on the crosstie someone had so thoughtfully hammered between two pilings, but angled at a crazy slant, the soles of my running shoes hot and slippery from the steel ties, splinters driving into my palms—the entire bridge alive with weight and motor noise, rattling my guts and bones and suspended thoughts, rattling my skull and teeth while blood streamed from a corner of my lips.

The train took forever.

It was by me in less than a minute.

The horn stopped its insane howl.

The engineer probably thought we were both dead.

No matter.

All my muscles had locked. I wanted to throw up but there was still stuff I had to do. I punched my arm and leg to release their lock, then edged forward along the crosspiece, which angled down to intersect another piling, and then along a lower piece, balancing briefly between pilings, shoes still slipping (I never bought that brand again) until I was within ten feet of the tidal flow, and I just gave up and fell back, closing my eyes—

Dropped and dropped.

Splashed down hard in the bath of the brackish stream, the shock spread evenly along my back and hips and legs. Water filled my nose. Eelgrass grabbed my hips and tried to hold me under, but I thrashed and broke free, found the mucky bottom, and shoved up with water streaming. The air brightened with diamond spray.

Only then did I look for Joe. He stood about twenty feet away, soaked and covered in mud, eyes and teeth golden through the muck. Both of us laughing. We had not stopped laughing since we'd seen the train, except when we were screaming.

"Fuck! I SAW YOU!" Joe shouted, turning the expletive into a buzz saw. "You were like RIGHT UNDER THE FUCKING ENGINE and I could see you fucking *vibrating like a GONG* and then—you . . . you . . ." He'd swallowed a lot of water and was spewing it up, saying between shuddering heaves how foul it was. We pulled our feet from the muck and finished crossing the lagoon, then stumbled through saw grass to the gravel bank of the highway. There we sat on the margin and leaned our heads back in the last fiery glow of the setting sun, suddenly quiet, laughter spent.

"Nothing better," Joe said hoarsely. "Nothing *ever* so great."

We sat beside each other for long minutes. The sun slid behind the far edge of the Pacific. Mud dried and stiffened our pants. The chill of evening made us shiver. We didn't care. We talked about trains and bridges, then about girls and drinking and movies and parties, then about cars and how we were no longer alone in the universe, all that stuff, like we were adults, old wise men, until the only lights we saw came from cars rushing north and south and a high scatter of stars washed gray by the electric glow of San Diego and Del Mar. Mist from the lagoon cloaked everything.

By then we were so cold we had to move. We got to our

feet, shoes squelching, and walked into Del Mar—miles away, not hitching, just walking, drawing out our time of being alive after what had happened, clinging to that feeling that we had survived something amazingly stupid and really, *really* great. This had just happened to *us*.

This was *Adventure*.

Walking backward ahead of me, Joe looked up and raised his hands to the dull orange-black sky.

"What's it like out there, Vinnie?" he asked. "We've sucked this planet dry. Nothing better here, just more stupid stunts."

"Great stungs," I said. I had bitten my tongue jumping from the bridge.

"Great what?"

"Great *stunts*," I corrected.

"What's waiting out there? What's *way* out there waiting to happen to both of us?"

That was the night Joe Sanchez and I told each other we would enlist. We wanted more stupid joy and danger and the sheer, druggy rush of survival. We wanted as much of that as we could get, the real thing. Wanted it over and over. God, how I loved that whole stupid day and chilly night.

We were idiots. But we were also young gods.

I SAW THAT in an old movie.

Coyle!

This time the word balloon fills in. I roll over, look up from my tangled bed, and glare at the ceiling. "It was real. It happened to me—to us." I can feel her, recognize her—almost hear her voice. "I don't know what you're doing in here! You're fucking *dead.*"

And you're fucking stuck in a cheap hotel. But not for long.

That makes me angry. "Get the hell out of my head!"

And what is this about you and Joe and a mummy? *That is just creepy. If you want original, you should see what I'm seeing. And by the way, I like Corporal Johnson better than you.*

"You mean, DJ? Where is he?"

Then—Coyle's voice dusts up and away, before I can even decide whether I'm still dreaming.

DAY 123

The stainless steel shutters behind the thick window hiss and click and slide open. A new guy stands behind the glass while the suite's little buzzer attracts my attention. He's alone. He looks around, sees me standing in the door to the bedroom. I'm still wearing my bathrobe.

The new guy's in his late fifties, bald, skinny, with a peach-smooth pink face and small, bright eyes. He's something of a sloppy dresser and wears a gray wool coat over a worn green sweater. He fastens those small bright eyes on me and smiles. Pink lips, tiny, perfect teeth.

"Master Sergeant Michael Venn. Vinnie," he says, though nobody around here has earned the right to use that nickname. Any other time or place, I'd look right past him, but there's something about this new guy, like close-mortared bricks or a finely fitted rock wall. He's confident, in his element, with the creepy manner of a civilian who can make generals wait in the lobby.

I get it. I'll play along and see what transpires.

"My name is Harris," he says. "First name Walker. I'm not a doctor but the docs talk to me. They tell me they're just about finished with your CDE."

Command Directed Evaluation.

"Oh?"

He smiles reassuringly. "They tell me there's no evidence of a maladaptive and enduring pattern of behavior destructive to yourself or others. In short, you're fine."

"Why did the docs take so long to make up their minds?" I ask.

"The stories you told were interesting. Fantastic and interesting."

"You're Wait Staff," I say.

"Some call us that," Harris admits. He releases a dry chuckle and then his eyes scrinch down. "You claim to have been influenced by a green powder you encountered inside an intriguing geological formation on Mars."

"Not just me," I say.

"Right. Another soldier, Corporal Johnson—DJ. Pardon. Another Skyrine. We needed to check out the stories, and so we have. I'm about to deliver a report to a trio of Gurus. They work in threes, you know."

I did not know.

"They interact with us in threes, that is, to avoid making mistakes, I suppose. I've been working with the Gurus for ten years—eleven, actually—and I am still amazed by how little we know about them. How little *I* know."

"Inscrutable?" I ask.

"Like open books, actually—but printed in a foreign language. Well, our local trio has expressed great interest in your story, what you've told us. Our doctors and scientists have finished their analyses, and the upshot is—the final report is going to read—I am going to *tell* the Gurus directly—that nothing significant about you has changed." Walker Harris touches the bridge of his nose, sniffs lightly, and concludes, "You are not contagious. Never have been. Nobody should feel concern. The green powder appears to have been innocuous. Maybe it was just dried algae, residue from the attempts to fill the old mine with breathable atmosphere. Don't you agree?"

I don't say a word. Maybe they'll let me out. Maybe they'll let me get back in the fight. It's all I know, really. All I've ever been good at.

"As for the dreams you've been having, we've been tracking your thought patterns, even translating some of them, and I'm told they're vivid, imaginative. But your dreams are neither based in mental disorder or referential to another reality. Certainly not an ancient moon's reality." Having doubled down, he waits for my response. I give him a twitch of one finger, which he focuses upon like a targeting system.

That look, that expression—

Is this guy human or machine? I have to ask. But I don't. Could be *maladaptive.*

"Your time here can't have been easy."

"No complaints," I say.

"Remarkable presence of mind. Though I understand you've been visited by a friend." His targeting system homes on my eyes. "A dead friend."

This gives me a jolt. I haven't told any of the docs about Coyle. My skin heats, my face flushes. Walker Harris watches with sympathetic concern. I murmur, "I miss my buddies. Nothing out of the ordinary."

"And nothing to be ashamed of," he says. "We remember our dead in so many ways. As for the experience itself… What little I've managed to understand of Guru metaphysics is a puzzle to me. They might or might not deny the possibility of life after death, but you understand—in *our* military, in our security forces in general, such an experience does not inspire confidence. Still, MHAT is prepared to evaluate and clear you quickly if it's just a stress-related interlude."

"Yeah," I say, "but I never expected a visit from Medvedev. Vee-Def, we called him. He hated my guts."

"Paradoxes and surprises abound," Harris says. He's giving up nothing—or he doesn't know. He's like a watchful barracuda, perfectly happy to find blood in the water; any excuse to tear me down and eat me up. I'm thinking maybe Walker Harris is borderline maladaptive.

"But given the trials you've been subjected to, and the length of time you've been isolated with little in the way of human company—and given that most of these contacts have been *scientists*…" Harris's smile could chill a side of beef. "I can arrange for all of that awkwardness to be ignored." His cheek jerks. He's lying.

"Good to hear," I say. "What else have you seen, looking into my head?"

Harris appreciates the chance to show off. "The compiled profile shows an intelligent and resourceful warrior with fewer stress-related issues than might be expected. A warrior who could return to service very soon and be a valuable contributor to our war effort. Which is entering a new and interesting phase."

"Titan," I say.

Harris nods with a tight little fidget. "We have yet to

broadcast these actions to the general public," he says, "but you've drawn conclusions from what little you've heard, and they are not wrong."

"How long have we been there? Fighting?"

"Two years."

Again, he's lying. Based on what the gray-haired secretary said to me outside SBLM about her son's death, I think maybe four or five.

"The Gurus must have given us new tech," I say. "Otherwise, it would take a decade for space frames to reach that far, even with spent matter drives. Out to Saturn and back."

If they come back.

"Very good," he says,

"How's it going out there?" I ask.

Harris purses his lips and presents his profile as if looking at someone beside him—a theatrical pose that tells me our little session is almost over. "Thank you for your patience, Master Sergeant Venn."

I approach the window. "I was told I'd be taken to see some Gurus."

"That meeting is not necessary."

"Pity," I say. "All my dreams, my other life—just made-up shit?"

"Pure and simple."

I manage my best boyish grin. "Good to know," I say.

"I suppose it does bring relief." With a ramrod break at the hips, meant to be a respectful bow, he motions for the shutters to close.

All lies and deceptions, of course. I know things I can't possibly have made up, things I learned in my other life, if I can just remember them clearly, make them stick down like wallpaper over *this* life; things I will apply once I get out of Madigan, if I ever get out of Madigan, if this isn't just a prelude to Zyklon B being pumped into my suite....

The rest of the afternoon passes, my lunch arrives on schedule, I eat and don't die. No poison gas, no quick and dirty end. The window remains closed. Another day passes. And then another.

Inside I'm buzzing. I know that feeling. Something scary incoming. I'm on the fork of two futures. In one, I'm dead. In the other, I would rather *be* dead. Balls-up or balls in a vise.

For a Skyrine, having any choice is outstanding.

SNATCH AND GO

I'm a light sleeper, when I sleep at all. Hours later, something jerks me out of a warm doze. The alarm clock on the bedstead tells me it's four in the morning. The door sighs and clicks.

Not the window shutters.

The steel door.

I push my hand between the foam mattress and the bed frame, wrap the improvised sap—a twisted bath towel with one end tied around a clutch of nuts and bolts—around my wrist and through my clenched fist, and move in a flash through the bedroom door to crouch in front of my reading chair. I swing the sap around and around. The lights blaze on. Blinking, I sway on one knee, buzzing with adrenaline. A tall brunette stands there, dressed in a green flight suit. She looks at me, at the dangling sap, then back to my eyes, which are vibrating madly. I can hardly see straight.

"You're kind of strung out," she says.

I raise the sap.

"Keep that, if it makes you happy." She points through the steel door. "Ready to get out of here?"

I remain on my knee, evaluating.

The brunette tightens her lips. "The Wait Staff ordered you to be killed. I'm your last hope."

My shoulders sag. I lower the sap. I have to chuckle. "Jesus Christ! 'Come with me if you want to live.' "

"Exactly," she says. Her dimples vanish. "Coming?"

"Shit yeah. Where to?"

"I'm not sure."

"Under whose recognizance?"

"Mine."

"And you are . . . ?"

"Commander Frances Borden, USN, Joint Sky Research Center, Mountain View, California." She taps a finger on her watch. "We've got maybe ten minutes. Get dressed."

I pick my day clothes off the desk, shed my pajama bottoms, put on pants and shirt, and stuff the sap in my pants pocket.

"No jacket?" she asks.

I shrug.

"All right, then."

One foot after the other, more than a little skeptical, I walk behind the commander through the open steel door. There's nobody in the big chamber outside the black-barred cage that surrounds the suite, and nobody guarding the outer lock doors that keep negative pressure on the whole shebang. I've never seen all the shit meant to keep me sealed tight until now, and it's hard to believe one Navy officer could have arranged for everyone to just vanish, but we're moving smooth and fast. No guards. No alarms. Nobody seems to care. Scary, but certainly *different*, and for anything that's truly fucking different, after 124 days in stir—I'm game. I'm up for a change.

"This way, Venn," Borden calls as I lag behind, caught up in the drama of how important and dangerous I am. "We've got five minutes before this place screws down tight."

"How do you know about me?" I ask.

"You passed a tight little cylinder to a Corporal Schneider, who delivered books from the base library. Corporal Schneider passed it to me. The lab evaluated it, then sent it on."

"What was in the cylinder?" I ask.

"A tight little manuscript, and a metal disk. A coin."

"Did you read it?"

"I did not."

"Did they get to Joe?" I ask.

"How the hell should I know?" she says.

We jog past a reception station, through double glass doors, and outside the main isolation building. I glance back, of course. It looks like a huge aircraft hangar, big enough to hold a hundred suites.

Borden grabs my shoulder and points to an electric Skell-Jeep idling in a red zone in the front drive. No other vehicles. Nothing else even *parked*. Like a dream.

I stop, hands by my side. Only now do I reach into my pocket and drop the sap. It jingles on the concrete. Nothing makes the least bit of sense. "Just who the hell are you, ma'am? And what is this, a blind date?"

Borden climbs halfway into the driver's seat. Her eyes go flinty. "I am geek steel," she barks. "And *I am your superior officer*. Don't forget that."

I want to smile, to reassure her I'm cooperating, but her

expression tells me this is a bad idea. "Apologies. Permission to return to your good graces—ma'am."

She lifts her eyes. "Just *get in*."

We're out under the early morning sky: light deck of clouds, blinking stars, crescent moon fogged by high cirrus. The whole base looks deserted. Borden drives the Skell diagonally across several McChord-Field runways, over grass and gravel medians, between long rows of blue lights. Absolutely nothing in the sky coming or going.

"Why no planes, no ships?" I ask as the wind rushes past.

"Broken quarantine," she says. "Incoming load of hung weapons. Whiteman Sampler."

"Whiteman Sampler" was a legendary incident from ten years before, when a whole Hawksbill filled with spent matter waste destined for Whiteman Air Force Base in Missouri got mistakenly diverted to Lewis-McChord. And came too damned close to contaminating the entire Pacific Northwest.

"Really?"

"Take your choice," Borden says. "I don't know, they didn't tell me."

I look up, unconsciously suck in a deep breath—and hold it. We're not heading for one of the long strips where Hawksbills land but toward a cluster of five circles radiating from a shorter taxiway.

Borden thrusts up one hand and grabs my jaw. "Breathe!"

I open my mouth and breathe.

"It's going to be close," she says.

The Skell hums toward the northernmost circle, where squats a dark gray, bulky shadow. It's an old Valor—an antique V280 tilt-rotor, used nowadays only for training. As we rumble out of the darkness, the Valor whines and coughs and begins to spin up its awkwardly massive black props. Borden cuts the Skell's motor, slams on the emergency brake, and jumps out even before we stop.

"Go! Go!" she calls. I follow, but not too close, as we run for the descending rear hatch.

"Taking me to Joe?" I ask.

A quick hard look. We ascend the ramp. Palm leaves cover the rear deck, along with boot- and tire-impressed cakes of mud. Could have been flown up from California. Could be from Pendleton. The leaves and mud crunch and crumble as we squeeze forward and take our seats. The whole frame of the Valor vibrates, the cabin sways back and forth, doesn't feel reliable, doesn't feel good. Behind us, the ramp rises with chuffing, shuddering slowness.

I buckle in. "Something's screwy!" I shout over the roar. "You couldn't do this without major pull. But all I see is desperation."

Borden looks sideways. She doesn't like looking right at me. She's scared of me. "Smart boy!" she says.

From the flight deck and the copilot's seat, a red-lit profile turns and stares back at us—calm, cool. High forehead. Paki or Indian. My interrogator.

The chief wizard.

I lunge. Borden shoves her arm across my chest. "He's why you're here!" she shouts over the roar. "Right now, he's your best friend."

My tormentor languidly blinks.

"I don't even know his fucking name!"

"He's Kumar," Borden says.

I thump my head back against the rest. "Fuck this, begging your pardon, ma'am. Let me know *something*! Where are you taking me?"

Borden shakes her head. "Away," she says.

The Valor lifts from the ground—barely. My stomach doesn't like the suspense. Then the engines rise in pitch and the vibration smooths, the rotors tilt forward, and we're really *moving*, soaring lickety-klick over airfield, farmland, highways—mountains—above a big, ghostly, glaciered volcano, like God dropped His ice-cream cone—

The whole beautiful, wide-open world.

Despite everything, I have this insane grin on my face. Away is good. Away is fucking awesome.

AN HOUR IN the air. I manage a sweaty little nap. When I come awake at rough air, I sit up and lean to look out the port by my right side. More farmland and rocky knolls, all golden in the morning sun. The sleep has improved my mood if not my outlook. I look at Borden. She's slumped, also sleeping. The Valor shudders and makes a wide turn, and the rising sun blasts her with light. She jerks up like a startled doe and rubs her eyes.

"Good morning," I say.

"Coffee and newspaper?" she grumbles.

"I'll ring the butler."

I'm rewarded with a wan smile. She's rank and geek steel, but she's the only female I've seen in months, and she's not bad-looking. Kumar, if that's his real name, leans back again, surveys us with those shining dark eyes, and says, "Barring difficulty, we will take you to Oklahoma. From there, we will all transfer to another conveyance and fly to South Texas."

I lean forward and say, louder than strictly necessary, "When do I get to beat the crap out of you, sir?"

Kumar doesn't bat a lash. "No foul, no regrets. I'm way outside your chain of command."

"Wait Staff?"

"No longer," Kumar says.

Borden leans over, says, "He might make a decent piñata, but if you treat him right, he'll shower you with candy—no need for the stick."

This provokes a twitch of Kumar's lips. "I'll apologize if you desire," he says with that same slow blink. I think it over. Amazing how long-held emotions vanish when plucked out of context. I may yet beat the crap out of him, but for now I shift my shoulders and release my death grip on the seat arms. Breaking me out of Madigan could be apology enough. Everyone on this aircraft is taking a huge risk.

"No need, really," I say. "What's in Texas?"

"Blue Origin Skyport."

"Fifteen minutes," the pilot announces.

I settle in and look at Borden. "What's going on out there? I've been cooped up for months."

"Nothing you want to hear about," Borden says.

"I'll be the judge. Tell me."

"Everybody's happy," Borden says. "Economy is booming. Hardly anyone complains."

"The Gurus have asked that we offer up a new religion," Kumar says. "It's becoming quite popular."

Borden looks like she doesn't think this discussion is strictly necessary.

"It's not too bad, actually," Kumar says. "Unifying, really."

"Gurus want to be gods?" I ask.

"No. They insist that worshippers of this new religion respect all other religions. No prejudice. Choose and let choose. All equal."

"So?" I look between them. "How's that bad?"

"We are to worship the *electron*," Kumar says. "Apparently all electrons are the same, they just swap out around the universe, so the One Universal Electron shares all points of view, everywhere, across all time. Voilà. Deity."

"God is a minus," Borden says.

"God is a diffuse cloud, sometimes a wave, sometimes a particle," Kumar adds, sort of getting into it. "Physicists in particular are pleased."

"Wow," I say. "I didn't see that coming. They still hate us saying 'fuck' or otherwise disrespecting sex?"

"Still," Kumar says.

"So watch yourself," Borden says, expression sternly neutral.

"Joe had a story about *fuck*," I say.

"Later," Borden says.

In a few minutes, Kumar says to Borden, "Time to speak of Wallops Island. Before we land. Might bring some clarity to our situation."

Borden twists in her seat. I'm peering across her sight line, out the opposite port, so again she takes my jaw and rotates my head a couple of inches, then asks, "What do you know about the silicon plague?"

I like being touched. Not this way, but it's better than nothing. Long swallow. "Is that its name?"

"Among several. Tell me."

"Sounds like what happened to some of our Skyrines when they tried to lay charges in the Drifter, in the Church. They turned hard and dark, inert—but with lights inside. Then the lights faded. Dead, I guess."

Or maybe not.

"Could it have been some sort of defensive mechanism?" Kumar asks.

"We thought so," I say, unhappy to relive that shit and be reminded of even weirder shit. Then I get it. The docs kept asking if I or anybody I knew brought back specimens from the Drifter. "Wallops Island got infected?" I ask, looking between them.

Borden dips her chin. "Thousands of square kilometers are under quarantine. No flights, no entry, a tight cordon for fifty miles around the entire facility. They shoot and collect animals exiting the area, but there isn't much they can do about insects, the ocean...dust in the air. They're pretty damned scared."

There goes my Virginia Beach apartment.

"What happened?"

"Somebody on Mars bagged and returned a piece of the black stuff. Somebody else tested it for potency. It was potent. Now they're in panic mode. That's probably why you were scheduled to be executed." She looks to Kumar, who nods: She can tell me more. "They call it 'turning glass.' Sky Defense has canceled all transfers or drops on Mars for the semester. No more offensive or defensive actions."

"What about the Antags?" I ask.

"Quiet, but beyond that, nobody knows," Borden says.

"Anyway, the question you should be asking is, how far is this crap going to spread?"

"Turning glass?"

"No. Executing recent visitors to Mars. Quite a rift has opened up between Wait Staff and Sky Defense. And that is one reason why we're hauling you cross-country."

"I was once in command of Division Four," Kumar says. "Division Four went against the express orders of Division One and ordered your release."

"Good," I say, just to be agreeable. I haven't heard of Division Four or Division One, or any division, for that matter. "What are they?"

Kumar ignores me and looks forward.

The rotors tilt back for vertical landing and that damned shudder returns. My mind is going like I've just been dosed with post-drop enthusiasm. I think on Joe and DJ and Kazak and Tak and Vee-Def and all the others—on Captain Coyle and her team—all of us who were in the Drifter.... I had been worried about the green powder. Hadn't thought much about the black, shiny stuff. I am remarkably dense.

"Touchdown in two," the pilot announces. "Ground crew wants a quick transfer. They're armed and anxious, so make it clean."

Borden tightens her belt and says, "For what it's worth, you'd be glass by now if you were contaminated... right?"

"Sure," I say. But I'm ignorant. Ignorant, unshaven, wearing rumpled civvies... I could be a paranoid homeless guy wandering the streets of Anytown, USA.

The Valor bounces and sidles before settling. We're surrounded by anonymous figures in severe orange MOPP gear.

Three big green Oshkosh fire tenders stand by, foam guns ready—whatever the hell good that will do. We run under the shadow of the rotating blades to another Skell—me, Borden, and Kumar. Borden advises me not to make any sudden moves. "They'll blow us off the runway if you so much as cross your eyes."

"Got it."

Our transfer is swift and clean. We pile in. Borden drives. I watch the nervous crews part to let us out of their cordon. Even through their thick visors, their eyes flash fear and even hatred.

An odd look crosses Kumar's smoothly calm features. "Getting interesting, Master Sergeant?"

"Yes, sir."

"That's what the Gurus like. They like it *interesting.*"

Our next ride is a low-slung private jet shaped like a manta ray with a fin coming out of its head. On the fuselage below the fin I read *Blue Origin Texas.* We enter through the tail hatch and find comfortable red leather seating near the front, behind wide windows facing forward, not apparent from the outside. The comfy seats wrap around our legs and middles and cushion our necks. A sweet female voice tells us we'll be in Texas in less than forty minutes. Sounds too pretty to be real.

The rear door seals, the jet spins about, and in a few seconds we're in a steep climb. The jet is a drone. It feels smooth and expensive.

"We'll be hitching on a Blue Origin lifter," Kumar says.

"Why not ISD ships?" I ask.

"If you haven't noticed, we're off the grid," Borden says.

"At the end of all our careers, I'm afraid," Kumar says. He arranges his hands neatly in his lap. "But if promises get fulfilled, we'll get a lift to LEO, transorbital to a Lagrange station, and from there—if we're *really* lucky—a high-speed shuttle."

"To where?"

"First stop, Mars," Borden says.

I've guessed it all along—felt it in my bones. Back to the Red. Unfinished business.

"Courtesy of some very brave CEOs," Kumar adds, "a couple of senators, and more than a few generals and colonels."

"Sounds like a full-throated conspiracy," I say.

Kumar demurs. "Let's just say a number of us have become dangerously curious."

A little vanilla-colored cart tracks up the aisle and offers us coffee or juice. I take coffee. Borden orders orange juice. The cart dispenses our drinks in blessed silence.

"Mr. Kumar provided the Chief of Naval Operations with your evaluation, as originally submitted to the Wait Staff," Borden says while we sip. "Your psych chart has some interesting bumps. The Office of Naval Research put me in charge of evaluating those bumps."

"Arlington?"

"Right."

"Someone's skeptical about what the Gurus have been telling us?"

"Draw your own conclusions."

I raise my cup in toast. "They need you to find out why I dream about being a bug."

Borden shakes her head. "That is beyond my mandate," she says. "I was given another assignment. Not to beat around the bush, we hear you have visits from the dead."

I'm silent for a few seconds. "Walker Harris told you?"

"I don't know a Walker Harris," Kumar says.

That's about to drag me through another line of questions, but Borden interrupts, "Was your experience informative? Real-seeming?"

I look out at the pretty cloudscape. "No. Yes."

"Can you tell me who it was you thought was visiting?"

My throat tightens. "Captain Daniella Coyle."

"Were you and Coyle close professionally or otherwise?"

"We were in a bar fight at Hawthorne years back, some sister Skyrines and Coyle and my training buddies. She went Special Ops and we didn't see her again until she arrived at the Drifter with her team. They carried bags full of spent matter charges."

"Enough to collapse the Drifter."

"Easily."

"She turned glass? Describe that again for me."

Reluctantly, hands clenching, I recount the last moments of Coyle's transformation in the heart of the Drifter—the Church—in the looming presence of that crystalline pillar. The blooming spikes, the weird little lights chasing inside her like fireflies in a black night. "After that, the rest of us were in a hurry to get out."

"Understandable. Are you sure she was dead?"

"I'm not sure about anything."

Borden's expression stays cool and firm, but there's something in the way she moves her eyes, looking away, then back—her first tell. Psych evaluations are standard for Skyrines. Trips to Mars and back are expensive and the brass does not want damaged goods fucking up an otherwise orderly drop.

"I was in a transfer once where a Skyrine lost it after we entered orbit, in cleanup," I say. "He came out of the Cosmoline screaming, then started crying like a baby. We weren't told what the corpsmen did with him."

"I don't think that's at issue here," Borden says.

I shift in my seat. "Yeah, but what *did* they do with him? I've never bothered to ask, maybe I don't want to know—"

"Tell me what happened after you returned and were taken to Madigan. No diversions. Straight out."

This is it, then. It could all end right here. "And if I don't pass your exam—Kumar sends me back to the shithouse?"

"You've never experienced visions before? Contact with spirits, ghosts?"

"Not out-and-out. Dreams, sure, but nothing real."

She doesn't want to hear about dreams. "Tell me what happened when Captain Coyle visited you."

"It's pretty fucked-up. Pardon me. Crazy."

"Let me be the judge."

Maybe Gurus are watching everybody on Earth, writing down our stats in dense little Guru charts, and holding back is silly. And so I lay it all out. "I think Coyle was trying to tell me something...pass along some sort of crucial information."

"You could see her?"

"I could *feel* her."

"How?"

"Well, a little protective voice woke me up in the middle of the night and said, 'Captain Coyle is *here*.' It seemed surprised."

"A protective voice... War sense? Battlefield angel?"

"Whatever. Me and it are not used to having dead people show up in our head. My head."

"And then?"

"I could *feel* her, sense it was her—or a dream of her, though she seemed pretty real. But when she tried to speak, there was just this word balloon filled with scribbles. Like those wind doodles all over Mars..." This makes my neck hair bristle. I look hard at Borden. "A few days later, I could actually understand what she was saying. A real pain in the ass. But what's it to *you*? Why track something so crazy?"

"Corporal Dan Johnson reports the same phenomenon."

This is the first time she's mentioned DJ. "He's alive?" I ask.

"So I've been told," Borden says.

"He hears from Captain Coyle?" Coyle had told me she liked him better. Sometimes I have a hard time putting two and two together.

Borden nods. "Nobody has answers, but it could be part of a pattern."

"Do my buddies dream of being bugs?"

"Some of them, something similar," Kumar says.

"Wow," I say.

"*Wow*," Borden echoes dully. She looks out through the little port, angles her head to see better.

"We'd all like more clarity," I say.

Borden nods. "Yup."

I'd section 8 myself if I was in charge. "Maybe we should ask the Gurus. Walker Harris told me the Gurus might allow such things in their metaphysics."

"As I said, I do not know a Walker Harris," Kumar says.

"He claimed to be Wait Staff," I say.

"Other than me, you were never visited by Wait Staff," Kumar says.

"Well, that's what he called himself. And he pronounced me cured. Safe."

"Right before they finalized orders for your execution," Borden says.

A FEW MINUTES later, we arrive at a broad, tan stretch of long-gone prairie, sun high overhead, a few cotton-ball clouds pieced out along the horizon. The jet lands on a long runway and swings about to a small terminal. We exit from the rear. The Texas air hits us like a hammer after the cool inside the jet. Heat rises from the concrete in rippling waves.

A few klicks to the north, alongside complexes of support hangars and fuel depots, lines of squat, blunt-nosed heavy lifters rise from concrete pads like the columns of a roofless temple.

"One of those is our next ride," Kumar says.

We're met by a small blue bus. "Apologies for the heat, folks," the bus says; again, no driver. "Please climb in! It's cool inside." Not a human in view besides us. The entire spaceport seems to be automated, at least for this launch. Borden lets me go first up the step and into the bus's air-conditioned interior. I settle into a seat, looking around with that feeling of extreme displacement I've had since leaving SBLM....

I hear a low murmur from outside. Kumar is conferring with Borden. I can't hear what they're saying. They look serious. I don't care. I'm floating, in a way: a worrisome lightness.

"Good for you, too, Bug?" I ask my inner crustacean.

"Yep," I answer for the sublimated presence. "Pillar of fire, then orbit, and after that—we're going home, right?" I have no idea how true that's going to be, and how soon. "In your opinion, Bug, am I fit for *any* sort of duty?"

Kumar and Borden put their conversation on pause and join me on the bus.

OH FOR COSMOLINE

The compact passenger cabin of the Blue Origin lifter—accessed from a cherry-picker elevator carried on another truck—is trim and comfortable. Kumar peers in from the elevator door, observes as Borden and I are strapped in by our seats.... And then, a little awkwardly, he crawls behind us, barely avoiding my nose with his knee.

"It's been a few years since I've crossed the vac," he confides.

The cabin is too warm. Noises rattle up from the structure below—pops, clangs, something like a vat of gurgling, ricocheting ice cubes. All chemical. Hydrogen and liquid oxygen. Old-school, low pollution. As we're lifted into space we'll leave behind a plume of steam.

A ride up on a Hawksbill is a sweet, high-g swoop from the skyport runway, then—*froomb*! Spent matter boosters take us through eight g's to orbit in a few minutes. Guru tech aplenty. But here—no spent matter, no re-ionizing shockwave and sound dampers—proudly, purely human. Early century twenty-one. We had heard about some civilian launch centers shying away from Guru advances but never quite understood why, and our briefings never touched on those matters—any more than we received detailed briefings on Muskies. Not our concern. If companies want to be wallflowers at the Guru orgy, they have that right; the Gurus do not complain, nor should anyone else. Survival of the fastest, right? Yet here are twenty or more Blue Origin lifters, capable of running themselves and apparently in fine condition. Making money. Surviving outside the orgy. I find that reassuring.

The hatch seals. Lights flicker around a wide touch monitor. Another small, sweet voice instructs us. From side pouches on our armrests I extract goggles for an external 3-D view. Borden leaves hers in the pouch. Behind us, Kumar is goggled and smiling. He looks like a mad scientist.

The elevator pulls away and the hatch swings in and seals. Cool air quickly fills the cabin. I wait for the noises below to settle into a musical routine. A couple of seconds later, the popping and gurgling stop. Almost immediately, we hear a thin whine—pumps, I assume—and then a low, bowel-loosening growl. The candle is lit! We're enveloped by a ragged, powerful animal noise that ranges high and low, through bass and treble, into *power.*

We're pressed back, and in four smooth shoves, Texas dwindles beneath us until it's barely visible through a hot blue and orange corona of chemical thrust. The sky turns black. Old-fashioned is kind of a sweet rush. I like it.

But once the rockets cut out and thrust drops to zero, Borden decides to be violently ill. Kumar stretches forward, releases a convenient mask cup, and reaches around to press it over her face before she spatters.

I'm doing okay. I feel superior, happy—for about five minutes. Then it's my own dry heaves for the next hour. Borden starts up again midway through my torment. Humans don't belong in zero-g. That's why Skyrines soak in Cosmoline during the long haul upsun and back.

DAY ONE

Goggles tell the tale: Our lifter is entering orbit at about three hundred klicks. Minutes later, the lifter shudders and we hear another series of echoing rattles and clangs. The small sweet voice says we've hooked up with a transorbital booster. Borden is no longer sick, but she's irritable. We don't say much. A more gradual boost again presses us back. The weight feels good but doesn't last. After twenty minutes we coast. We've reached escape velocity. My stomach is done twitching. Through the port, I glimpse that we're pulling away from Earth. The motion is barely obvious.

"What next?" I ask.

"Six hours transit," Kumar says.

"Love these antiques," I say.

"You'll soon feel more at home," Kumar says.

Borden closes her eyes and takes a deep breath.

"What's our next ride?"

Neither will go into details. Maybe they don't know. Little tubes pop from the sides of the neck rests. I suck on mine.

It supplies a sweet reddish liquid. No food. That's fine. I'm not going to be hungry for a while. Borden's eyelids flutter like she's dreaming. Her skin is pale.

"Problems?" I ask.

"Nothing you want to hear about," she says around an acid *urp.*

"Try me."

"Too damned warm in here!"

"Shall we crack a window?"

She opens her eyes, stares about wildly, and fumbles for the belt clasp, but it refuses to open. This really pushes her buttons. Her hand clutches at the straps, then at her neck, and I get concerned. But she forces herself to relax. Takes another deep breath, this one squeaky.

"Enjoy the moment," I say, not trying to be cruel. "Try the little tube."

She fumbles the tube between her lips. Her cheeks dimple.

I turn away with mixed emotions. "Five and a half hours," I say. "Right?"

"That's all," she says around the tube. She folds her arms and keeps sucking. That's almost more than I can take. High cheekbones, deep dimples.

"First time?" I ask.

She pulls the tube out. A little red liquid sticks to her upper lip, like wine. "Obviously."

"Did you volunteer?"

"Yup."

"Why?"

"The Gurus have been lying to us for thirteen years," she says.

"Gurus lie?" I tsk. Still, the confirmation isn't pleasant.

"About everything," Borden says. "I've spent the last four years gathering evidence and convincing the right people. Now, I have to get up here and see for myself."

"Well, the Antags like to kill us," I say. "That much is true."

"How many Antags have *you* killed, Master Sergeant?" Borden asks.

"A few."

"Did it always make sense, the way this conflict has played out?"

"No war makes sense. Not if I read history right."

"You're invested. You're well paid."

"Could be better." I'm just yammering to keep her talking. She might spill facts I shouldn't know.

"They caught us in a velvet trap," Borden says. "We fight and die for a cause, we're paid in beads and trinkets, and we think it's a fair trade."

"Then why blow up the Drifter?" I ask.

She shakes her head. Maybe she's already said too much.

"Isn't that the heart of the argument?" I say. "There's something in the Drifter that neither Gurus nor Antags want us to find."

Another shake.

"You must have *some* reason to stay so close to me. You're not in love, and keeping me stupid won't help, will it?"

Her jaw muscles shape little ridges. I'm not making this easy for her.

"So...?"

"If I had all the facts, and proof of what I know—and if I could make it all make sense—I'd tell you. But what we've put together is crazier than a sack of spiders, and twice as unpleasant to pick apart."

"Spiders," I say. "You have something against bugs?"

This elicits a weak smile. Her jaw relaxes. "You never said you dreamed about being a spider."

"More like a big crab."

"Not quite so creepy," she says. "You think you can see everything from the crustacean perspective?"

"Not really," I say. "All that is remarkably vague, for being so weird and important."

She's settled now and focuses in. "The Drifter. The crystal pillar. The green powder. The silicon plague. Your dreams... Captain Coyle."

"Not just delusions?"

"We don't think so," Borden says. "We've convinced the CNO." Meaning the Chief of Naval Operations—a four-star admiral. "And we're working on SecNav. Next up the line, SecDef—but he's Wait Staff."

I look to Kumar. "Tougher nut?"

"The toughest," Kumar says. "To the positive, the top brass and governments of three signatory nations seem to agree with us, as well as your vice president."

"Not the President?"

"He may be persuadable," Kumar says, "if we can bring back proof. And cancel out the messages coming from the Secretary of Defense."

"Proof...from where? Mars?"

Borden points up, around, shifting her shoulders. Then she slips on her goggles and motions for me to do the same. "Ready for something special?"

I goggle up but can't see much, so instinctively I strain against the belt as if to peer around a corner. The external cameras are still seeking. Then they find their targets. Below us, still only half visible, is a tight cluster of large, featureless cylinders. Tough to guess size from where we sit but the cluster looks about four hundred meters in length and half that across the beam. Larger, but not so different from the space frames they pack us into to go transvac. Above that, relative to where my butt is planted, rises the limb of the Earth, now slipping into night. I can make out southern India, Sri Lanka.

The lifter's voice tells us a passenger tub will arrive in the next few minutes to ferry us to our next ship, once the arrangements have been made. Boarding fees, tickets stamped, visas presented to the proper authorities?

Usually Skyrines crowd into a sheep dip station to get sedated by the transit crew, after which we're bagged and slipped into tubes. The tubes are then inserted into the rotating cylinders that make up the rotisseries. After we're loaded, the rotisseries are arranged by number on their respective frames, and that determines how and when we disembark and drop. Before that, we indulge in mostly blank sleep until we arrive. Warm sleep, some call it.

Now we can see what's on the other side of the cluster. It's something new, to me at least, and by looks alone makes my body feel numb and my brain more than a little left out of the bigger picture.

"What in *hell* is that?" I ask.

Borden shakes her head.

Kumar leans forward. "Some call it the Spook. Perhaps the prettiest of our new toys."

Spook—fine name, I hate it right off—is a triplet of very

long white tubes almost obscured by longitudinal sheets of glowing, pearly film. The sheets are attached to the cylinders and each other by thousands of twinkling strands, like nothing so much as burning spider silk. Whether the sheets are made of matter or energy is not obvious. All together, Spook—if it is one ship—must be over seven hundred meters from stem to stern. The sheets ripple slowly, like a flowing skirt in a slow breeze.

I've seen it before. But it wasn't me. *Coyle* saw it. Rode on it. No words this time, but she shares a glimpse of a line of soccer balls where you sleep on the way out to…

I desperately try to ignore her input. "How does it move?" I ask. "What pushes it?"

"She is called *Lady of Yue*," Kumar says. "I do not know what makes her go. She has been traveling back and forth to Saturn, carrying soldiers and machines, for over five years."

Carrying Coyle, apparently. That means Coyle made it to Titan. Why return to Mars? Why not cash out and retire a fucking hero? I wonder when the captain will deign to fully manifest and completely clue me in. "Is *she* our ride?" I ask, my voice barely a squeak. Coyle aside, it all scares the bloody hell out of me.

"No," Kumar says. "Not this time. Perhaps soon." He gives his finger a twirl. We're still rotating. A shadow passes over our little ship as something even larger, *much* larger, passes between us and the flare of the sun. We're swinging into view of an object at least five times the size of the Spook, in any dimension—and vastly greater in volume, like a gigantic, silvery Rubik's cube with the different faces separated and expanded. Between these faces twinkles more silken fire. This cubic monster is at least four thousand meters on a side.

Our rotation locks, but one last wobble gives us a slender glimpse of what might be the business end of the cube. It's black, no details visible—shadow within shadow.

"What's this one called?" I ask.

"Some call it the Big Box," Kumar says. "Larger than previous versions, and special to Division Six. I know very little about it."

"Tell me more about these divisions."

Kumar turns aside and says nothing. He looks like he doesn't want to be reminded of something.

I look to Borden.

"Six divisions of Wait Staff report to the Gurus," Borden says. "Together, they carry out the Gurus' instructions, plan big plans, and interface with governments and leaders."

"What's Division Six?"

"Logistics and other affairs internal to Wait Staff."

"Mostly civilians?"

"Mostly," Borden says.

Kumar sinks deeper into his gloom.

"What kind of civilians?" I ask.

"Some were part of the original greeting parties, back in the desert days. Others were selected by the Gurus after the revelations, with special assignments and privileges. Division Four was like PSYOP."

"Oh," I say. "Who controls the war effort?"

"Division Four," Borden says.

"The war is part of PSYOP?"

Kumar closes his eyes and looks sleepy.

Borden says, "Yeah. All meshed together. Eventually, some of us got tired of our own bullshit and started asking questions."

"Enough about our questions," Kumar says. "All will be obvious soon enough."

I doubt that.

Hissing and clicking noises starboard. We resume our rotation. In the final quarter of our turn, with no more surprises possible this side of something really weird—hyperspace, electron spin space!—I see a much more familiar sight, three space frames tied to a big spent matter booster. Looks like we're in for prep tanks, rotisseries, tubes...

I let out a groan. "*That?*"

"Our troops are already aboard and asleep," Kumar says. "We'll join them in the next hour. If all things work well—"

"Which they rarely do," Borden says.

"*If* we get our job done," Kumar persists, "then one or both of those other monsters might join us and carry us farther out into the solar system."

"Why all the show, then?" I ask, trying to be blasé and not succeeding.

"Different kind of war out there," Borden says. "The weapons are big. Everything is just... big."

"What the hell are we up against?" I ask, glancing between them.

"Nothing much, at the moment," Kumar says. "Right now Titan is undefended. Few if any surviving Earth forces, and apparently no Antags."

"Something pushed a big button," Borden says. "A button marked 'delete.'"

"Or 'reboot,'" Kumar adds.

"Some*thing*?"

Borden lifts an eyebrow, like maybe I have an explanation. A *clue*. That really makes me sweat.

Our lifter falls into deep shadow. We've closed the distance and now we're linking up. More hissing and grappling. Long guide ramps swing around and lock on to our craft, and with a scrape like fingernails on slate, the transfer tube fastens around the hatch. The hatch slams open. My ears go through their usual discontent, and our seats release us with reluctant sighs.

"Time to go," Kumar says, pushing past.

Borden looks ready to be sick again, but manages to keep it down.

The rest is familiar—to me. Humans take over. Prep teams float us to a pressurized work tank where cordons of vac techs, hooked foot and hip to cables that run the length of the tank, administer injections and brusquely ask how we're feeling, in general, whether we've eaten in the last few hours, how much alcohol have we consumed in the last week, do we have allergies, have we experienced adverse reactions to Cosmoline?

The techs tell us to strip. Personal effects will not be preserved—should have left them home. Too easily, I fall back into the old, old routine. But it's brand-new to Kumar and Borden and they look like sheep being prodded down the chute to slaughter. Rugged. And gratifying, sort of. Still, I know nothing about our mission. I have yet to get my orders, much less any sort of decent briefing. We're heading somewhere—presumably Mars—and when we get there we will do *mumbly-mumble*—and then if that all turns out well, maybe we'll go somewhere else. Somewhere far away. Maybe on the creepy-looking, beautiful Spook. Or inside Box.

The cordon pushes the three of us along none too gently, despite the fact that for the moment we're the only victims in line. Rank hath no privileges here, and after the first few injections we're propelled by casual, expert hands toward a slowly rotating bank of transparent cylinders at the aft end of the tank. One by one, techs fold our arms and legs, tell us to hold still, and prepare to slip us into bags. A pipette not-so-gently squeezes past my ass cheeks and shoves into my rectum. A hydraulic mask clips over mouth and nose. Nozzles on the bag poke out to receive Cosmoline. With a couple of brisk pinches, a head clamp settles around my ears and I feel thick gel worm into my ear canals. I don't mind. I'm already dopey, feeling no pain and not much concern, except for the usual hope that I don't wake up before it's over. I've taught myself to play blackjack in my head, but pretty soon I can no longer keep track of the cards.

Then the old cool goop slurps into the cylinder and smears out against my skin. I smell cloves and lemon vodka—the usual. Soon I'm chilly all over. Then everything warms nicely. Warm and cozy.

Hello, sleep! My old friend...

Sweet dreams—long and dark and slow.

THE NEXT THING I know, I'm being decanted. My bag is popped and stripped and I'm hauled aside. Rough hands throw me into the car wash, where rotating cloths slap me awake and sponge off the goop.

Groggy, I look for my squad, anyone familiar.... Where the hell are they? Lots of faces! Grunts aplenty, and then I stop seeing triple and realize there's maybe twenty of us, male and female, several different races, about half Asian—all naked, tense, shivering, and complaining, some loudly.

I recognize one officer from training in Hawaii—try to recall her name. Naveen something—Naveen Jacobi. That's it. Slender, blond, close-spaced black eyes, corded shoulders and arms, long legs. Tough and distant.

One Asian is a Winter Soldier. Almost half of her body—one arm, one leg, half her head—is composite or metal. She's cut her hair to match the plastic fuzz-lines on her composite cranium. Her organic eye is wide and very black; maybe she's tinted the sclera. The fake eye is closely matched. She must have survived horrible wounds somewhere on Earth—maybe in training. We don't bring them back from the Red when they're that badly injured. She's sleek, shiny, modesty minus. She'll never really be naked again. Hard time peeling my eyes away. She sticks close to two females and two males. They fought or trained together. Typically, they've tattooed dead buddies' names all over their torsos and legs. Tough crew.

Also waiting to be processed are four males, two young and skinny and scared, two in their late twenties or early thirties who look elaborately bored. Small load. Peewee drop. Usually, each decant delivers two hundred and females fly separate from males, but we've been given special dispensation.

As my eyes focus, I see Borden join the lineup. She's five grunts away, beside Jacobi; the commander has nice but not spectacular breasts. Tries to cover her privates. Good luck with that. I turn to find Kumar. There he is—pale and pudgy. Makes no attempt to cover himself. Who the fuck cares. He seems just a tetch peeved, like someone's delivered his Scotch sans rocks.

More techs in padded outfits like dog attack suits move down the lines. Grunts fresh out of Cosmoline can behave poorly. Sometimes we bite. Anyone who misbehaves will be spun like a top and pushed out of line to a recovery team—which injects more enthusiasm—and gradually, if not under control, will be spun into another tank, smaller, older, smells different—smells less like Cosmoline and more like shit and sweat and despair. But everyone's tip-top. No wingnuts and no spaz. And so we're rewarded with skintights dispensed by another pair of techs, blank-eyed and long past weary of slapping and sponging and injecting—looking forward to end of watch, to finishing this tour and hooking up with the next return shuttle. Maybe they go easier on each other when they return. Probably not.

O, pass a bull to the butcher,
Then pass the butcher your brother—
Butcher takes care o' the one
Same, same as the other....

Old Corps tune. We like 'em tasty.

We're wedged into stalls. Two techs reach into a carousel and distribute helms. The techs help Kumar and Borden put on theirs; the grunts and I do our own, with critical squints and finger tests for seal flex. We work fast. The quicker we're down on the Red the better. We close our faceplates to test suck. Borden and Kumar get help doing that. Finally, all our elbows and ankles cinch tight. Diagnostic lights flick on beside each grunt. Next step, I'm thinking, a puff pack, another round of enthusiasm, then getting cannolied—stuffed into a delivery tube—and the big drop. Burning puff all the way down.

But that's not the way it's going to be. Not this time. Not

for Commander Borden, Kumar, or me—not for any of our grunts.

Borden grimaces as suit techs pluck us from our nooks, rotate us like bags of sawdust, and push us past a short lineup of impatient pilots and chiefs to an accordion tunnel and another ship. But what kind of ship? A passing, spinning glimpse through a narrow port shows us a command orbiter snugly secured to the accommodating flank of a big lander, side by side with an impressive transport sled strapped to another lander. Such lovely accommodations. Orbiters usually fly high, under threat of Antag G2O—Ground-to-Orbit bolts or other weapons. Even command orbiters are generally about half this size and never fall below fifty thousand klicks. By itself, our next ride confirms there have been big changes on Mars: total G2O fire suppression, apparent theater domination—

Or one of those big old reboots. Both sides on pause—Antag and Earth. Maybe we won the last round after all.

The weapons techs are busy finishing inventory. They look up from their slates, expressions neutral, but I sense their scorn. I'm obviously Skyrine—semi-shaggy fuzzcut, wide shoulders, a Virginia Beach tan around my arms, mostly faded—but I'm not dropping in puff, I'm descending to the Red in luxury. I feel like a fucking POG: *Person Other than Grunt*. Nothing lower in Skyrine hierarchy than a POG.

The burly drop chief meets us at the end of the accordion. Blaze reads CWO 5 Agnes Chomsky. "Twenty-three for command descent," her voice booms in the confined space. On seeing me, her expression sours. I've passed her way five times before. "Limo to the Red, ladies?" Chomsky grates, waving a big hand as we pull ourselves to the lock beyond.

Her smirk is a masterpiece of contempt. I glide past. "What, no tip?" she sneers.

"No tip, *Chief*," Borden says, coming next.

"None deserved, ma'am," Drop Chief agrees with no sign she feels the bruise. Her voice rises to crescendo. "*Move it out*, VIPs! Ten minutes to clear lock." Even the grunts wince. They're strapping on blazes, printed and handed out by the chief as she confirms inventory. I do not get one. Tourist. Fucking POG.

Kumar hands himself along a guide wire to the far side of the lock. Borden and I follow, then the first six of our squad—if they are a squad and not just random reinforcements. I note the Winter Soldier is named Ishida—Sergeant Chihiro Ishida. She's tight with Captain Jacobi and four others, including two sisters—Tech Sergeant Jun Yoshinaga and Sergeant Kiyuko Ishikawa—and two males, Gunnery Sergeant Ryoka Tanaka and Master Sergeant Kenji Mori. To me, they look integrated and aware, like they share unseen scars.

Jacobi seems to be in command of a highly trained squad with four snowballs, one truffle, and seven caramels—Asians who speak American with no accent. Our Japanese sisters go through hell in two countries to get where they are in the ISD Skyrines. Two decades ago, Japan fought China for three months in and around the Senkaku Islands. Thousands died. The old Bushido tradition was revived in Japan with a stacked deck of consequences. For these sisters, combat training of any sort, but especially in the USA—I've heard from the likes of Tak—makes returning to a normal life in a more and more conservative Japan unlikely. So they phase American, more American than me, probably.

And they fight like furies.

We pass through the lock in two packs. The passenger compartment of the command orbiter, a cramped cylinder, is grand by Mars standards but still no one's idea of a limo: a crowded, cold jumble of crew spaces broken up by surveillance gear, sats stacked like tennis balls in a tournament launcher, emergency pods jutting halfway into the main hull—but compared to a space frame, this is luxury.

"Do they serve tea?" Jacobi asks.

"No, ma'am," calls a hoarse voice forward. From between two pod shrouds, a lieutenant in pilot blue pointedly salutes as Borden grapples past. He watches with no visible joy as she inadvertently knees herself into a half spin followed by three painful collisions. Me, however, he tracks with a critical eye. He's a small, wiry guy with a trim shock of black hair, olive-colored eyes, and a softly drawn, mouse-brown mustache. His blaze says he's *Pilot: Transfer: 109—Jonathan F. Kennedy*. JFK. PT-109. Cute.

"Coming with?" I ask him.

He shakes his head, unwinds, and emerges. "Just next door," he says, and swoops a forefinger full circle. "I'm solo on the sled. They'll release me at ninety klicks, I'll spread chaff, see if there's G2O, then drop first. If I make it, you're next."

"Brave fellow," I say.

"Any clues?" he asks.

"I wish."

"Pure fucking snake," he says. By which he means BOA—Brief On Arrival. At least that's familiar. Kumar floats a few meters ahead, knees drawn up and ankles crossed in a kind of lotus. Drop Chief Chomsky emerges last from the lock and pulls herself forward. Her voice is almost gentle now; she's filling couches and assigning escape pods. I've never heard of anyone using a pod. Taking a big Antag bolt is decisive.

I have more time to check out Jacobi's Skyrines. Goddamn, they sure do look like Special Forces. They all move with a freakish physical poise that reveals absolute conviction the rest of the world is their own pre-shucked, swig-'em-down raw oyster. We have seven sisters and eleven brothers—four corporals, three more sergeants, three engineering chiefs, four majors, two captains, two lieutenants. As a full commander, Borden seems to rank. All the Skyrines appear totally down with the program, however unfamiliar and risky. Can't let Navy see them sweat.

The orbiter pilot, also in light blue, emerges from the cockpit after Chomsky has finished. He's a junior lieutenant in his mid-twenties, olive complexion, balding, bigger than the norm. He grabs a brace and stays to one side as Borden salutes in passing, then he lifts a lumpy, soft-sides bag containing the *real* pilot: a preprogrammed Combined Software Navigator: Astral—CSNA. These units are replaced by fresh tech every few weeks, hence the bag. No peeking.

"Welcome aboard, frequent fliers," he says. "I'm Lieutenant JG Clover. Our trip tonight nets you three hundred million bonus miles, good for a free trip to the beaches of Pearl-Hickam, with no return." The joke doesn't raise a grin. "Wunnerful audience. Please be seated. Separation from cluster in five. We'll be on the Red inside twenty. Drop Chief, cross-check and link skintights. We're on ILS for the remainder of our trip." ILS = Internal Life Support. Borden has been assigned the couch next to mine. Jacobi straps in opposite and introduces herself to Borden, then to me—meaning she doesn't remember. No matter. Officers rarely pay attention to noncomms. She's out of Skybase Canaveral and tells Borden this is her fourth drop.

"My first," Borden admits.

"Welcome to Vertical Limit," Jacobi says, then settles in, closes her eyes—clams up. No sense getting acquainted. In a few minutes we might all be dead.

Up front, the cockpit hatch is open. I see Clover strap in and expertly slide the navigator into its slot beside his couch. He looks back, flashes a nerveless smile, and says, "Release in two."

The hatch to the cockpit slides shut.

Chomsky calls out, "Suck guts and grab ankles, cadets!" She settles back, seals her faceplate, and closes her eyes. We seal our own plates, hook patch cords into the couches, bend until helms touch a rear seat pad, shove both hands between our legs, grab our curtain handles, and finally, lay thumbs over the plastic covers on the emergency switches—the diddles.

With a jerk, the couches whir and roll into landing config, spaced around the cylinder beside assigned pods variously at eight, ten, twelve, fourteen, and sixteen of the clock.

Drop Chief, eyes still closed, runs down the seconds to release. The whole damned orbiter makes scary noises, and they're getting louder.

"Crap," Borden murmurs.

I ignore the angel boot-up rolling across my faceplate. Focus on my gloves. Flex my fingers. Steady respiration, *in* one two, *out* one two. Even. Calm. God, I hate physics. From here on down, physics *is* God.

"Orbiter checks prime," Clover announces through our helms. "Sled checks prime. Lander checks prime plus. Release from cluster... *now.*"

The orbiter shudders and lurches free. I feel motion along

the axis between my shoulder and my butt. I'm good that way; I somehow know which way I'm going just from sensing inertial vectors. Our descent is smooth, only a little buffet. Then—a low, piggy groan, filled with hypersonics, chords, nasty little demon tunes—

We tense.

And shoot off toward the Red. Our plunge takes five minutes. When upper Martian air begins its low banshee wail, I look left through a palm-sized port and watch the ionized glow, like dying coals, torch to brilliant cherry. Inside, all is smooth and cool and dull. Dropping in puff is so *much* more amusing. Grunts have all the fun.

"Down in three," Clover says. "Sled reports no G2O. We'll descend through our corridor until we pass two klicks—then hard DC. Stay strapped until I give thumbs-up. If we get painted in corridor, tug on your grips, flip the plastic cover, double press the diddle—curtains will drop, you'll spin into your pod, pod will punch free—orbiter will be history. Be ready for anything."

As always.

"Sled is safe on the Red," Clover announces.

Final DC—deceleration—rattles my bones like a cartoon skeleton. I hear the lander stage interact with the orbiter, loud squeals and nerve-racking *bangs*, like maybe it wasn't strapped on too well. Spent matter plasma retros deliver a final quivering kick up my spine, all the way into my skull—

Our backs and butts sink deep into the couches—

The lander shivers like a horse stung by a bee—

Drops a meter or two—

And settles with a deep, final crunch, like a boot stomping gravel.

"Beautiful!" Clover shouts over the mournful decline of the plasma turbines. "Exceptional if I say so myself. And I *do.*" His relief is a little obvious. Follows ten seconds of comparative quiet while angels assess our health. "Will three of our passengers kindly remove their thumbs from the diddles?" Clover requests. "That's two demerits. We're down firm, we're alive, and better yet, we've been recognized by resident authority. Such as it is. Welcome to Mars."

The pods retract. Rope ladders unwind and fall down the core between the couches. I look at Borden and Jacobi, peer around my seat and along the pods—rubberneck fore and aft. Behind her faceplate, Borden is pale and shiny. Kumar looks asleep. Beyond them stretches a descending spiral of impassive grunt faces, all the way down to the Winter Soldier. We're all going to be great friends, I just know it.

Thanks for the excitement, thanks for liberation from Madigan, thanks for saving my life, maybe—but even with all that, I just want to know why the fuck we're here.

BATTLEGROUND

First we tap up from the orbiter's gasps and sips, each of us making sure we get a day or so if the welcome wagon doesn't show. We pass through the orbiter lock in phases and I stand in a group of six on the fenced-off platform between the lander and the orbiter, feeling the cozy warmth radiating from the lander's rainbow-scorched skin.

A metal ladder unspools and our group descends. I reach bottom, third in line after two Skyrines, then step back to let Borden and Kumar join us. Next group, and then the last, until we all stand on the dust.

Our skintights hold suck. Readout is optimal. The angel in my helm—quiet until now—perks up with a puzzled report that all is well but there are no instructions, no maps, nothing. As the sled pilot said, pure snake: Brief On Arrival.

I have to note again that I have never dropped like this in my life. All told, it's less exciting than aero and puff and no doubt more expensive. Plus sheer group suicide if the Antags are waiting.

I look through heat shimmer over the pebbly ground and locate the sled about a hundred meters off, still vertical and attached to its lander. The landscape is eerily familiar. Flat—monstrously flat, with high, filmy ice clouds obscuring much of the pinkish-brown sky and more than the usual number of dust devils twisting far to the south. I know this place. This is where I was hoisted from the Red over two years ago, right in the middle of a pitched battle with the largest force of Antags I'd ever seen. On the northwestern horizon lies scattered wreckage: Tonkas, Chestys, and Trundles broken and burned in a ragged line about a klick and a half away.

We're back on Chryse. Our dead are still out there. Hundreds of them. My whole body shudders. We'd just broken out of the Drifter, or what was left of it—trying to avoid flying, crushing chunks of rock as everyone in the universe seemed dead set on blowing that old piece of moon to rubble. We beat a retreat, leaving a lot of comrades behind. Skyrines can't bring back the fallen with the fidelity we once guaranteed our troops on Earth. I've said that before, but you just may not know how much it hurts.

I slowly turn, letting my helm map the local features. Angel also tallies the wrecks in the middle distance, those that can still be identified.

Borden leans in like she's going to kiss me and taps her helm against mine. "War grave," she says.

I'm too choked to answer. A lot of Mars is sacred ground.

FORMING A THIRD point with the two landers is a half-buried line of red-and-tan depot storage tanks, like those erected when a base plans to stick around a few months. Beyond the tanks are revetments like molehills that probably conceal fountains, used to draw moisture from the Martian atmosphere. But there's no sign of domiciles. Maybe they're dug in away from the depot. I picture the enemy sitting like Indians on the surrounding hills, but there isn't much out there in the way of hills, and as cavalry goes, our force is puny compared to the Antag brigades that once smothered this theater.

The Skyrines open belt pouches and strap on their combat blazes. I have no blaze but everybody seems to know me, like they've been shown pictures.

They gather around Borden. "Time to share, ma'am," says First Lieutenant Vera Jennings. Jennings sat to the rear of the orbiter, showing a strong instinct for self-preservation, however misapplied. I remember her naked—stocky, heavy shoulders, fuzzcut pate streaked black and brown. Sharp gray eyes behind her plate. She tries to be heard through her helm—she assumes we're in blackout mode. "Where's our camp? When do we get logistics?"

But Borden's comm pings and our helms link to hers. The Skyrines give each other skeptical looks. No blackout, no cordon, no sentinels—nothing?

Borden announces, "I've got daylight, just a little. This is a temporary resource depot, set up here to take care of us and our landers. Nobody stays long."

"Sappers?" Jennings asks.

"Probably," Sergeant Ishida says.

"Too exposed," says Tech Sergeant Jun Yoshinaga. She's small, so small her skintight has cinched up around her knees, but from what I saw during transfer—smooth, flat abs; round, tight lumps of shoulder; huge forearms but long fingers like twisted rope—I wouldn't willingly match up against her.

"I don't know," Borden says. She looks around as if expecting company. The horizon is mostly empty, but I can't see beyond the clutter of charred vehicles. "We're scheduled to rendezvous with friendlies. They'll transport us to a relocation camp, where we'll pick up additional personnel."

"Who's been relocated?" Jennings asks.

"Settlers," Borden says. "They're being protected by our forces."

We all note that she doesn't say Joint Sky Defense—JSD.

"You mean Muskies? Why?" Captain Jacobi asks.

"Muskies, as you call them, are the reason we're here," Kumar says.

"This is Mr. Aram Kumar," Borden says. "He's part of Division Four, our civilian command. I'd listen to him."

That's keeping it simple. The rest of the grunts turn.

"Who gives a fuck about Muskies?" Jennings asks.

"They may be the most important people you'll ever meet," Kumar says.

Jacobi puts on a wry expression and looks my way.

"We have three missions," Kumar says. "We are to investigate the remains of the mining operation called the Drifter and assess its condition. We will then proceed to the relocation camp and evaluate those individuals who have been exposed to the interiors of the old mines. And if there is time, we will organize a travel team to visit where mining continues on a second remnant of old moon. Division Four believes our work there is critical."

"Sir—Kumarji—what about security?" asks Sergeant Chihiro Ishida—the Winter Soldier.

Kumar actually smiles at her, perhaps at the honorific. "For now, according to our best information, the last of the

Antagonists on Mars have retreated to the northern polar regions. As for their orbital assets, they have either scuttled or withdrawn them to Mars L-5, shielded by one or more trojans."

No cracks about being shielded by Trojans. He means asteroids. Mars L-5 is the trailing Mars Lagrange point. The trojans—small *t*—are asteroids stuck at either the leading or trailing Lagrange points in the Martian solar orbit. I thought we had scrubbed them years ago—Operation Rubber or something like that. I guess not.

Borden extends her arm northwest. Four Skell-Jeeps, three Tonkas, and a Russian-style Trundle, a TE-86, have skirted the charred wreckage and are cautiously rolling in. "Those are for us, I think," she says.

"They don't look good," Ishida says.

We magnify and inspect. Ishida has at least one very sharp eye—all of the Skells, the Trundle, and two of the Tonkas have suffered damage. One Tonka is rolling on four out of six wheels, and the Trundle still smokes where something took out a corner of the cabin.

"They're painting us," Jacobi says. Our helms confirm—we're lit up. No alarms, however—friendlies, right?

"Hey, they've charged bolts and slung the ballista!" Ishikawa calls out.

The Skyrines reach for their spent matter packs.

"Don't charge, damn it!" Borden barks. "Keep your weapons slung!"

Slowly, all comply—against instinct and training. I look at Kumar to see if he's reacting. He is—just barely. His hands curl into fists.

"Fuck this," Jennings mutters.

Two of the Skells and the fenders of the four-wheeling Tonka are smeared with freeze-dried blood.

"Casualties," Ishida says.

Our group tightens.

"No Ants, right?" Ishikawa asks.

"Nobody make a move," Borden orders. "Let me do the talking, but stay on my band."

The roughed-up vehicles pause at fifty meters, then, after thorough inspection, wheel forward at the same measured pace. They still light us up. The vehicles are naked of insignia, not unusual on the Red, but I see the Skells are driven by Russians—helm colors and skintights obvious—and I see Russian colors moving as well through the narrow windscreens of the badly damaged Trundle and the Tonkas. My faceplate manages to capture and magnify a couple of their blue and gold blazes. Special Ops—Spetsnaz, I'm guessing Russian Airborne. We trained with 45th Nevsky back at Hawthorne—not always on good terms—and fought together during my third drop. I might know these guys. I itch to communicate and ease things back, but this is on Borden's plate.

Dead silence on the comm. Nobody looks happy—nobody looks like they know what to expect.

"*Cold and calm*," Borden says. "Do not stare, do not charge weapons or make a move to target."

"No, ma'am," Jacobi says.

"Don't even *twitch*!" Borden's eyes are like a hawk's intent on a distant mouse. Our unhappy grunts keep their hands low and weapons slung or holstered.

Finally, wide comm pings and Russian fills our helms.

A smooth, deep male voice identifies himself as Polkovnik (Colonel) Litvinov and asks who is in charge. Borden raises her hand. Follows a direct burst of data from the Trundle's laser to Borden's helm.

Borden visibly relaxes. "These are our escorts. They didn't get notice we were arriving until last sol. They've been traveling since. They were hit four hours ago, probably by Antags—about fifty klicks from here. Four dead."

That gives everyone pause.

"How can they not *know* it was Antags?" Jennings asks nervously. "Who else would it be?"

Jacobi nudges the back of Jennings's calf with her toe. Jennings shuts up.

The vehicles stop again. Polkovnik Litvinov steps down from the lock of the damaged Trundle and pulls a soft brown cap with a green and gold eagle cockade from under his right shoulder strap, then perches it atop his helm.

Borden crosses to meet him. She opens the conversation with name and rank, says she's glad they're here, commiserates with their losses. None of us have twitched but the rest of the Russians keep to their vehicles, ready to return fire if we offer any trouble—ready as well to depart in quick order.

"You are first in three months," Litvinov says as he studies the way we're grouped. Jacobi has spaced her Skyrines into five fire teams, weapons visible but not at ready. The rest of us hang apart, very still.

Litvinov's sharp eyes miss nothing. "We too are glad to meet. It is confused on Earth, last few months. I learn to pick and choose which instructions to obey. Not good for peace of mind."

I'm guessing the chain of command up here is missing quite a few links. I do not like this one bit, and neither does Borden.

"Sorry to hear that," Borden says. "Our primary instructions are clear."

The colonel points toward the sled lander. "Is that for us?"

"We've been told to make a delivery, yes, sir," Borden says. "In exchange for transport and assistance."

If they want what we have, and don't want to give what we need, things will happen soon and they'll happen fast. The colonel, however, walks a few deliberate paces away from the Tonka and toward Borden, putting himself in any feasible line of fire. "Yours is unauthorized operation, no?"

Borden keeps quiet.

"Division Four?"

"Yes, sir," she says.

"Important division—newly disruptive. Puzzling." He walks by the commander and into the shadow of our orbiter, studying our Skyrines. Ishida's mechanical arm is steady. Her real arm has a light quiver.

"Yes, sir," Borden says.

The colonel's a bold one. Passing me, he leans in with a wolfish grin. "Are you called Vinnie?"

"Yes, sir," I say. "Master Sergeant Michael Venn."

"We are Russian Airborne, Aerospace Forces, Detached—45th Nevsky. Do you recognize us?"

"Yes, sir."

"Good to be memorable. We are told to expect you—in particularly, *you*, Master Sergeant." Litvinov slings his rifle and cuts bolt charge. The Russian soldiers stand down. "We are to protect and deliver you to specified location. Mutual colleague pays respect. Says hello."

I ask, "Who, sir?"

The colonel reaches into his belt pouch and withdraws a worn photo. He holds it in front of my plate. It's Joe, wearing gray long johns but apparently none the worse for wear. He seems to be standing inside a cluttered, crowded domicile, and looks apprehensive but not under duress. Joe just doesn't like having his picture taken, underwear or no. He's beside someone so tall her head almost doesn't fit in the photo. Someone I've been thinking about ever since I departed Mars. Tealullah Mackenzie Green.

Teal.

Borden and Kumar step in to peer at the colonel's picture. Kumar nods to Borden.

"You recognize?" the colonel asks me.

"My friends," I say.

He pockets the photo and examines my face behind the plate. His eyes are determined, sad. "They are twelve hours away, if we encounter no other setbacks. Which one is Skyfolk agent, Guru man name of Aram Kumar?"

Kumar says that's him. The colonel compares Kumar's face with another photo extracted from the same pouch. "Our orders were to come to site of previous hero action, where depot has been dropped months past, with fountains to collect fuel. Here, the orders say, we will take passengers, reinforcements, and supplies. Yet why drop depot so far out there, I ask? And I am told, to allow passengers to conduct recon of former site of moon fragment. Is this correct?"

Borden nods. She's hearing what she wants to hear.

"Then comes complete blackout, no more orders, no other explanation, and so we travel on faith, and already we have paid dearly. We get our supplies?"

"Absolutely," Borden says.

Ten more Russians climb down from their worn and damaged vehicles. Most are sergeants or lieutenants. One is a captain, another is a major. Several are female—I think. The Russian skintights are not flattering and carry heavier armor than ours—useless in my estimation, but maybe reassuring to them.

Lieutenant Kennedy has exited the sled lander and joined Borden and Kumar. Borden tells him to unload the sled, and Kennedy hustles back with a few experimental leaps—which the Russians scrutinize like weary dogs tracking a squirrel—to let down the high, broad white cylinder. The sled angles away from the lander until its support rails crunch on the hard ground. Then it pops its round cap and begins to roll out vehicles. When the vehicles are out, a pallet of supplies in four plastic containers—about a metric ton's worth—is winched down from the lander's cargo deck.

Kennedy then returns with his little slate. Litvinov studies the slate briefly and signs off. Formalities observed. Apparently even under the current circumstances, and even on Mars, we're still bound by paperwork.

Jacobi's Skyrines have stood in place, observant but hardly calm or patient. Jacobi, Jennings, and Ishida now huddle to speak helm to helm. Borden notices but lets it go. I'm a couple of meters away from this triad of discontent, but I can just make out what they're saying.

"I don't see it," Ishida says.

"What's our *real* goddamned mission?" Jennings asks.

"Looks to me like the only way they could get these dudes to come out here was by promising resupply. I'll bet the settlements are down to pucker."

"And what's that crap about no Antags within three thousand klicks?" Ishida says. "If not Antags, what hit the Russians? We're in eclipse and carrying an Ugly tight with Blue—that's fucking off the drum." By Blue, Ishida means Navy—Commander Borden. I'm the Ugly—Ugly fucking POG, a stick-beat off the drum and maybe even a Jonah.

Jacobi catches me looking their way and ends the confab. They split with dark glances. Nobody wants to talk to me. Cheery times.

More Russians depart the vehicles. There are twenty-five altogether, more than doubling our force. We're going to need the new transports.

Within a few minutes, four Russian *efreitors*, or lance corporals, led by a slender female *starshina*, or sergeant major, have sliced away the plexanyl packaging and taken charge of a new Trundle, two Tonkas, and a Chesty replete with righteous hurt. The supply pallet is hoisted by crane onto the back of the Trundle.

Litvinov steps back and pings his troops. "Welcome to our American comrades!" Half of them salute without enthusiasm. The others just stare or glower.

A pair of tech sergeants with black, bug-green, and gold blazes—spent matter specialists—prepare to set charges to destroy the damaged Russian vehicles. Once the charges have been placed and primed, Litvinov assigns the four *efreitors* to drive or push them half a klick away—what he seems to think might be a safe distance.

Litvinov's second-in-command, Major Karl Rodniansky,

a squat, bluff-shouldered rectangle with white-blond hair low on his brow, arranges with Kennedy and Clover for transfer of depot fuel to the lifters. "Use it up!" Rodniansky tells Kennedy. "Cruel bastards out here. They do not deserve."

I'm not sure if he means Antags.

Both landers will lift off once we're clear. The sled will be left behind. Thousands of such sleds litter Mars—along with as many artifacts not our own.

The colonel, satisfied that orders and obligations are being fulfilled, returns to Borden and Kumar. "We are told Antags stay up near northern frost," the colonel says. "Maybe that is true. Our attackers use human tactics, not like *Antagonista*. And why do they not take out depot?" The colonel points to the poorly camouflaged tanks and fountains. "*Antagonista* would not need this to get home. But *others*..."

"Sappers," Jacobi confirms with a sour face. She doesn't seem to catch Litvinov's total message. Maybe she doesn't want to.

"Why not both?" Ishida asks. "We're special. Everybody's out to get us."

Nothing better.

Litvinov turns and moves his head close to mine. "Master Sergeant Michael Venn. We have history, you and me," he says. "In Nevada, at Hawthorne dive bar. Like Old West rowdies. You throw me in filthy alley. Remember?"

"No, sir," I say. I don't remember the colonel, but I remember the wicked, navy-issue Iglas the Russians waved in that long, antique saloon. The colonel could still be carrying an Igla and a grudge. Borden is sticking to my side like a shadow. And I notice Jacobi is alert, too.

"Good fight," Litvinov says. "We were green, brash. We

learn well—and months later, join and share hero action on the Red. Now you remember?"

"Yes, sir."

"Venn," Litvinov says, getting closer, "we have fought against and alongside. You swear to me, we speak truth, nothing else?"

"I'll do my best," I say.

His brows compress. "Swear to me on famous Marine's grave," he insists. "Tell me *only* truth, not Earth bullshit."

"On General Puller's blood-soaked grave, I swear to tell only truth," I say.

"Chesty Puller! Namesake, real bastard in Nicaragua, true imperialist American villain. Is good. *Damned* good." Litvinov shakes my hand. He means it. I mean it. Funny how you can feel such things.

Then he gestures for Kumar, Borden, Jacobi, and Rodniansky to join us. We touch our helms, excluding the others. "Two relocation camps have been attacked and evacuated," Litvinov says. "Many settlers die. Witnesses, survivors, say it is not *Antagonista*—it is humans in small teams, well supplied. Fast ships, small ships, arrive, depart, carrying these teams. I know they are not Russian. That leaves same forces that worked to destroy mine in old moon—multinational, American-commanded Skyrines, like you. Kumarji, you are servant of Skyfolk—but top commander in Division Four?"

"To our purpose, yes," Kumar says.

"Is destruction of moons and camps ordered by Gurus?"

"We think so," Kumar says.

"So, safe to say, other divisions on Earth do not approve of your actions?"

"That is safe to say," Kumar confirms.

"*Chërt voz'mi!* Deeper and deeper pile," the colonel says. "Our commanders long suspect Gurus not on up-and-up. Last orders from Rossiya Sky Defense instruct to cross desert and escort new arrivals to resettlement, to what Skyrines call Fiddler's Green—and protect Master Sergeant Michael Venn *at all cost*. Sound like Russians belong Division Four?"

Everyone looks at me, but Kumar answers. "I believe both the Russians and the Japanese have signed on to Division Four and its goals."

Litvinov shakes his head. "But not Americans?"

"Not entirely," Kumar says.

"Not yet," Borden adds.

"Then future is unpredictable. If most Sky Defense signatories want us dead, what if someone here, among your squad, *this* squad, agrees?" the colonel asks. "What if *your* troops turn weapons, finish what others could not?"

Kumar faces Litvinov's sad, serious gaze. "These men and women were handpicked, and all are determined to do the right thing." Echoes of civilian corporate bullshit. Kumar isn't used to hanging out with warriors, much less reassuring them. The morale here is nonexistent. He needs to up his game.

Litvinov looks out from under those tight, shadowy brows, straightens, and scoffs. "*Fuck* right thing," he says. "We do this to piss off goddamn Skyfolk! They treat Rossiya different from UK and USA? Hold back secrets, let us die wholesale—poor rewards, not same prize as America! Again, Slavs are disrespected. *Pfahh!*" He grinds his thumb against his forearm, then lifts his chin and shivers off that long, bad history.

This done, the colonel says, "We stay until ships launch—

then roll to Fiddler's Green. Name of afterworld where dancing and singing never stop, favorite of American warriors—true?"

Borden darts her eyes between Litvinov and the other Russians. We're on margin here, but Litvinov seems to be well in control. Everything depends on him, then—and not on Kumar's social skills.

The Skyrines line up to climb into the assigned vehicles. Ishida and Jennings scope me again, but Jacobi refuses to look at me. The Russians' mood is infectious, and Skyrines despise poorly defined relationships as much as they hate unclear missions and muddled orders. Litvinov—a Russian!—picked me out of the crowd. What am I—hero, MacGuffin, prisoner, or worse, a renegade? Somebody who fucked up so badly they locked him away at Madigan, just to measure how screwy a Skyrine can get?

Makes my cockles warm to think of how much they could end up hating me if things turn bad.

FIREWORKS

The Russians finish laying charges in the damaged and stripped vehicles. The muffled crumps unite into one impressive, upward-flaring blast. Fragments fly off mostly to the south, but a few flaming scraps loft over us. Oops. One piece of fender tinks from the side of the orbiter but causes no damage—though much concern to Kennedy, who prances and rants. But quickly he decides it's not major. He hastily preps to depart. He wants off this rock bad.

The busted and damaged TE-86, Skells, and Tonkas smolder and join the wreckage of the Chryse hero action. The one still useful and four new vehicles form an outward-facing cordon around the landers as the pilots perform their preflight check, all this under a sky graying rapidly to night.

Kennedy informs Borden that the depot has enough hydrogen and oxygen to get the ships to orbit on burn alone, without dipping into spent matter reserves. That improves their chances of getting home in a timely fashion. As well, the depot resupplies our vehicles—and by extension our skintights—with fuel and water and oxygen. A couple of hours more for each of us. No gas stations between here and Fiddler's Green. Last gasps and sips for six hundred klicks.

Twilight is short on the Red, mere minutes in a low-dust sky. It's remarkably clear and cold. Walking around in skintights is a mostly quiet affair. Loud sounds come through, but blunt and dreamlike; other sounds simply don't cross the distance. Brief digital snaps of radio comm are restricted to necessities. Not much in the way of chatter. I stick with Borden and a couple of Russian corporals not the least interested in striking up a conversation, possibly because they don't trust angels to adequately translate their anger and resentment. Dead friends. I get that.

Borden's head is on a swivel as she checks out everyone and everything. I have to say she's adapted quickly to walking on the Red, an economy of motion that speaks to training back on Earth, possibly in harness at drop school—or maybe she's just a natural.

I still don't know what to think of Kumar. Skyrines have never been happy with civilian authority. But alien authority? Are the Wait Staff civilians, prophets, or demigods? Going along with Borden and Kumar has gotten me out of Madigan and transvac and down on the Red in relative comfort. And a chance to meet up with Joe and Teal. I don't deserve to feel resentment against anyone here, except Kumar, and other than being scoped as a POG—but I do have doubts. Deep, severe doubts. My thoughts are an unruly churn of speculation lit up by sharp flashes of dread.

So far, at least, no more Captain Coyle. But there is just a hint of *other*, inside, that I can't give shape—can't make out or force to come forward. Brain is *still* not my friend.

Finally Litvinov breaks from yet another huddle with two of his captains and tells Borden, Kumar, Jacobi, Jennings, and Ishida—and me—that we'll ride one of the new Tonkas, now rolling forward. "Keep group tight-knit, no?"

A gruff, hatchet-faced Russian chief named Kalenov finishes passing out vehicle assignments. The rest of our U.S. and Japanese Skyrines will ride in the second Tonka with three more Russians and the driver/shotgun. Litvinov's being extra prudent. None of our Skyrines will ride in the Chesty or the Trundle, denying us immediate access to decisive weapons. For the time being, we're passengers.

As ALWAYS, THERE's a delay—the landers have to wait for something, the pilots don't say what. A few Russians get picked for sentinel duty. Most of us climb into our assigned vehicles to stay warm. It's toasty inside the new Tonka, toasty and stuffy and boring. The sisters are making small talk in the back. They seem to be picking up from a previous conversation.

"Meeting *the* guy just before you go transvac," Jennings says to Ishida. "*That's* luck."

"Is he nice?" Jacobi asks Ishida.

Despite myself, I'm fascinated—their talk is low and private, but I can still wonder how a Winter Soldier gets along that way.

"A little," Ishida says. "He was curious at first. Then... after, very gentle, sweet. Yeah. Nice."

"I'll *bet* he's curious," Jennings says. "Shiny sister, strong like tank."

"Fortress heart," Jacobi says.

Ishida takes this stoically. "Right after, he asked about my nick."

"Did you tell him?" Jennings asks.

Ishida suddenly looks forward and sees I'm listening. She leans in, looks sharp straight up the aisle, and says loudly, "It's Gadget, *sir.* Inspector Gadget. Like the TV show."

The others raise their eyes to the roof. I am such a perv. I want to say something clever and complimentary to make up for my blunder, for being who I am—make up to her for what she has become, but really, that's not in it. I don't know what I want. I'm like a kid caught staring into the girls' shower in high school.

"Athena, bringer of victory, whose glory shines in war and peace," I say. "None dare look on her nakedness without fear and envy."

A long, stunned silence. Borden regards me with honest pity.

"What the *fuck*?" Ishikawa says.

"Cut the guy some slack," Jacobi says. "You'd blast him like a stump, Gadget."

"I would, wouldn't I?" Ishida says, languorous.

I lean back, scorched wasteland. Victory is theirs.

I USE THE next hour to close my faceplate and study the battle reports screed to our helms. Some are still locked, orders of Commander Borden. No doubt she wants to explain them to us personally, with Kumar watching over her shoulder. There are a few open launch and landing reports, however. We didn't see any of the first part of the so-called Battle of Mars, since my platoon arrived later and was spread out across Chryse by a badly broken drop. I flip back through the logistics, looking for Russian and Korean launch dates. Their fast frames were sent out *after* our own frames departed from Earth orbit, but arrived nearly a month earlier. As some of us surmised, command on Earth—generals? Wait Staff? Gurus?—had decided something big had to be done and done quickly—and so they had arranged for a major and very expensive push.

And fucked it up.

ELEVEN HOURS. EVERYONE's asleep in the Tonka except the Russian shotgun. It's totally black out. Low clouds obscure the stars. One small moon rises, a swift, misty little ball. I catch a light doze myself.

Then Litvinov radios that the ships are leaving and we're about to move out. Everyone rouses. One of the Russian corporals, perhaps fresh from a good dream, rubs his eyes through his open faceplate, bumps arms with me, smiles. He has a clean, square little-boy face. I return his smile. He sobers, looks away. Warm and cozy in here.

We focus on the growing roar outside. Two brilliant blue torches rise through the dark on silvery plumes. Vapor drifts back in the diminishing glow and freezes to a fine, powdery snow, like confectioner's sugar, vanishing before it touches the dust. We're on our own.

The perimeter guards climb onto the Skells. We begin to roll. Kumar keeps his eyes on the dark flats out beyond the wreckage. The first Drifter—what's left of it—is about ten klicks away, maybe fifteen or twenty minutes. I'm not at all sure I want to go back. Our fallen are still out there, freeze-dried into rag-shrouded jerky....

Or buried deep in the Drifter.

I keep expecting Captain Coyle to fill in more word balloons, to call out for vengeance from her grave. But I still don't feel her. Maybe I left her back on Earth. How do ghosts find their way around?

The cordon forms a loose W with Skells taking the rear and sides, the Chesty and Trundle on points, weapons bristling, and Tonkas rear and center. Litvinov rides in the Chesty—namesake of imperialist bastard. I would, too, if I had a choice. Chestys are packed with good, strong hurt. I don't see the point of returning to the Drifter, really; if the bombardment was anything like what I remember, and went on after we departed, we'll find nothing but a big ditch. But Kumar's goal is clear. We're here to see for ourselves.

He wants *me* to look.

MESSAGE UNCLEAR

Morning begins with high, pale clouds turning orange before light touches the land. Winds are at work up there, cross-shredding the clouds into faded lace. Then the flats of Chryse emerge from darkness. We're rolling at about thirty klicks over smooth basalt, but that's going to change; I remember the terrain, some of it, far too well.

Wind doodles are everywhere. Dust devils scour random lines across the flats like phantom fingers. I count seven through the windscreen: thin, high, twisting pillars, bright pink this early, far out near the northern horizon as dawn throws rosy light through the Tonka's side ports. They've been scribbling on the Red for billions of years and nothing comes of it, they never remember what it is they really want to say, but they never get bored trying.

Our ride turns bumpy. I move away from the pilot's nest and peer through the dust-fogged plastic of the nearest side port. The landscape looking west is rugged and fresh. Recent craters dimple the basalt, bright at the center and surrounded by silver-gray rays. More chewed over than I remember—what little I remember before we were lifted off.

"Familiar?" Kumar asks.

The entire cabin listens.

"I don't recognize any of it," I say. "Too much has changed." It's not hard to figure out, from the nature of the craters, that a lot more heavy shit fell from on high, whether comets or meteoroids or asteroids, no way of knowing. One crater on our right is easily three hundred meters across. "Must be Antag bombardment," I say. "We don't drop comets... do we?"

Kumar shakes his head.

We're passing signs of less cosmic conflict: blasted revetments, crushed and burned space frames, the melted ribs and skins of big vehicles: Chestys, deuces, Trundles. We roll past six slagged weapons platforms in a hundred-meter stretch, just off the path we're following, which curls through the worst of the wreckage. I assume this action took place not far from our retrieval. But it spread over dozens, maybe hundreds of klicks.

"What were they fighting for?" I ask. "To hold ground, repel occupation?"

"I thought you could tell us," Kumar says.

"I didn't see that much. But this was big. This was *nasty*."

Is Kumar trying to draw me out, open up my head and see if I know important shit but am too stupid to realize it—just as he did back in the cell at Madigan? He's still the whirly-eyed inquisitor. He can't help himself. My gloved fingers form claws. I work to maintain.

"After we left, there must have been more campaigns lasting weeks, months," I say. "They wouldn't have kept concentrations of troops or stable positions. They would have moved, or been lifted out, then replaced by more drops—"

"Was four battalions," the Russian driver says in heavily accented English. We look up front. His blaze identifies him as Sergeant Kiril Durov. This is the first time he's spoken. He looks to be in his late thirties, with a rugged, finely wrinkled face and experienced brown eyes. He and the copilot, Efreitor Igor Federov—riding shotgun on a bolt cannon—scan the terrain, perhaps remembering the carnage. "Hero action. We do not bury Antags, what are left. But many."

We pass within meters of the remains of a big Millie—an Antag millipede transport—carved down the middle, broken and burned, windblown dust obscuring the low-lying pieces of hull and canted wheels.

"Why Chryse, why the Drifter?" I ask.

"I cannot speak for the Antagonists," Kumar says, "but Sky Defense was told that control of this sector was important enough to mount a major invasion force, earlier in this extended season than any of us had believed was even possible."

Borden says, "They were instructed to defend the site and deny it to others, or, failing that, to render it inaccessible."

Beyond the Millie lies the wreckage of six more Skyrine deuces, then, half-buried in dust and chunks of rock, a command orbiter and its lander, not unlike the one that brought us here but in no condition to ever fly again.

We *must* be near the first Drifter, but I don't see any rocky swimmer trying to complete a billion-year backstroke. The mounded head, shoulders, and sheltering arms must have been hammered over and over—

Shoved under and drowned.

Kumar gestures for Jacobi and Borden to take the seats across from us. Soldiers and Skyrines rearrange. Here it comes.

"Commander Borden has thoroughly studied what some are calling the Battle of Mars," Kumar says. "Before we arrive at our first stop, we should refresh ourselves on how it all transpired. Commander?"

Borden stands behind the pilot's nest and releases the data loaded into our angels. As she speaks, we view diagrams, short vids, approximations.

"There were at least three major bombardments by Antag orbital forces—two comet strikes followed sometime after by a carpeting with megaton-class spent matter charges," she says. "The first comet strike consisted of seven objects, all presumably redirected or harvested from the Oort cloud. These were the impacts that Master Sergeant Venn experienced on the surface, along with his comrades."

"You were in the open?" Jacobi asks.

"Pretty far away," I say.

Jacobi looks at me, solidly neutral. That's an improvement.

"The first strike took out four settlements, including the largest Voor laager," Borden continues. "Some of the pieces seem to have gone astray, or were intended not for the Drifter but for the Muskies. We don't know, because of course we don't have access to Antag planning and orders.

"Surprisingly, about a hundred and fifty settlers escaped—including a group of Voors who were traveling to the Drifter. They encountered Captain Daniella Coyle's Special Ops team, and against their will, carried that team to the Drifter. Captain Coyle had been put on Mars with orders to destroy the Drifter, by any and all means at her disposal."

"Who gave the orders?" Jacobi asks. "I mean, at the top."

Borden looks to Kumar. Kumar hesitates but finally says, "The instructions were relayed by Wait Staff in Washington, D.C., to Joint Sky Defense."

"You, sir?" Jacobi asks.

"No. I was not in that chain."

"Coyle could have been me," Jacobi says. "That team could have been all of us. Best we get that understood now."

Kumar tilts his head.

Borden says, mostly to me, "Captain Jacobi trained with Captain Coyle. She was in command of the backup team."

"We'd have died inside there like Coyle, if we'd been picked," Jacobi says. Her comrades are somber. The Russians are quiet, attentive. All eyes turn to me, waiting for my reaction.

I look up and down the aisle. "Every one of you—Special Ops?" I ask.

"Yeah," Jacobi says. "Make you uncomfortable?"

"Fuck yeah," I say.

Jacobi leans forward. "We would have tried to kill *you*, Venn."

"That's enough," Borden says.

Strain to breaking. Better get it all out now. I clamp my jaw and look down at my boots.

Borden pushes on. "Captain Coyle was unable to complete her mission, and she and many of her team met puzzling ends within the Drifter's crystal chamber."

"The Church," Kumar says.

I've had quite enough. "They used lawnmowers on the Voors!" I shout. "They carved them into lunch meat!" The old anger, the disappointment—the sting of moral wounds. I was there. Now I'm here. So many aren't anywhere now. "But when they set charges, the Church—"

"You saw the Church, didn't you?" Jacobi asks, cool as ice. "You were inside. What was that like?"

I twitch along my entire back. "At the end, awful," is all I can manage.

"Blood and treasure," Jacobi says, with the respectful yet discouraged tone only an experienced warrior can manage. She gives me the benefit of another direct look, like a confession. I can guess what she's thinking. It should have been her.

But that's not it, not entirely.

I want out of this fucking Tonka. I'll take my chances on the Red. I do not want to be any part of this cabal of butchers, whatever their rank, civilian or brass or grunt—dead or alive. I jerk forward as if to get up—but then close my eyes and force myself back.

I wanted to return. I wanted to see what really happened, how it all turned out. Now I'm here. Eyes back to my boots. I'm okay. The cup of my helm is filling with sweat. The suit draws it back but can't hide my own stink.

I'm *okay*.

I can still feel Jacobi's eyes.

Borden continues. "The survivors from the Drifter managed to organize and break through Antag forces—a remarkable feat considering the pasting a fresh flotilla of our own orbital assets was delivering to the enemy and to the Drifter at the time. During a lull, with the Antags in disarray, landers were dispatched, and our troops were lifted to orbit and returned to Earth."

"Who ordered the pasting?" Jennings asks.

"Gurus," Ishida says. Jennings elbows her, but it probably

hurts—funny bone intersecting metal. "Everyone just fucking wants it gone!" Ishida insists. "Why? What's so bloody important?"

That conversation won't stop. The Skyrines buzz on. The Russians look aloof but don't convince. Jacobi keeps watching me. She won't give me a break. I'm the fucking linchpin.

We have to get this done.

"What happened to the Voors?" I call out, interrupting the others. "Litvinov carries pictures...."

"We're here now to protect the settlers," Borden says. By her look of nervous keenness, like a dog about to flush a partridge, she totally gets what's happening in the cabin, the danger and the opportunity. We're like a raw blade pulled from a hot flame. If she strikes with the right hammer, she's got us—she anneals and strengthens. But one wrong blow...flying shards.

Borden strikes. "Since there was no way to evacuate noncombatants to orbit, the woman known as Tealullah Mackenzie Green, who rescued some of our Skyrines, and whose camp was destroyed in the first strikes, was handed over to the surviving Voors. The settlers made their way across a hundred and fifty kilometers to an emergency cache they had established years before. Five of them survived the journey, and joined hundreds of other refugees from other camps."

"What sort of cache?" I ask.

"An abandoned domicile, associated with a mining operation similar to the Drifter," Kumar says.

"How many of these moon things are there?" Jennings asks.

"Fourteen fragments large enough to detect and map from orbit," Borden says. "Two have been investigated. The first was mined extensively by Algerian settlers, taken over by the Voors—then abandoned when it was flooded by an underground river, a hobo. That first mine was called the Drifter. The second...The Algerians dug some ways in, how far is unknown, before they abandoned it. The Voors were never able to get back inside."

"No coin," I say.

"Correct," Borden says.

"Master Sergeant Venn came into possession of that coin," Kumar says. "He found it in a pair of overalls in the Drifter. And he carried it back with him from Mars."

"Man of mystery!" Jacobi says.

I flip her off. She smiles sweetly.

"I came upon a copy of Venn's...ah, report, but not the coin," Kumar says. "Apparently, the coin itself was necessary to gain entry. And that was somewhere on Earth—so we thought. So we informed the Gurus, before Division Four made its move toward independence."

"Was on Earth?" I ask.

"The coin is now on Mars," Kumar says.

That adds further confirmation to Joe's picture in Litvinov's pocket. The somebody I trusted at Madigan managed to get it to Borden, who passed it on to Joe. Joe carried it back to Mars. That's what we all wanted, isn't it? Does *any* of it make sense?

"Why not just blow their way in?" Ishida asks.

"Huff and puff," says Corporal Paul Saugus.

Borden looks down the aisle. "Force has proven counterproductive in these locations," she says.

"Silicon plague!" Mori says. Jacobi steps on his boot, not hard enough to break anything. The others yammer until Jacobi pointedly shuts them up. Then she stands and braces against a roof beam. "Commander, who are we really here to serve or save? Nobody gave a fuck about the settlers in the beginning. Why all the fuss now?"

Kumar's eyes are hooded. "Because of Earth's embargo on communications from Mars, we knew nothing about these endeavors. When we revealed the existence of the first fragment and mining operation to the Gurus, they expressed interest. It seemed to me they were not surprised, though it is always hard to read their emotions—if they have any. Then—within weeks—the Gurus ordered us to locate and do all we could to block access to the mine, and to destroy it, if at all feasible. As well, we were ordered to locate and isolate settlers who had worked in or visited the mines. When we asked for explanation, none was given.

"At this stage, a number of Wait Staff in Division Four expressed long-simmering doubts. We wished to learn more about the mine before it could be destroyed—but made sure to keep our interest secret from the Gurus. Within a few weeks, two members of the Wait Staff in India and Pakistan, team leaders in Division Four, convinced senior officers in the Pentagon, U.S. Joint Sky Defense command. Those officers secretly ordered a number of Skyrines and other personnel already on Mars to investigate the mine, and protect the settlers if possible."

"Joe," I say.

"Lieutenant Colonel Sanchez. Your team was to supplement their operation," Kumar says. "Though you never received your final orders. Other divisions learned of those efforts, our officers were arrested, and their replacements ordered the training and fast dispatch of a Special Ops team. That team was commanded by Captain Coyle. They were to locate and destroy the Drifter, from within if possible. No one was to prevent them from carrying out that mission, including settlers and their fellow Skyrines."

"*Shit*," Jennings says, shaking her head.

"The competing forces arrived within weeks of each other, during a busy season of combat on Mars. They were scattered and disorganized both by internal sabotage and opposition from the Antagonists."

"The Antags also tried to destroy the mine—didn't they?" Jacobi says.

"That soon became obvious, and the size and strength of Antagonist efforts added to our suspicions. Why would two enemy forces in effect coordinate to destroy a potential source of fascinating data? With our efforts scrambled and conflict mounting within the Wait Staff divisions, we were forced to delay. Wait Staff gathered as much information as they could from the survivors of the Battle of Mars and devised a comprehensive threat analysis," he says. "I personally presented those scenarios to the Gurus."

"What did the Gurus say?" I ask.

"They expressed regret that the destruction had been delayed, then informed us that the so-called silicon plague might not be the greater worry. There was potential for the green powder inside the Drifter to become even more dangerous. Once we delivered our reports, orders were issued within days to renew our efforts to destroy the Drifter and its contents.

"By this time, a number of us within Division Four were firmly convinced that the Gurus were not being truthful. Then, somebody at or near the Guru level ordered the quarantine of all personnel returning from Mars—followed by select executions. They called them necessary sterilizations."

"*Fuuuuck!*" says Jennings, drawing the word out with mounting rage. Jacobi puts a hand on her shoulder.

"Master Sergeant Venn was the only one we could rescue. As we worked to establish a political counterforce, and absorbed the results of our few studies on the old ice moon, some of us drew further-reaching conclusions. We became concerned about the entire rationale behind our other ongoing conflicts, those in the outer solar system."

"Titan," Jacobi says.

"Yes, as well as several expensive exploratory expeditions to Europa, which seemed to come into focus as more than just idly scientific," Kumar says. "These orders were followed by promises of more advanced technology, even more powerful weapons and faster ships."

"We've seen some of those," Jennings says.

"Not all," Kumar says, then winces, as if he might be speaking ahead of his point. "Our forces were unable to complete their missions, but Antagonists were in a more advantageous position, and continued pouring down as much destruction as they could, plowing up the surface of Mars, then sending in additional battalions...no doubt depleting long-term reserves and putting them at a strategic disadvantage throughout the solar system. Why put themselves at such risk? Perhaps because they, too, had been ordered to do so.

"When the activity subsided on Mars and Titan, Division Four split from other Wait Staff and started reaching out to those we suspected or hoped were in agreement. They turned out to be more plentiful than we expected."

"Split command. That's fucked-up," Jennings says.

Durov and Federov divide their piloting attention to look

back down the aisle, as if checking mood and temperature—or just observing a greater awakening to some new truth.

"Who's giving the orders now?" Jacobi asks.

"Division Four no longer takes orders from the Gurus," Kumar says. "We are an independent authority."

"What about the Russians?" Jacobi looks forward. Russians and Skyrines exchange glances. Federov keeps his gaze on the Tonka's cabin.

"On the fence," Kumar says. "But so far cooperating, perhaps to gain traction for some of their own initiatives."

"What about Jacobi's squad?" I ask.

Borden answers that. "Captain Jacobi and her team have agreed to the new command."

"You trust them?" I ask.

"Fuck you," Jennings says.

"Silicon plague turned everything upside down," Ishida says. "Every one of our sisters who came back got locked up—and then executed."

Pause on that.

"Enough *trust*, asshole?" Jennings asks me.

"We couldn't save them all," Borden says.

Another quiet spell.

"None of that tells us who's in charge of the sappers," Jacobi says.

Sergeant Durov says, "We return fire and kill. Not to ask or to think."

"Why rations with vodka," murmurs Federov.

I'm reminded of the MREs attached to the bunch of Russian tents that saved our asses last drop. Vee-Def straggled in off the Red and invaded our tent, scaring us and waking us up. He stuck a piece of reindeer sausage up his nose as a joke, then snorted it out, covered in snot. That nose is still out here somewhere. Along with the rest of his head. So why doesn't Vee-Def talk to me, if I'm being haunted by dead Skyrines?

Because he did not turn glass.

That conclusion is so stunningly obvious that I wonder at my stupidity not to have thought of it before.

The Tonka rumbles and jounces over deep ruts.

"We should be in the Chesty and the Trundle, on weapons," Ishikawa grumbles from the back.

"Our best soldiers man weapons," Durov says. "*Polkovnik* riding with them, keep you safe. In good hands. He is why you are not dead."

The Tonka slows and runs alongside a high gray ridge that stretches across our entire field of vision. We swing left with a shudder and a couple of slams and roll up a rise of undulating, cracked basalt about half a klick long that forms a bumpy ramp to the crest of the ridge. The Tonka noses down and halts. Sergeant Durov has expertly arranged to give us a tourist's vantage. Skyrines and Russians crowd up front or glim through the side ports.

Jacobi, still brooding, is invited forward by Borden—a crook of one gloved finger. She squeezes in between me and Borden. Doesn't want to touch me if she can avoid it. Weird fucking emotions. I did not know about the other executions. Somehow, I always assume my misfortunes are special. I'm suspect in part because I'm not dead and some of their friends are. Better and better.

Through the dusty plastic, we see the rim of the biggest crater we've yet encountered, maybe eleven klicks across, a massive, scythe-shaped upthrust that mingles old surface basalt and lower crust. The crater's far wall is an irregularity along the horizon, interrupted by a dark, jagged peak that rises a few hundred meters out of the center.

"This is the Drifter?" I ask.

"Until recently," Borden says.

"It's *gone.*"

"Huge impact," Borden says. "The smaller surrounding craters are backscatter, ejecta. The prominence is the central peak. There's still a big portion of the fragment left below, but it's pretty shook up."

"With more activity than anyone could have expected," Kumar says.

"Perhaps due to nitrogen from cometary ammonia," Borden says. For the moment, I ignore that as irrelevant—though a conversation flashes into memory: the old Voor talking about essential ingredients, *stikstof*—nitrogen.

I make out a series of beige level surfaces this side of the peak. Could be lightly dusted frozen lakes—something I've never seen on Mars.

"The hobo is still flowing," I say.

Kumar agrees and points. "Look there. And there. Those are not dust devils."

Beyond and to the left of the peak rises a thin white plume, and then, almost invisible, four or five more. Venting steam. The magma under the Drifter is still hot, still coming in contact with the hobo. But it's no longer capped off, no longer sealed under the fragment of moon.

"There's magma close to the surface," I say. "Too hot for Voors or miners. All that's left down there is probably dissolved or melted."

"Possibly not," Kumar says. "As we said, there is still activity. We do not refer to seismic activity."

"Everything in that hole is brown or gray but the center," Jacobi says. "Why's that peak so dark and shiny?"

"We think not everything in the mines below was destroyed," Borden says.

"But what's up with all that black shit—sir?" Jacobi asks.

Kumar is about to interrupt when comm crackles and Litvinov demands entry. He passes through the lock and the Russians brush him down before he carries forward a steel bottle and offers us hot coffee. The Russians distribute tin cups. Our Skyrines join in with the sudden manners of polite society. I don't ask where the Russians got coffee.

"No doubt you see water and heat," Litvinov says as we sip. "Before last and biggest impact, we sent exploration team inside Drifter—down deep. Instructed to bring back specimen from crystal pillar. Some brave fool attempted to cut away pieces. He turned dark glass—what you name silicon disease."

"The sample that caused so much trouble—was it from here?" I ask. "Was it your soldier?"

"It *is* him," Sergeant Durov says, and taps his head. "We bring him back, but do not touch him—very difficult. He is filled with lights. No lights when we pack him on return lifter." The colonel's look is intense. "He is dead—but I feel him. Do you?"

I shake my head. The shotgun, Federov, holds his finger to his lips, lightly grips Durov's arm. What's that about? No speaking of the dead? The undead in our heads?

Follows our fourth silence. The Russians are stony, mostly,

but the square-faced soldier clutches his cup and weeps. He's not afraid—he's sad and bewildered. He reaches inside his helm and brushes away tears, then looks aside, ashamed.

"Satellites reported big incoming. We evacuate Drifter," Litvinov says. "Before we get all out—biggest comet does *this*. Half of team, far enough distance, survives... Other half still inside." He swallows hard. These are hard men and women, I know that—but what they've experienced is more traumatic, in some ways, than what our Skyrines went through. "Have you study mountain at center?"

We lower our cups, close our faceplates, and magnify that view. The central peak is not just dark. As Jacobi observed, it's black—with shiny surfaces.

"*That* happen after comet. Everything in center of impact is black glass."

"They blew it the fuck up," I say. "It felt threatened."

"*What* felt threatened?" Litvinov asks sharply. "It is rock! How can rock know fear? You are to give answers! Is it angry at us, Venn?"

"I don't know," I say. "I don't know if anger is part of it."

"I say it *is* angry, deep down," Litvinov insists. "Everything it touches... black glass." He lifts his bushy eyebrows into an arch above his thick, broad nose. "We leave here now. Too dangerous. Too *strange*."

"I believe we've established that nothing practical can be done here," Kumar agrees.

"You know madness from inside," Litvinov says to me. "Old moons, crystal towers, make many things, dangerous, strange, and special. Including, what did you call it? 'Ice Moon Tea.'"

"That was DJ—Corporal Dan Johnson," I say.

"Affects a few of my soldiers. What is it doing to them?" Litvinov asks.

"I'm not sure, sir," I say. "It could make us sensitive to something old. Something still down there."

"Our dead?" Litvinov waves that question off. The colonel's not a believer, and Durov isn't going to convert him. "No understanding, no sense," Litvinov says, then instructs Durov to back us off the rim and begin the long trek to Fiddler's Green. "I will stay with you," he says. "Best soldiers in Chesty, put on strong weapons."

"Good to hear," Kumar says.

Borden quietly observes that central peak until it's out of our sight. I wonder what she knows—what she thinks she knows and how that fits into why I'm here. "What do you see out there?" I ask her.

"Same things you see," she murmurs.

"I do not like being kept ignorant," I say.

"Neither do I. When I know for sure what I'm seeing, I'll tell you. And you'll tell me. Deal?"

"Yeah," I say.

We backtrack, then head northeast. In the rear of the warm Tonka we absorb ourselves, hide ourselves, by finishing the cooling coffee.

Once we are well under way, Litvinov arranges his words carefully, with a tinge of bitterness. "Where we are going, three camps have been attacked and destroyed. For safety, some settlers and your people move into second mine. We delivered to them your token, Master Sergeant Venn." Litvinov reaches into his belt pouch and brings out a quarter-sized circle of inscribed platinum. I recognize the spiral of numbers. It looks like the coin I brought back from Mars, hid from the medicals, then smuggled out to Joe, along with my notes.

"I don't know who it belongs to—I found it in—"

Litvinov waves that off as well. "Joe Sanchez tells me to give it back, so you will know," Litvinov says, and hands me the coin. "Reminder of hard things yet to do."

I'm trying to remember how well the colonel fought back in the bar at Hawthorne. Funny—that stuff is less clear to me than what it feels like to be ridden by a smart parasite under a hundred klicks of ice. I'm thinking the Wait Staff had good reason to be concerned and keep me locked away.

I might not be human much longer.

ACROSS THE DUSTY DESERT

We're twelve hours crossing the huge basalt plain. The going is smoother the farther east we move, away from the battle zone. Kumar is awake but unfocused. Borden spends most of the time sleeping. I've napped and played a little helmet chess with the *starshina*, a slender young woman with small green eyes named Irina Ulyanova, who in other decades might have been a ballerina or a gymnast.

Even the thought that I might see Joe and Teal again is darkened by the realization that it's been a while since we were here and so many things could have happened. Teal could have been forced to mate with one of the Muskies, the Voors—one of de Groot's sons—and squeeze out that fabled third-gen baby, momma and poppa and then infant double-dosed with Ice Moon Tea. I do not want to think about that.

Joe's being here—and Joe himself—are complete ciphers. Was he ever really back on Earth? Alice said he was, but could I trust anything Alice was telling me, back in the condo?

After all, I ended up in the hands of the Wait Staff. I never made it to Canada and freedom.

You don't know folks until you've fought with them. In large part because of my relationship with Joe, fighting fills the list of important things I've done for twelve years. It's all I know, really: how to train to fight and travel to fight and arrive to fight and then just *fight*. Make scrap and stain on the Red. I'm sick and tired of fighting. I want to be done with it. Don't we all. I'm avoiding the main issue, aren't I?

It *really* disturbs me to think about Teal and what might have been. It disturbs me more that I wasn't here for her, but what disturbs me most is the uncertainty she would even have wanted me to stay and help in the first place, or the second place—or any place.

I don't know nothing about anything.

And I'm hungry.

The wind is blowing strong enough to rock the Tonka. There's a light patter on the outer skin.

"What's that?" Borden asks.

"Storm," Litvinov says, hunching his shoulders. "Strange weather always now."

I lean over and look through the windscreen. Little hard bits of white are striking the Tonka—hail. I've never seen hail on Mars. The wind picks up.

Borden becomes sharply interested. "It's because of the comets," she says. "More moisture in the air." As if in a trance, she tries to get closer to the windscreen, but Federov holds out his arm.

"Two kilometers from mine camp," Durov announces. "Going dark fast."

Litvinov squats behind Federov to study the forward view.

The silvery light through the windscreen darkens from pewter to gray steel. The line of vehicles keeps rolling, but this degree of wind and hail is not part of our training. Nobody's fought on Mars during such extreme weather.

The Tonka sways as if kicked by a big boot.

"Tornado!" Durov shouts. The dust devils have given up scribbling and combined to form a Dorothy-sized funnel of dirt and rock, swaying and touching down to our left, rising and wagging like the tail of a huge dog, then digging up our right. I don't know if it has enough strength to lift us—the air is so thin! I can't work up the brainpower to understand how the hell this is even happening—

Then I hear another voice, clear but far off—far *inside*. Bold but also scared:

Let me hook you up to the straight shit, Skyrine. There's a lot to see, but they won't let me do it without you, and I'm getting bored.

I jerk and look around, but nobody's playing a joke, the others are as quiet as little packaged lambs. I stare at Borden. She's focused on the storm. The Tonka shudders and the steely sky flashes. A brilliant white arc moves from left to right across our path.

Sergeant Durov shouts back, "Bolt!"

Litvinov drops his hand. Everyone in the cabin charges sidearms. The *whee*s of ramping energy are painful in the enclosed space. Durov turns the wheel hard left. Through curtains of hail, we see the Trundle in front go just as sharply right. The line is splitting to form a perpendicular to the arc of the bolt, a decent enough maneuver for running over flat and open, if one shot is the only info you have as to location and concentration of opposing force.

Federov returns fire but his choices are few—his targets unseen.

Another bolt. The Trundle on our right erupts in a brilliant violet flare, lighting up the storm and flinging molten chunks of fuselage and frame, then veers toward us and slams our tail, front wheels chattering against our bumper and almost locking before the pilot torques us right and we're free again. We've all sealed our faceplates. We know what's going to happen next. We're sitting ducks in here.

"Outside!" Litvinov shouts. The airlock hatch blows and we push through and jump free, trying to find someplace, anyplace, to lie flat and return fire. The hail is pea-sized and falls faster than it does on Earth—really stings, even though it weighs less. There's a wall of dust and what might be mud spinning off to what I think is the south, obscuring the outline of the big Chesty, which is now laying down a series of sizzling purple barrages.

Then something over to our left fires a volley of chain ballistas, designed to take out vehicles—the double strike of a first charge hitting one side and six meters of thin, strong chain swinging the second charge around to the other side.

One of our guns? I don't think so.

Chain ballistas tend to belong to Antags.

Jacobi is right beside me and Borden is opposite. We all go flatter than flat as two more of our vehicles, right and left, are blown to hell. Sizzling blobs of aluminum and steel and flaring pieces of composite drop all around.

Jacobi's Skyrines disperse into three fire teams, arranged in a spread-out triangle. My status puts me as a fourth wheel on the short team, and Borden thrusts a pistol into my hands.

The hail and wind blow up and away, exposing us to

anyone who cares to look (of course). The air is amazingly clear. Sizzling, popping ice litters the dust—hail drying faster than it can melt. Jacobi sticks up like a meerkat, surveys the flats from her full five nine, then swings her right arm to the northeast. I see our enemy, too, bobbing black dots out there at maybe half a klick. Jacobi pivots and swings her hand southeast—more dots. Things with ill intent fill fighting holes on both sides of our line of travel, as if they knew we'd be coming.

A bolt lifts up and screams to hit not twenty meters off, upending the flaming chassis of the Trundle, which emits that ghastly, up-smeared glow of spent matter depleting all at once into the sky—the vehicle's energy rising in controlled detonation. Three surviving vehicles—two Tonkas and the Chesty—roll around us, any minute *over* us, firing with all they've got at the same targets Jacobi has spotted—quick curves of rising and falling bolts, the straight-out, washboard-roaring, nauseating rip of lawnmower pulses, whiz-screams of disruptors, concentrated on the fighting holes. Two broad patches become flaming blue-green luaus.

Then our team leaps as one and crazy-jogs the distance to where we saw heads bob. I take the run with Ishida and Jacobi. We square off at about ten meters and stoop. Something in the hole is blasting our direction without taking aim, single weapon sputtering half-charged bolts—down to almost nothing. I'm hit by a smoking green blob that tries to burn a hole through my chest but can't do more than crisp the upper layer of skintight. More green blobs lob from the ditch—

One brighter than the others passes over my right, and the

Skyrine behind me—the gunnery sergeant? Tanaka?—keels over flat with fire twisting from his back—

We're within three meters of the ditch, staring down at a fucking Antag sprawled on its back, wings out, doing a dust angel, faceplate fogged, low on gasps, and scared shitless—even so, aiming its bolt rifle over the rim of the hole to zero us if it can.

Ishida drops to her knees, the pair of us behind her follow, and together, we all pump the hole with bolts and a lawn-mower beam until dust and dirt and charred bastard kibble blow from the ditch like the plume from a small volcano.

Another brighter bolt flies over our lowered heads from the Chesty, I hope, and blows the ditch all to hell, knocking us back on our lightly padded asses. We're kept busy for a few seconds cursing and brushing each other off, tamping out the smoking shit with the backs of our gloves. A comic display of self-concern before we even know the fight is over, but what the fuck, it'll be over for *us* right now if our skintights don't hold suck.

I've somehow hit the deck again and spread out. Borden has her arm over my back, cozy-protective. I try to shove her off but she stubbornly shields me. Jacobi stands again, slings her bolt rifle, daring more fire—she'll take it or she'll know where the fuck it comes from, and I admire that, I really do.

Then, "Thirty it. We're done," she says over comm.

Surrounded by little whirls of smoke, in the middle of our own fading dust devil of soot and flakes of enemy, we stop, lift our heads, look around, assess....

We're alive.

Some of us.

I roll out from under Borden's arm but we wait another few seconds to rise, not as ape-shit brave as Jacobi. And perhaps not as sensitive to when the action is over. I'm out of practice, I tell myself—but truly, I accept that Jacobi is superior, I'll follow her anywhere, even knowing we're going to die in the end, because she's so fucking awesome.

Borden shadows me, just inches away. Our brand-new Tonka is behind us, flaring and slumping into puddles of silvery metal. I see maybe three crispy critters within the collapsed and sputtering frame. We are left with two intact vehicles and perhaps twelve Russians and as many Skyrines and of course Kumar, he made it, I've made it—

Shit. I'm pumped, I'm scared, I've pissed and filled my drawers—I've become shit sausage. My skintight works frantically to process what was once safely wrapped in bowels and bladder, as well as filtering the salty, smelly fluid leaking from all of my pores.

All I can say to Borden is "Stinky."

Big-eyed, she nods.

Litvinov and three of his soldiers join us. The Russians take a knee and view the scene through scoped bolt rifles. I hear little seeking *whee*s and clicks.

I can still hear. That's good. One thing about air on the Red is—

Fuck that.

Litvinov sends four more soldiers across the flats to make sure the opposite attackers are down and scrapped. They drop and zig-crawl, rise and run hunched—a talent in low-g, where any little toe jab can loft you like a clay pigeon. When Jacobi gives the all-clear, we cross the dust and join them.

Along the horizon, as if nothing's happened, rise more of those goddamned drunken pillars of dust, reeling and scribbling in Mars's diary: *What you say, Bwana? Bullll-shee-it. Don't look at us. We're busy.*

Jacobi kicks her boot at a piece of charred reddish-gray fabric that barely covers what was once the arm or wing of an Antag warrior. Another step and she nudges a helm, weirdly intact after all that energy—a cup cradling the four-eyed, beaked head of a warrior who came all the way from the distant stars to die right here on the Red. This one looks at us with a lazy, crowlike leer—or maybe not—through two large outboard eyes and two smaller eyes above the bridge of the beak. The eyes are frosting over and shrinking now that the big heat is gone and moisture is being sucked away. Its raspy tongue is frozen between the open halves of the beak, like a bird's, but studded with what look like teeth. Ishida comes over and pries open the beak. Inside—flatter teeth for grinding. It chews with its tongue. More like a squid or a snail, somehow.

Ishida mocks a gag and backs away.

As if conducting a tour, Jacobi joins Ishida and both wave us forward, then jump into one of the Antag fighting holes and pull back strips of camouflaged cover, sliced into six-inch ribbons by our lawnmower. The strips barely conceal a small pressure tank and a broken-bladed fan—a small fountain. For gathering sips and gasps and fuel from the thin atmosphere. The Antags weren't many, at this point in their mission, but they were here for the long haul. And they knew they would die.

Litvinov approaches, opens comm, and turns to me. We're wearing weird little skull grins, both of us; our cheeks hurt,

Momma says our faces will freeze this way—but we're alive, and it's either grin or bawl like a baby, even the big, tough colonel.

He says, "Bet you other *Antagonista* soon come and finish. Is it bet?"

"House always wins," I say.

"Truth," he says. This is afterglow, we're stinky and jazzy and fear isn't in it, not now. We're beyond that sour shit into hypercalm or just plain hyper, a weirdly happy state almost like an out-of-body experience. Like the Antags in the trench, we know we're going to die out here. Nobody fucking goes home.

The colonel scans the smoking wrecks and our own charred dead. Skyrines and Russians join to assess our losses. Taking names and blazes if any. We've heard that Russians reduce their dead in place. There's little oxygen for cremation so bolts do the work. Litvinov's soldiers start that process, shooting energy into the shattered Trundle and two Tonkas, taking care of their dead and ours as well. The vehicles flare purple-white. The corpses wither and smoke. Bits of char and ash top our helms and shoulders. We brush them off.

"Waste of energy," Jacobi says. Hard sister. But this hurts her. It hurts her bad. Including the Russians, we're down by half. Twenty-four of us climb into the Chesty and a Tonka, the only vehicles still functional and carrying charge.

Borden and Kumar, Ishida and Ishikawa, Jacobi, the square-faced young *efreitor*, and the chess-playing gymnast, Starshina Ulyanova. Litvinov. They've made it.

Jennings, Tanaka, Yoshinaga, Mori, Saugus, the pilot Durov, and his shotgun Federov—all dead.

Inside the Chesty, with the Tonka trailing, we cross the

last two klicks. The Russians sit toward the rear, near the lock, shivering and talking about what, I don't know, just talking. I want to talk as well. Screw propriety and courage. Screw everything.

"I heard the captain back there," I say to Borden. It's something to mention, something random that may or may not be important.

"I didn't hear anything," Borden says with less than her usual focus.

"I mean Captain Coyle," I say.

She stares.

Litvinov lifts his gaze. "Ah," he says. "You hear ghost."

"She's not a ghost," I say.

"No? What, then? Others return, you know. Not just your captain. Federov heard! Now he is ghost, too."

Kumar watches with sleepy eyes. He's in shock, I think. He's not hurt, but that doesn't matter.

"If not ghost, what?" Litvinov asks.

"Bored," I say. "Waiting for shit to happen."

"On Mars, dead get bored fast," the colonel says, then adds, in passable American, "*Ain't it the truth.*"

The Chesty's driver calls out in alarm. Through the side port, I see burning hamster-maze domiciles laid out on the brown rock like PVC piping hit by hammers and torches. The camp's temporary housing has been opened to the sky.

I drop my chin and swallow hard.

ARRIVALS AND DEPARTURES

Rather than pass through the Chesty's airlock, we hunker down and the driver opens the side loading hatch. There's a brief gale, a frosty puff, and Borden, Kumar, and Litvinov exit first.

The resettlement camp is in ruins, all but for a single quarter, which is surrounded by a couple of dozen Russian dead, Antags, a small Millie that seems largely intact but empty, until we walk around to the other side and see it's been opened up as if by a can opener and scoured by lawnmower beams. The insides are gruesome.

"They wanted the settlers dead, all of them," Kumar says.

"No shit," Ishida says. "Willing to fight to the last warrior." Jacobi touches her shoulder. She shrugs it off and takes point automatically, leveling her bolt rifle. I almost expect Coyle to add something, but once again she's gone silent. No words, no word balloons—not even static.

Borden watches me like a mother hen over a piebald chick. We walk through a little arched gate, very pretty, that once led to an outdoor tented garden, now flat and torn. Someone dug trenches around the revetments, which look to me as if they're protecting the domiciles and not vehicles. Someone, probably Litvinov, decided on a strategy of mobility and rapid response: Keep vehicles and fountains below ground level, dig fighting holes around the perimeter at fifty meters, prepare the ground to protect what's important.

Six Russians emerge from the forward trenches to greet us. They're all that's left. They gave everything they had pushing back the Antag offensive, and Litvinov isn't bringing them good news, except that—maybe—the last of the enemy have been dispatched.

"All bad guys, toast," a Russian says in passing, shouldering his bolt rifle and accepting a spent matter pack from Ishida. Unless there are human sappers out there with their own orders, ready to move in next. If I had any creep left, I'd be creeped the hell out.

The Skyrines load up from the Chesty's reserve. I'm left with the pistol. Litvinov barks instructions. Vigilance. No rest for anyone. Another Russian comes around the far end of the domicile carrying two lawnmowers, both blinking red—depleted. She stumbles along, worn down, a sticky wrap around one arm and another around her leg to help her suit hold suck. Without a word, she hands me one of the lawnmowers and Ishida the other. I hate lawnmowers as a matter of principle. I hate the noise they make, I hate what they do, and I've never used one in combat—trained with them, of course, back at Mauna Kea—but I'm glad to have it. The lawnmower means I'm no longer a fucking POG. Ishida passes me two spent matter packs and we lock and heft and wait for the lights to go steady green, then dark blue. Borden watches. No objections. She lends four Skyrines to the Russians. Jacobi goes with them and instructs Ishida and Ishikawa to follow Borden, Kumar, and me to the last intact domicile.

Litvinov waves for Ulyanova to unlock a small fountain. We climb down brick steps to the tap. "Take what you need," the colonel says. "The mine is two klicks north. We stay here."

"Understood, Colonel," Borden says. "Apologies, but we're taking the Chesty, sir."

Litvinov shifts his boot in the dust. "We do our best," he says.

At Borden's nod, Ishida hands back her lawnmower. The Russian *efreitor* who gave it to her, in hopes perhaps that the Chesty would now be available, receives it with a side look at the colonel. Borden then gestures for me to give my lawnmower to Ishida. I hand it over. POG again, but it's all good and we're good to go. Six of us climb into the Chesty. All but three sentries head for the domicile to rest and organize. The domicile has a big lock on the north end, sadly adequate to pack them all in at once. Clearly we're not taking time to stop and compare notes. I wonder who's left inside. I wonder who's at the mine. The second chunk of old moon.

Jacobi drives. Kumar takes the side seat. Borden sits beside me. Ishida and Ishikawa take seats on either side of me. Nobody says a word.

Ishida periodically taps her mechanical arm and grimaces. The wrist is softly clicking. Whatever tech they give Skyrines never works as advertised. I wonder what it's like to be made one with your equipment.

You'll find out.

Quoth Coyle. Only that, and nothing more.

BAD MOON RISING

The ride to the mine is quiet and swift. We seem to have temporarily run out of things that want to kill us. The weather gets weirder, however—spooky fog lies in a fine, low carpet over the basalt and dust, a few rocks poking through like tiny islands. Briefly, looking through the Chesty's narrow slits, I feel like we're in a jet cruising above overcast. Then, as if at the snap of a magician's finger, the fog bristles into spikes and vanishes. Poof.

We climb a rise. Ahead is a sullen gray promontory, blocky and crenellated like an ancient castle, about a hundred meters broad and thirty high. Not as impressive as the Drifter's old swimmer, but more than enough to draw attention on the monotonous plain.

As if pointing an accusing finger, a dust devil rises over the castle's brow, dances a gray little jig, touches the Chesty's nose, then picks up its skirts and dissolves. A scatter of sand rattles on the windscreen.

"Coin?" Borden asks.

I take it from my pouch and hold it up for her inspection. As returned by Litvinov, perhaps at Joe's request. She says, "Good. Now we see who we can trust."

Jacobi draws us up onto a cleared square of brushed lava and gravel in the shadow of the castle. She parallel parks, as hidden from the sky as possible—and shuts down the main drives but leaves the weapons on full charge. Again, we disembark through the wide side hatch, never having pressurized the interior. Out of habit, I check the Chesty's water and oxygen supply, prominently displayed beside the hatch. Levels are at one-sixth. Quick calculation tells me that if there's nothing left in the mine, no taps and no reserves, and somebody finishes off their work at the camp, we'll have about four hours of sips and gasps. Jacobi notes this as well. Our eyes meet over the helm readout. She gestures for me to follow Borden. Ishikawa and Ishida flank us as we step down. A tight little cordon. I feel like a Roman emperor. Speaking of Rome, I could use a good orgy. Wonder what Ishida's skills are in that regard—that little conversation—

Don't think I'm a nutless, squeaky-clean Skyrine. I hope Coyle isn't rummaging deep in my basement, and not because I fear she'll run into old shellfish. Wonder if they all mix it up down there. Ghosts who aren't ghosts, bugs who aren't bugs, squared off in a primordial do-si-do.

"Venn!" Borden calls out over comm. She's found a tall inset in the rock, mostly hidden by shadow. A quick sortie by Ishida shows us, using her paler silhouette for scale, that the cavity is about ten meters deep and nine high. There's a rusty steel hatch about the right size for a buggy or a bus, and a smaller personnel hatch beside it. Architecture may vary from mine to Muskie mine, but the basics are the same. Now to find the lock. We step into shadow and search around the hatch. Ishida finds the little panel first, on the right, behind an inset, spring-loaded push-plate that opens with a strong poke. The others form a cordon. I approach the panel, coin foremost, wondering if we could ever find it again if I fumbled—here in the gravel and dust—

The insertion point is obvious, like a slot in a coin-operated clothes washer. Nothing fancy. Might be molecular-level recognition of the coin's metallurgy, damned difficult to duplicate, plus the number spiral—an encrypted description of the coin itself—

Maybe. How should I know? I am more nervous now than I was getting out of Madigan. Back there, I had adrenaline pumping and the sheer joy of breaking out of stir. Here—

I'm down to piss, no vinegar. Don't know what we're going to find. Joe, Teal, the Voors—maybe the old bantam himself, de Groot, herding his sons around in the dark—

Or everyone dead? Turned to black glass?

The wide hatch shudders but does not open. Instead, the little personnel hatch creaks and shoves inward, giving us access to the smaller lock beyond. Bet it all. We push through, leaving the Chesty with just Ishikawa on guard—packing the bolt rifle to protect the Chesty's weapons, in case we need to make a hasty retreat. Ishida carries the lawnmower. Within the walk-in closet of a lock, we brush off and cycle through. The inner hatch opens and, as always, our ears pop. On the other side, a long garage has been carved out of lava and sealed with plastic sheeting. There's room for three buggy-sized vehicles. Currently the garage holds one buggy, plus, on shelves to our left, the suits and gear of the current inhabitants, which I estimate number forty or fifty. No names on the folded and packed skintights, just numbers. Farther back in the shadows, I make out plastic cargo modules, their transparent sides revealing hints of steel and round green surfaces, square gray surfaces, in-between bits filled with pipes or wires.... Equipment. Tons of it. And beyond those crates, a stack of more crates emptied, folded, and compacted. At some point, the mine received a lot of support.

Kumar and I open our faceplates. The air inside is clean. Kumar sneezes, which is impolite up here. Colds that can't be suppressed by antivirals spend about two weeks infecting all before they burn out their host reservoirs, kind of like brush fires, and we're the brush. A cold in a skintight is less than optimal. Snot has nowhere to go—nowhere good—and sneezing is painful.

"Just dust," Kumar says, looking around. "I'm fine."

Funny how the trivial magnifies. We'd rather be thinking about cold viruses—not so much about turning glass.

"Sir, Venn," Borden says, "please close your plates. We keep sealed until we learn what's happening."

"Of course, yes," Kumar says. "Apologies."

We seal up again. Typical that those instructions weren't made clear from the beginning. Then again, for me, does it matter?

The garage's far steel hatch opens with a clattering hiss, and a ruddy, middle-aged man in a white tunic steps through. He looks like a Greek in a college play. I don't recognize him. "Welcome to Fiddler's Green," he announces in a voice at once oily and assured. "We hear you've had a bit of a trek!" He looks beyond Borden and Ishida and spots Kumar. His smile inverts and his face becomes a drawn olive mask. "Kumarji!

You have finally decided to break with your masters and join us. Perhaps it is not too late."

"You left me in ignorance!" Kumar says, and moves through the press of Skyrines toward tunic man, who, as the distance closes, looks less and less sure of himself. Kumar backs tunic guy up step for step, until he's against the plastic-wrapped rock. "We were attacked," Kumar says. His head moves as if he's examining the path of a fly zipping around tunic guy's head.

"What could you expect? I told you not to force their hand!" Tunic guy draws himself to his full height, hands clenching a fold of dingy cloth before his crotch as if afraid Kumar might punch him in the 'nads. "Division Four was in disagreement, we could not be sure you would accept. You were the last—"

Kumar suddenly swoops. "You *idiot*!" he shouts and slaps tunic guy square on the face. He reacts with a snort, then leans against the wall. "If I could, I'd throw you out on the Red," Kumar says. "I'd leave you out there *naked*. After you gave me your assurance we would work in tandem, stay in touch..."

"How could I know? Division Four was split from the start," tunic guy says.

"We hadn't finished our work! You always were a grandstanding son of a whore!"

Tunic guy drops his gaze.

Jacobi whispers to Borden, "Who the fuck is he?"

Borden replies, also in a whisper, as Kumar and tunic guy continue to argue, "Krishna Mushran, head of Mumbai Research Authority."

"Wait Staff?" Ishida asks.

Borden nods. "One of the first to be invited to meet with the Gurus."

Jacobi makes her mock-impressed face—eyebrows raised, lips pinched—and says, "Terrific. What now?"

Kumar looks back to the rest of us, who are either increasingly concerned (Borden) or neutrally bemused (the Skyrines), and says, "Will someone please detain this man.... Is there a brig, a cell, a goddamned *hole* into which you can stuff him?"

"You have no such authority," Mushran says, rubbing his cheek. "And we are past that now. I have—"

"You've been out of touch for months," Kumar says. "Division Four is united and more powerful than ever. We've done your work for you."

"Did he order the attacks on the Russians and the camps?" Ishida asks Borden. The commander shakes her head—she doesn't know. None of us moves.

Kumar looks over his shoulder again at Borden, a kind of expectant glare. Borden rouses and says, "Captain Jacobi, please take this man into custody."

"Yes, ma'am. Where shall I put him? And how shall I log his detention?"

"Just hold on to him."

Jacobi motions and she and Ishida flank Mushran, take him under his arms, and lift him until his feet kick.

"There is no need of this!" Mushran squeals. "Kumarji, our meeting brings good news—"

"No thanks to you!" Kumar growls. His eyes are actually popping a little and there's sweat on his cheeks. "Soldiers have died. *Wait Staff* have died."

"Not my doing!" Mushran says. "I came here and beyond to supervise a difficult situation, in order to speed progress! I have arranged scientific work, medical exams—all this is far more important than the Gurus let on!" Then he gives in to his own anger and begins cursing in Hindi, loudly and with some talent, if I'm any judge—curses being what I studied most back at Madigan.

Kumar steps through the hatch and we follow. Mushran and his Skyrine escorts come last. The tunnel beyond is bare reddish-black rock, no visible veins of crystallized metal. Little lights glow steadily in a shallow furrow along the ceiling.

"You can't begin to know what's down here!" Mushran calls out. Ishikawa clamps a hand over his mouth, but Borden shakes her head, not necessary. She doesn't let loose.

Then we hear the cry of a baby. Louder, insistent.

Mushran watches with concern as a trio of shadows emerges from the gloom at the end of the tunnel. The Skyrines raise their weapons.

"Do not shoot!" Mushran shouts through the muffling gloves. "Do not fear! They are no threat! The only danger down here is you!"

"Let us take this slowly," Kumar says. Borden waves for the rifles and lawnmower to be lowered, then signals hold tight. The squad stands down—slightly.

Two males and a very tall female pass from deep shadow to dim light. My heart skips a beat. I hope it's Teal and Joe and maybe Tak, or maybe Kazak—our old team regrouping on the Red—but my eyes are watering and I can only make out that they're all wearing white tunics stained with green.

Borden leans in close to me. "Muskies?" she asks. I squint and recognize one of de Groot's sons, Rafe, I think—and then

DJ. The tall female beside DJ is not Teal but could be her sister. She's carrying a baby, suckling now and quiet.

"All Muskies except for the skinny dude," I say.

"Hey, it's Vinnie!" DJ calls out, and steps ahead from the group, approaching until Jacobi shouts, "Hold your ground!"

DJ looks surprised but stops.

Jacobi asks me, pointedly, "Do you recognize them?"

I nod.

"I need voice affirmation!"

"I recognize Corporal Dan Johnson, and I think that's one of the Voors—Rafe, Rafe de Groot. I do not recognize the female."

"So noted," Jacobi says, comparing DJ's picture in her helm with the living article.

DJ by now has realized how strung out we are. "Vinnie?" he says plaintively. "That *is* you, isn't it?"

I wave.

"Fuck, I knew you'd find a way back! Joe and Tak—they're here! We'll be a team again!"

Kumar observes our exchange as if we're all lab rats in a maze. Mushran also seems intrigued. At heart, both are still whirly-eyed inquisitors.

I say, "Your turn, DJ. Who's with you?"

"This is Camellia," DJ says. "And you remember Rafe. He's okay now. We're all a big family down here. This place is amazing, Vinnie. You got to take the tour."

Rafe is unhappy to see so many sisters packing heat. He remembers well and slowly edges back.

"Who else is in there?" Jacobi asks.

"Fucking everybody!" DJ says, grinning. "Everybody who counts. We'll show you! There's no danger, Vinnie, it's not like the Drifter—not like that at all. Everything's changing, active, but it's under control, it's friendly—no turning glass! We've accomplished awesome shit! Really! You need to see the stuff we've found. Come on!" He's like an excited little boy.

Rafe takes the opportunity to turn around and glide silently back down the tunnel. The rifles twitch but do not rise. The tall woman and her baby remain, curious, transfixed—fearless? Or just ignorant?

"Let him go!" DJ says. "He doesn't like you guys. He's okay, really."

Borden keeps her hand on my shoulder.

"Who are this infant's mother and father?" Kumar asks.

Mushran chooses to speak. "I may introduce Camellia Vanderveer, and her son, the second of our third-gen offspring."

"Where's the first?" I ask. Before Mushran or DJ can answer and dash my long dreams—

The hatch behind our welcoming committee fills with clambering, clacking clusters of shiny pipes like thick gray straw—translucent, cross-connecting into individuals, then letting loose. Kobolds, DJ called them—the self-assembling workers we found in the first Drifter. The unexpected and alarming mass is punctuated by beady black eyes like camera lenses.

Borden draws back, bumping into Mushran.

DJ says, "It's okay! They're here to help. We've made amazing progress—once we learned to listen to the tea."

I hear "the tea" as well—the gentle suggestion deep in my head that these assemblies, these *servants*, are no threat. They are familiar to a subset of the things that fill my cranium.

But Jacobi and Ishida and Borden have once again raised their weapons and aimed them at DJ, the Muskies, and the kobolds. Knife's edge, I think. Kumar seems fascinated by the entire mess. As if willing to let bygones be bygones, or at least to hold his anger in reserve, he moves closer to Mushran and tells Ishida and Jacobi to release him. "What is this... happening now?" he asks.

Mushran shakes out his arms. "I have not been treated with respect, Kumarji. Let this make itself known without my help!"

"Open your minds!" DJ invites the rest with a big smile. "Let the tea in! If the old moon likes you, things clear up fast."

Nobody knows how to accept his invitation. Nobody, I think, would even if they could.

"Suit yourselves," DJ says with a shrug. "I'll go tell Joe and Tak you're here. See you down deep when everyone's ready to have their minds blown." He steps back through the kobolds, who clatter out of his way and flow back into the darkness.

Camellia's infant has settled down to suckling at her exposed breast, hardly more than a bump on her ribs. The baby's pale skin is mottled with green. The tall mother seems reluctant to leave us—hungry for fresh faces, diversions, society. But finally, with spooky grace and composure, she pulls the baby from her nipple, to soft complaint—then folds up her tunic, turns, and follows DJ.

Mushran takes advantage of our divided attentions. He makes a cautious step forward. Nobody stops him. "There should be a meeting before we enter the preserve. We need to brief these fine soldiers. Please do not interfere with or attempt to damage the workers—the assemblies you saw earlier. That I implore! Am I understood?"

Borden says that no harm will be done to them.

"Good," Mushran says. "The consequences could be catastrophic. Much that is down here, and the reasons we are all here, needs be described. And I am owed explanations, as well, Kumarji. I need to know what has happened on Earth since I left, and since communication was cut off with Mars."

Mushran has adeptly put Kumar in his place, yet strangely, both former Wait Staff seem totally down with the reversal of mood and tactics. They've gone through these games before, I guess, like retainers sparring in a royal court—which is what they are. Or were. And their game is far from over. "First, since you insist on staying in your suits, we should provide replacement filters and top you up with the necessaries," Mushran says. "There must be a chance to rest and recuperate. Do any require medical assistance? Calming drugs?"

"We're fine, sir," Borden says. "We'll keep our filters and such for the time being. We'd like to move on to the next phase."

"Then please, come with me."

A LITTLE KNOWLEDGE

Mushran makes sure the way is clear and leads us from the garage and equipment hangar through rough-cut tunnels to a hemispherical chamber about ten meters across and five tall, which leads to three branching corridors—all lined with the same pale gray plastic and lit by strings of low-power lights. Kumar is content to be quiet and follow, so Borden and the rest of our group follow as well. Mushran turns into a broader corridor, this one square in profile, with two long, parallel grooves like guide rails cut into the floor.

The sheets of plastic come to an end, revealing that walls and ceiling and floor are no longer dark stone but almost pure nickel-iron, shiny and etched with sprays of big metal crystals formed over millions of years deep in the heart of the old ice moon. The way the lights reflect on the buffed walls, we seem to walk in a shadowy fog. I remember that from the Drifter.

Mushran leads us up a gentle incline and then through a dogleg into a narrow, long room lit by three lamps on stands.

I could be getting closer to seeing my buds again, and closer to Teal. Things might be moving forward at a real clip. And something inside me is reacting positively, as well—*not* my inner shellfish. Captain Coyle. If she thinks we're making progress, finally getting somewhere, I have no idea how I should feel, because she's past cark and care, right?

I am not a fucking ghost, Venn. Got that? And what the hell does cark *mean?*

All righty, then. The word balloon has filled in very clearly, accompanied by a voice that sounds at least vaguely female.

I'm not alone, wherever the hell I am. This place is full of extremely weird shit, the kind of shit nobody can train for—nobody has ever prepared for—and I'd like to know what the bloody hell is going on.

"Yes, ma'am," I murmur. "Me, too."

Borden sees my lips move. "You okay, Venn?"

"Yes, ma'am," I say. "We're fine." Borden doesn't even favor me with a pitying look.

Mushran has pulled a flat rectangle out from the wall. I wonder if it's a door, a hatch, or maybe something exotic. It's giving him difficulty, wedged behind a flap of insulation, catching on a plastic strap. We watch with wary fascination. What's this fucker up to? What magic trick is he going to demo to our amazed and childlike eyes? If it's a door, is there something weird behind it—more kobolds, or worse, something we've never seen before? The long rectangle is not cooperating. "Just a moment," Mushran says, and gives it a jerk. It clatters back, rattles against the wall, and teeters loose into his hands.

Everyone lifts their weapons.

"Here it is," Mushran says. "Not a problem."

"God*damn*," Borden mutters through her teeth.

Mushran frees the rectangle from the strap, lowers it to the floor, then looks up at us. "Some assistance, please?"

It's a folding table. We're all pretty strung out. All but Kumar, who has kept this disembodied, steady smile on his face the whole time, observing with his big, warm black eyes.

"A little help?" Mushran asks again around the group of stock-still Skyrines. "I believe there are chairs over there—behind those boxes, perhaps."

Borden tips her head. The Skyrines fall out and chip in to set up the makeshift conference room. When the table and enough chairs to seat eight have been unfolded and arranged, Borden acts as mother and decides who sits where. She puts Kumar at the head, which Mushran accepts without protest.

I notice Rafe has joined us again. He's standing in the doorway, listening.

"Mr. de Groot—please, come in," Mushran says.

De Groot gives me a look, as if trying to think why my face should be familiar, then sits at the far end. He doesn't like Skyrines. No reason he should. The sister who's taken up lodging in a corner of my head would have killed him and his entire family. And after listening to Teal's story, maybe I would have as well.

This is getting cozy.

"I will begin," Mushran says. "Some years ago, a settler at Green Camp reached out to ISD troops and passed along descriptions of the Drifter and several other mines, which he thought might be of strategic importance—for their mineral stores."

I assume this was Teal's father. For his pains, he was eventually put out on the Red—left to die by the Voors.

"He thought that Earth would lavish more money and attention on the settlers if they knew of their expertise regarding these resources. The news caused a stir throughout Wait Staff. Contradictory responses emerged. The division charged with strategic planning for the war against the Antagonists expressed interest in exploring the old fragments, and in recruiting the settlers to help us secure their resources. But another division took a quite opposite point of view. They began to plan for the complete destruction of the settlements and any settlers who had visited these sites. No explanation was given, and such was our loyalty to the Gurus that none was requested."

Rafe clenches his jaw.

"But some pushed forward a more reasoned plan. Before any drastic action would be taken, it was decided that a reconnaissance survey on Mars had to be conducted. The Gurus did not seem to object. As part of a larger strategic push, select groups of soldiers would be tasked with finding and describing the old mining sites. Despite our best efforts, however, our planning came a cropper."

"What does that mean?" Ishida asks. "I don't know that word."

"Fucked-up," Jacobi says.

"Yes. That." Mushran continues: "Antagonists shipped many divisions of troops to Mars, along with a tremendous increase in orbital assets—and finally, a barrage of comet strikes. What appeared to be an attempt to disable or totally destroy our forces seemed, under closer observation, to more plausibly be an attempt to render the Drifter—the primary old moon site—inaccessible.

"Some of us—I credit Kumarji here—found this coincidental focus on the Drifter by both the Gurus and the Antagonists to be suspicious. Why would the Antagonists not want to exploit all available resources? Their supply lines were even more strung out than ours.

"And then, we discovered that those in Division Four responsible for long-range strategic planning—"

"And clandestine operations," Kumar says.

Mushran defers. "They ordered that Special Forces be trained and sent to destroy the Drifter. Perhaps not coincidentally, my original division—Division One, release and promotion of technological benefits—was kicked into high gear to make available the technology necessary to produce far more powerful spacecraft. High-speed probes sent to Jupiter and Saturn added to our knowledge of distant moons with deep oceans of liquid water, encased in shells of ice. The same sort of ice moon that once fell on Mars. The technology used on those probes was expanded. When the first three ships were finished, because of their configuration, they were referred to by our construction teams as Spooks. The Russians called them Star Gowns."

"There was one in orbit around Earth, last we saw," Kumar says. "Along with a very large Box."

"Yes. Well, each of these Spooks carried four divisions of Skyrines and forty scientists out to Saturn. The journey took three weeks. All in secret. We soon discovered that Antagonists had already begun extensive operations on Titan."

"Old and cold," I murmur.

"Old and cold," Mushran agrees. "The Gurus insisted

that we could not allow Antagonists to exploit the resources of the outer solar system, any more than we had on Mars. Our troops were supplied with very large, specialized weapons and vehicles. They journeyed down to Titan and soon engaged Antagonist forces on practically equal terms. That front heated up until it consumed more than half of our resources, which put a strain on our Martian operations.

"To some of our brightest minds, the coincidences became too great to be ignored. It seemed the Gurus were feeling more threatened by the old moons, or something they contained, than by Antagonist domination. What could this possibly be?" Mushran looks around the room. He must have been a teacher once. He's enjoying the chance to play professor.

"Turning glass," Jacobi says, lips pursed behind her plate.

Kumar folds his arms and surveys the dark metal ceiling.

"Most interesting," Mushran says. "But not our primary concern."

"Shellfish," I say.

Jacobi gives me a disgusted look, like I'm the snotty kid acting out in class.

"What the hell does that mean?" Ishida asks.

But Mushran agrees. "Indeed, the former inhabitants of the old moon that fell on Mars. Powerful and consistent visions were being supplied to a few settlers, as well as a small number of our troops, after exposure to the contents of the Drifter."

Jacobi asks, "Why bring Venn here? What does he know about it?"

Rafe has been tapping his finger on the table, a hollow drumming signaling his impatience. Kumar ignores Jacobi's question and turns toward the Voor, who shoves back his folding chair and rises. "Time a look-see," Rafe says. "Everyone as thinks they wor masters, powered an' wise, come a with." He sounds more like Teal now. I'm not sure I like that. What the fuck does it mean that his accent has changed?

"Lead on," Kumar says.

OLD AND IMPROVED

"Two hours before we need to hit the taps," Jacobi reminds Borden. The commander nods. That's a kind of time limit, then, to determine what our options are—whether we go all in and throw in our lot with the settlers and Joe and DJ and whoever else is here, or get back outside, decontaminate, and...

What?

Another possibility presents itself. If this mine is the wellspring of an undesirable variety of madness—uncontrollable shit that nobody wants to deal with, worse than turning glass—then we'll simply be cut loose. The next step—whatever that may be—will be made without us.

At the head of a widening tunnel, Rafe is joined by three other men I don't recognize, all dressed in the same white tunics streaked with green. No introductions are made. Rafe speaks to them in that bastard version of Dutch-Afrikaans affected by the Voors. Two break off and head down a side branch into a shadowy gloom with a white glow at the end.

Jacobi arranges her sisters in a spaced V, as wide as the tunnel allows. I itch to join their formation, but despite our action on the Red, she doesn't invite me. I do not want to be kept apart, but—

I get it. I hate it, but I get it. If I were Jacobi, I'd distance myself both from Borden—Navy rank—and me, shithead, VIP POG, as far as I could run.

It's Ishida who haunts me in a way I can't define. I keep looking at her. Jacobi and Ishikawa notice, but we're moving too fast for them to call me out. I've met three Winter Soldiers in my years in the Skyrines—never in space, never in combat. We all wonder what it would be like to be torn apart and put back together, made into something not quite human—better than human, more than flesh-and-blood Skyrine, according to some reports from those who should know—but difficult to reintegrate with the Corps, a judgmental and suspicious culture that resists challenge and change because everything we go through and especially combat overloads us with challenge, drowns us in uncontrollable change. We *hate* change. We hate newbies because they replace people we were getting used to. What if the newbie is actually someone we knew who is now someone different? But my fascination with Ishida goes beyond that.

Is it because I'm not entirely human, myself?

You've got real problems, Venn, Coyle says.

There's that, too.

The tunnel has gradually expanded to about ten meters wide and five meters high as other tunnels combine, the supporting walls replaced by textured beams that then also go away as we're surrounded by solid ancient rock and nickel-iron, not going anywhere. Vetted by the best mining engineers on Mars. Maybe by some of our people as well.

The light brightens ahead. Mushran and Rafe lead the way around a broad, curving corner—metal phasing into rock, finally becoming rock all around, with the plastic cover going up again as a moisture block.

What stretches up and out beyond that curve has been lit up like a nighttime bridge on a holiday. Red, blue, and green lights rise in sweeping lines along ramparts that begin on a broad, flat floor, then gradually descend to wrap around and intersect more rocky pillars, creating an interwoven, maniacally complicated cloverleaf with nine or ten levels—dropping hundreds of meters below the firm, dusty floor into the heart of the old fragment—encapsulating and supporting great masses of diamond-white crystal.

Borden and Jacobi and Kumar stare in astonishment at this immense and extraordinary excavation. "Is this like the first Drifter?" Borden asks me.

"Yeah, but more."

The first Drifter's digs—what the Voors called the Church—had revealed a tall, intact chunk of white crystal, surrounded by braces and struts of rock. In retrospect, and seeing what has been done here, I think the goal of the kobolds had been, and still is, to expose as much crystalline surface as they can. Inside Fiddler's Green, at least three times as much has been revealed.

So it can make tea, Coyle says. *Tea to train kobolds.*

"Yeah," I murmur. "And us."

Just below the overlook, pipes spray shimmering liquid over the digs, uniting in a cascade that plunges three hundred meters to fill sparkling pools on the lowest level. Rainbows gather around the inset floodlights. This could be another hobo, an underground channel diverted with the specific purpose of giving the crystals all they require, encouraging the kobold caretakers to finish their work, whatever that might be.

Only two people I can see walk the ramparts below, checking and measuring columns and brackets, flashing their torches up faces of crystal. They wear black hoods and shoulder capes made of the same material as the plastic on the walls, like raincoats. They don't seem concerned about getting wet. One flashes a light up, then nods to the other. They link arms and vanish beneath a rampart.

"Got the layout?" Borden asks me.

"The water is pumped from below," I say. "It recirculates."

Kumar says, "Maximized production. I'm not sure this was ever authorized."

"Nothing in half measures," Mushran says. "Such was implied from the beginning, as soon as we parted from the other divisions. We *go for broke*, no?"

"Why are the Muskies helping?" Jacobi asks. "What's their take?"

"Division Four promised them relocation, supply, and defense," Kumar says. He doesn't seem all that enthusiastic now, seeing what's been accomplished. Jealousy—or too much of a good thing?

"This fragment sat here, inactive, nothing more than a mass anomaly, for over a billion years," Mushran says. "Until we were sent to work with the miners."

From an access hatch a few meters behind us, two men emerge, removing their hoods and capes. My spine tingles seeing them.

"Fucking Vinnie!" Tak says, coming forward and patting my skintight. "Why all the armor?"

Behind him, Joe steps forward, face wreathed in a huge grin. "Master Sergeant," he says. He wraps his arms around me.

"We're old friends," Tak explains. "Vinnie, introductions?"

I hesitantly make the rounds, naming names and ranks, introducing Kumar as former Wait Staff. "Met him at Madigan," I say.

Joe looks abashed. "Sorry about that," he says. "Alice told me you didn't make it across the border."

"I got you the fucking coin," I say behind the faceplate.

"And now we're here." He wipes his face with a green-speckled towel.

Mushran suggests that the tour continue, there is not much time. "Joe, would you carry on?" They seem on good terms. Kumar notes this with precise calm.

"Yeah, well, this big dig looks like we've been here forever, but it's only been a few months," Joe says. "We drilled from the galleries around the upper levels, down to where we hit crystal—then blasted fractured basalt and sandstone a few kilometers east of here, diverting an ancient aquifer until it found its way to Fiddler's Green."

"Deliberate," Borden says.

"Absolutely," Joe says. "When the water began to intersect the rocky layers containing nodules of crystal, it triggered the assembly of kobolds, which began to carve outward through the matrix. Reproducing what happened in the Drifter, but this time... quicker and, as you say, deliberate."

"Water was enough?"

"The comets might have helped speed things up," Joe says. "Lots more nitrogen in the atmosphere."

"The Antags seeded nitrogen…on purpose?" Borden asks. "How does that fit in?"

"There is some thinking that the Antags are also divided and in turmoil over these artifacts," Mushran says. "But any theory of such planned action is not yet widely accepted."

"Weren't you afraid it would make you different—less than human?" Jacobi asks.

"Some of us are affected," Joe says. "Kazak was. Others, like me, like Tak, don't seem to feel it. For us, it's just dust. Nobody actually gets sick because of it."

"Why doesn't all this shoot out spikes and turn you to glass?" Ishida asks.

"We're not trying to hurt it," Joe says, his eyes crinkling with amusement, or anticipating Jacobi's next question.

"So if it's not going to kill us, why would the Gurus want it destroyed?"

"It's older than the Gurus by a few billion years," Joe says. "Older tech. Maybe they feel outclassed."

"But it's *not* technology," Ishida says. "It's more like rocks."

"That's how the ancient civilization kept records," Tak says. "The one that lived in the old moon before it fell. We still don't understand the process."

I want to throw up, I'm so torn inside. Seeing DJ, Joe, Tak, waiting to see Teal—and everyone here is talking like this is a ride at Disneyland. "What happened to Kazak?" I ask.

"Killed when they attacked Fiddler's Green," Joe says.

"Who attacked?" I ask.

"Antags," Tak says. "We got most of them."

Kazak didn't make it. That fucking hurts. I was sure he'd survive everything and see us all home. My heart sinks.

Everything's falling away beneath my feet. I absolutely need to see Teal. I feel dizzy.

"Those crystals aren't, like, a diamond as big as the Ritz, or quartz—or anything like that," Jacobi says. "They're some sort of server—data storage made of rock?" She's working this over. The literary reference is nice—I did not anticipate that. Maybe I tend to think grunts are ignorant, too. "So the dust, the tea, is..." She looks intense and lets it trail off.

"Why not just let it sit here?" Ishida asks. "Why did the settlers dig it up?"

"Tell us, Vinnie," Joe says, with that provocative grin I know so well. The grin that got me into the Skyrines. The grin that ultimately brought me to Mars. "Why do the Voors think it's important—why are *we* here?"

"The green powder hooks us into something I don't understand," I murmur. "Something really old. Maybe more important than anything the Gurus have offered."

"Speak up, please," Mushran says.

"Origins," I say, louder, to get through the faceplate. "Access to the deep past."

"The wisdom of an ancient civilization," Mushran adds, with an upward look, as if about to pray.

"Is that what you feel, Vinnie?" Joe asks.

"Yeah. I guess."

Jacobi is taking this in with that same fixed intensity, and now she's watching me the way I watch Ishida. They're *all* watching me.

Three more men, two young, one old, all wearing capes and hoods, all tall and skinny, walk past with barely a glance at us and enter the hatch, which turns out to be the door to an elevator. I walk to the rim to watch the men emerge below. They go on about their business, surrounded by a flow of kobolds getting on with their own billion-year jobs.

"Where's Teal?" I ask.

"We're heading to the annex now," Joe says. "That's where you'll have to decide whether to strip and join us, or break it off and go home."

Which is why this charade is so ridiculous.

FAMILY UNIT

He leads us around the rim of the dig, through a low, flat cavern shored up with natural columns of rock and metal and braces of load-bearing concrete. The ceiling is a meter over my head. As I've said, I don't like deep mines and the suggestion of overburden. I can almost see the openness of the Red, the surface, and wonder what the weather's like. Probably weird. Safer down here. But I don't feel that way.

We walk through a shadowy, unlit zone toward three bright spotlights. As we close on the lights, I make out a steel hatch, like the lock hatches but thicker. There's a box with attached pad on the right side, at chest level. Tak takes out a platinum coin and places it in the panel. "We don't get many visitors," he says. "We're just being extra cautious."

"You don't want shit getting out," Jacobi says. Her eyes shift and her plate fogs. She's not handling this part of the tour well. Maybe she shares my dislike for low, flat places covered with billions of tons of rock. Or maybe she's been more thoroughly briefed than me. Maybe there are real dangers, and all these good folks are crazy, and we don't want to join them.

The hatch opens. I've been through so many goddamn hatches, if I never see another I'll be a happy man. But this is the sticking point, whatever the fuck that means. This is why we're here.

Coyle's gone back into hiding; maybe she doesn't like caverns, either—with better reason than most, right? Bug is silent as well. It's just me in my cranium, and to be alone is to be in bad company. Some Frenchman said that. Maybe Jacobi can tell me. Alice would know. Where the fuck is Alice? Right. She can't go transvac anymore. Bad solar storm, no more Cosmoline. I remember. I remember the apartment in Seattle, Joe's and Tak's apartment where I was invited to stay when we were all on Earth, nice place, with a view of the Cascades and Puget Sound and all the ferries coming and going. Why we fight. What the Gurus told us, gave to us—all that tech.

But the Gurus lied. Everything's a lie. And now, we're about to be led into...what, the truth? Or another kind of lie, even older, even more devious and dangerous? Maybe the Gurus know more than we do about what the tea does. Maybe they really *are* looking out for our best interests, and we're acting like upstart children. Moses after all goes up the mountain to see the burning bush and receive the Utterances, and down in the lowlands, his people get restless and start worshipping idols. Dathan, right? Edward G. Robinson orders the casting of the golden calf. Maybe we've just looked on the golden calf and now Moses is about to conjure the lightning to righteously teach a great big lesson. My chin cup fills with sweat. I want to open the faceplate. It's too late for me, why not just open the plate and take in more dust, finish the job?

I reach for my plate.

Borden grips my elbow. "Not yet, Venn," she says. I shake her loose, then turn and try to back away from the hatch. My step is spasmodic. I'm shaking all over. Tak has come up behind me, Joe is on my left.

"Let me go!" I plead. Tak and Joe move in close and put their heads—their naked heads—against my helm. They talk in low voices, tell me I have to maintain, it's important we all stick together and see this through, this is why we came to Mars. Joe's wearing his patent-pending skull grin, part determination, part sympathy, part bloody-minded stubbornness. I remember that grin and the first time I saw it. I remember that day back in the lagoon near Carlsbad. The day he and I scared the living shit out of each other, on a stupid dare, when we were snot-nosed kids.

"Relax," Joe says to me. "There's good stuff to come. Maybe good answers. God knows we've earned them."

"I w-w-won't be *me*," I say, maybe I *whimper*. Yeah, that was a fucking *whimper*. "I'll get sucked down!"

"I don't think so. You look *muy frio*, Vinnie. We'll get through this together, right?"

I feel my head shaking back and forth, then cycloiding to up and down, like I'm agreeing. That's the effect Joe has on me, but Tak as well; I don't want to play the coward or the fool in front of Tak Fujimori.

"DJ's waiting," Tak says. "I think he has something to show you."

"Yeah, but DJ's crazy," I say. They ignore that. DJ's always been crazy.

The hatch opens. A short, dark-haired woman pokes her head through, not as plump or as pretty as the last time we met—haggard and worn down, pale, but recognizable.

"You remember Alice," Joe says. He likes surprises.

"You can open your plates," Alice tells us, no prelims, no intros. She walks between us, fluttering her hands and looking a little disgusted. "Everybody peel and get cleaned up, replace those filters. Doc says it's okay."

"Who's the doc?" Borden asks.

"Me," Alice says. "Former first lieutenant Alice Harper, U.S. Marine Medical Services."

"You can't go transvac," I murmur. "You'd die, right? That's what you told me."

"I was wrong," she says. "After what we did to you. You getting picked up...The trip wasn't easy, but I made it. What's behind the big door is worth the risk. You know that—don't you?"

"Can you ever go back?" I ask.

"Maybe not," Alice says. "Can you?" She taps her cheek. "Go for it."

I reach for my plate. Borden shoves out her gloved hand as if to stop me, but Kumar says it will be fine, this is expected. Despite that, Borden signals us to wait. She opens her own plate first. When she still lives, we all break seal and breathe the air of Fiddler's Green, which is pure and sweet and alive.

Alice crinkles her nose at our waft. "Jesus," she says. Our skintights have been stressed to their limits. We smell of shit and piss and combat flop sweat. "We got soup and tea inside. Real tea. Mushran, is this fine Indian gent another master of the universe?"

"Yes, Alice," Mushran says, and introduces Kumar in a

tone that indicates here, in the annex, Alice Harper is running things, not Mushran, and certainly not Kumar or any other part of Division Four. No surprise, once they got her here—however they got her here—Alice put herself in charge.

Four tall young men and women wait in an alcove beyond the hatch and receive our shed skintights. The suits are racked and the men begin to replace the filters with fresh ones taken from a box. They must be in their teens—Martian years. Second gen? The women break away and hand us plastic scrub pads, then point us toward a wide, shallow tub, where we step under U-shaped pipes rigged to deliver spray mildly scented of soap. The women make scrubbing motions. Naked, we turn about, enjoying the warm shower. Ishida's skin and metal drips. Ishikawa has a broad grin.

"Scrub!" Alice shouts.

We scrub.

"Don't forget butts and privates. And chew this."

As we emerge, she hands us little lozenges. The lozenges taste of cinnamon. My mouth begins to effervesce. We've got foam on our lips.

"Lick it down and swallow. New bacteria, better than your own, believe me. And fresh breath. Your tummies will ache for a couple of hours, but after that, you've never felt better."

"Alice," one of the men says, shaking his head in disgust, "te suits want disinfect and patch."

"Do it," Alice says.

They haul away the skintights. Tak has a stack of white tunics over his arm and starts handing them out. Children's sizes, considering how tall the Muskies are. Mine drops just below my ass, like a hospital gown, but feels clean and cool against my drying skin.

Still no Teal. I made sure of that before I entered the showers. And no DJ this time. What's he up to? Is it possible that here, inside Fiddler's Green, DJ has found a place where he can avoid being the total goofball? Astonishing. I'm starting to feel better about this. Clean makes a difference.

"I got to go topside," Alice says. "Joe will take you from here. Congratulations, Venn. See you in a few." She touches fingertips with me and smiles, then moves off. "Say hello to Tealullah," she adds over her shoulder. "I don't think she likes me much."

I watch her fade into the tunnels. "Why's that?" I ask Joe.

"Because Alice took her kid away," Joe says.

Joe and Tak stick by me. Borden sticks by me. Kumar has conceded his flanking position to Joe and Tak. I got a posse. "All right," I say. "We're here. Where's Teal?"

"In the annex," Joe says. "Let's go."

CHOSEN BY THE TEA

We look like patients in a mental ward, walking away from the shower room, chewing our gum, foaming and licking, but everyone is dressed the same so we fit right in.

"What was it like at Madigan?" Joe asks.

"Great," I say. "Docs took good care of me."

"I'll bet," Joe says.

"Sorry we couldn't get to you in time," Tak says.

"Hey, no problem. I screwed up," I say. "Talked to a secretary. Used my finger to pay for a cab. Nice apartment, though. Alice..."

"She's our Dorothy," Joe says. "Keeps all the Tin Men and Scarecrows organized."

I think of all the twisters outside. "Wasn't sure I could trust her... Still not sure," I say, time and imagination skewing in my head. Someone's rummaging in my memories again. And to confuse me more, I'm remembering stuff that never happened. Or looking at things from points of view not my own. Like the bar fight at Hawthorne.

"She's tough," Tak says. "Maybe a little too tough."

"Teal had a baby," I say. "And they took it away from her?"

"Him, actually," Tak says.

Kumar and Borden and Mushran are a couple of steps behind, listening.

"Let's go grab a beer and talk about it," I say, in my best "where the fuck am I" tone.

"Beer on Mars is crap," Tak says. "They tried brewing it from sawdust and yeast, so Rafe says."

"What the hell is he doing here?" I ask. "The Voors would have shot Teal."

"Voors live here, remember?" Tak says.

"The elder de Groot was a piece of work," Joe says. "He's dead. There's only eight Voors left. About a hundred died when Ants hit their caches two months ago. Rafe saved Teal, but he couldn't save her husband."

"Husband?" I'm used to bad news, but this mix of good and bad leaves me hollow. My stomach starts to ache. "I thought…"

"Do we ever get what we want, Vinnie?" Joe asks.

"You seem happy," I say.

"Weirdest thing is how happy Joe is," Tak says.

"I'm a happy guy," Joe says. "You met Kumar at Madigan, right?"

"Yeah." We look back at Kumar, walking between Borden and Mushran. Behind them I see our Skyrines, Jacobi and Ishida leading the way. "Real head-fucker. What the hell is this place?"

Joe ignores that for now. "Back at Madigan, they tested your blood and shit. You came up triple cherry. The tea had done a real number on you, strongest they'd seen off Mars.

So Kumar decided you had to be brought here, or the Wait Staff—the other divisions, still mostly in control—would kill you for sure."

"Venn was high on the list," Borden says.

"Which pushed everything forward faster than they wanted," Joe says. "Kumar was still playing faithful servant to the Gurus. And second fiddle to Mushran. Mushran gets around. It's weird how he gets around."

"Why not wait until I got back to Mars, for Teal…?"

"Elder de Groot wanted to breed a master race that would understand everything there was in the Drifter. He thought that would make him the ultimate power in our big old war. No good if the baby is fathered by a Skyrine, and besides, how would he know about you? Turned out none of his surviving sons were suitable, so he found another Voor who was."

"I don't understand any of it," I say.

"Good. Clear out the bullshit and think fresh thoughts. Where we're going…"

We enter another wide room, with a ceiling only marginally higher than the last one. The natural gloom here is broken by chains of lamps drooping from the roof. Rows of folding tables are spaced between rock columns and plastic braces, and where possible laid end-to-end beneath the brightest lamps. A few of these are attended by scruffy Muskies, not as tall as Teal. Shorter folk. Uglier, I think, but I'm irritated the Voors married one of their own off to Teal. Joe's right. What was I thinking? Joe's always right. Nothing better.

I look into a corner and see DJ working away madly at one of the farther tables, hands racing over sheets of gritty beige paper, covering them with crude pencil sketches. Scraps and wads litter the table and the floor. Where they got the paper,

I have no idea—but what he's doing is important enough that someone found it and gave it to him.

As I walk over, DJ glances up, eyes crossed, face pink, feverish, looking even more of a dumbass than usual, like he's on drugs—and I suppose, like me, that he is. "Hey, Vinnie!" he calls out. "It's coming in a rush. I can't get any of it right! Come help!"

"Sure," I say, lifting a page. The sketches he's making are from the time of the old ice moon, and they're not half-bad. DJ has drawn the gnarled outer shell of a big, regal-looking bug, rearing up to show its underbelly—which is uglier and more complicated than its upper parts. I recognize the triad of large eyes, and behind those, peering over curiously, another triad—the smaller passenger. Partners. Parasite-friends.

"That's the boss, but in my head, he's not just one bug—he's like a composite memory of a thousand or so, spread out over centuries, I don't know which one he is, really. Recognize him?"

I shake my head. "Sorry. Shouldn't that be 'it'?"

"Definitely *him*," DJ murmurs, returning to his drawing. "Do some more tea. Come back when you feel it stronger. Man, this sucks, this really sucks—who the fuck *are* these guys, and why are they all lumped together?"

"Maybe it's a dynasty," I suggest. "You know, inherited rule."

DJ shakes his head. "No way," he says. "These guys are way more Spock than that. They were better at running things than we've ever been. Good guys, inside—really."

"They're dead, DJ. Extinct."

"Not in here," DJ says, tapping his head.

I back away, a little spark jogging up my back.

"How many here like DJ?" I ask Joe.

"Before the strikes, we had six, including Kazak," Joe says.

"Now we're down to DJ," Tak says. "And you. Maybe."

"He looks pretty strung out."

"Screw you," DJ says, fingers dancing over the paper. "This is power. This is knowledge."

"I don't feel that devoted," I say.

"Give it time," DJ says.

"What about the kids? The third-gen babies? Where are they?"

"They're not here," Joe says. "Lifted off Mars forty sols ago. Moved to safety on Earth."

"Earth! What about the Gurus, what about Wait Staff who aren't going along?"

"They won't know," Kumar says.

"Yeah, *right*. That's insane!" I say.

"Safest place for them," Joe says. "Far safer than here. The only kids still with us are the Voor and Muskie children—those not affected."

I'm fuming at this bit of news when I hear and then feel someone on the opposite end of the workroom. A clear, throaty female voice followed by a soft padding of feet. "Who's all t'ere?"

Three tall women walk together, heads nearly bumping the lights. They look much alike: thin, worn, mousy fine brown hair cut short, skin pale, eyes wide. They all wear tunics that drape to their knobby knees. Green-stained tunics. They've come from the mine pit. We stare. None is the woman I saw earlier carrying her baby.

Joe whispers, "Recognize anyone?"

I don't, at first. The two women on the outside of the

group hold out their arms to guide the woman in the middle. She looks lost, out of place, as if focusing on things we can't see, people not here. As she's helped forward, I make out scars around her eyes. They outline the edges of a faceplate. Flash burns. She's blind.

"Say something," Joe says.

"Is t'at Michael? I feel him," the woman says.

Behind me, the Skyrines push up close, I don't know why, instinct maybe, even now, even with my being such an asshole—we have to stick together. Or maybe they just want to see the tall women and figure out what this means.

"She's been asking after you for months," Joe says. "Talk to her."

They've taken Teal's child away and now she's here, she's trying to find me, and I barely even know her. "Why?" I ask. "What good am I?"

Teal raises her head. "It *is* Michael!" she says. "He's here!" She bumps into a table. The other women guide her. I want to run. God help me, we've made these poor people suffer so much.

"Vinnie, if it's you, come a here!" Teal says, her voice bright. She gives her most radiant smile and holds out her arms. I remember that smile. "Come a me. Talk a me! So long, so much a tell!"

JOURNEYS NEVER END

With no tact at all, Kumar and Borden and Joe separate me and Teal from our protective posses—Teal from her helpful tall friends, me from the Skyrines, who all of a sudden want to stick like glue. Borden tells them, and Joe confirms, that this is okay, no harm, we need our privacy, Teal and I, and then we're shepherded across the workroom to a small side cubby with chairs and a small table—a single lamp. Isolated and quiet.

The look on Kumar's face is intense. Borden is trying to be discreet, but Kumar doesn't give a damn—he might as well be watching porn and jerking off. This is why we're here. This is why he assigned Borden to me and brought me here.

Then, Joe and Borden and Kumar withdraw like matchmakers leaving on cue, but I know they're just outside, listening. I get it. We're big investments. Prize Thoroughbreds.

I gingerly sit across from Teal. I have no claim. That passing spark of connection, that slap across my face, sharing her grief and fear at the appearance of the Voors—no right to think I did anything major to protect her or keep her from harm—did I? I imagined it all, right? Even so, I want to bathe in her presence. I could be a ghost and I'd still just want to be here and watch her.

Teal stretches her hand across the table.

"I am such a shithole," is the first thing I say.

"Hush t'at," she says.

I reach out. She hears flesh rub on plastic, grasps my fingers, then lays her palm over mine. Her touch is dry. Jeweler's fingers, long and strong but delicate. I remember that fine strength. She pushes at the table, trying to get closer, so I move around the corner, kneel beside her.

"Let me feel you!" she says. She brings her face close to my head, hands hovering beside my cheeks. Her nostrils flare. She's smelling me. "Hasna't been hard, hasna't?" she says, eyes moving as if they can still see. I wonder if somebody will replace her eyes, like Tak's, and I think it could happen—but not here. I want desperately to get her to Earth, to a hospital, to fix her and make her whole again.

Back to see her child.

"So sorry a be this way," she says, and touches the scars around her eyes. "Went hard for us."

"I know," I say. "Not your fault, not ever."

She raises her chin. "You're alive a-cause me, remember?" she says, teasing a little, but full of joy, of pride. "I saved you."

Tears drip down my cheeks. "You sure did," I say.

"I was sa glad a find ot'ers. Never touched you, dinna know your feel, just far looks," she says, and her long fingers stroke my cheeks, my lips, the orbits around my eyes. I don't remind her about that slap. "Dinna catch your smell, 'cept sweat, fear. You're afraid now." She touches the moisture on my cheeks. "Na tears. So much a learn!"

She takes my hands and raises them to her own face. I touch her skin. It's the first time I've actually felt her so intimately, flesh, bone beneath, warmth, and her scent comes at me from different angles.

"They say you feel strong te tea," she says. "You know te old moon's life. What do *you* see, Michael?"

I don't know how to say it. The silence grows and she frowns. "It's na wrong. Fat'er felt it. First gen gets it strong, second less. T'ree strongest of all, t'ey say. He use a give me stories. I t'ought t'ey were odd, but beautiful."

"You didn't tell me that," I say.

"Being in te Drifter weird enow," Teal says. "What happened after you went back a Eart'?"

"I need to know what happened to *you*," I say.

"Sure," Teal says. "Te Voors took me back a te main cache, t'rough te fighting. Only five lived, Rafe and de Groot and Aram and me among 'em. T'ere wor ot'er Voors and settlers at te cache. De Groot took lead, organized, tried a open te second mine but dinna have te coin.... Still, t'ey took me in, made me one a t'eirs. Te women fit me, de Groot got his way—I wor married. I wor married—Michael." Her eyes try to search me out, to see what I'm thinking. Her hands twitch. She wants to feel my expression, but she's afraid.

"Was he a good man?" I ask.

"He wor chosen by de Groot, one a te Voors but not one o' his sons," she says. "None of his sons felt te old moon strong. De Groot chose a man wit' a strong sense. Not cruel, not stupid." She turns her head. One ear got nicked, I see under the short fringe of hair. My whole body aches. "Te babe came quick enow. T'en Joe and DJ and Tak returned wit survey team a open te second mine. Joe had te coin."

"The one I found," I say.

"We returned a digging, all a us, and t'en, good time, fine mont's—t'en, Far Ot'ers came and hit us, we t'ink. Houses split open a dust and sky. Husband died. I nearly died. Alice and Joe send away te babies. After, we divide from t'ot'ers, live in te mine."

"Amazing work here," I say.

I hear a commotion outside the cubby. Kumar and Joe and Tak are arguing.

DJ enters, breathless. "It's gonna happen!" he says.

Joe pulls him back. "We got hours yet," he says, and drags DJ away. Harsh whispers out of our sight.

"What's that about?" I ask.

Teal's face firms. "Tell me about you," she says.

The little room feels close and dense. Everything feels fragile, temporary, I don't know why. And then...

I do know. The mine, the *contents* of the mine, senses time is getting short. I can picture it, maybe the same picture DJ has. The Drifter turned glass right to the central peak after it was hit.

And that's not a bad thing.

Coyle didn't die, not completely.

Teal pats my hand. "We're a get evacuated, some a new camp, some a Eart'. But tell me afore we ha'a go." She grips my hand firmly, brooking no dissent. The people outside have fallen silent. Maybe they've gone away. Maybe they're decent enough to give us privacy.

I stumble through my story. My life has been empty compared to hers, and what's the point? What are we expecting? Weren't we supposed to get together and produce the third-gen child? Was that the plan or just my fantasy? What the hell happened? I don't say this, but I think it as I speak, and maybe it paints over my words and makes her sad. She leans her head to one side, listening with that nicked ear, spidery hands moving slowly on the table, trying to find mine again, which I've put back in my lap.

I describe the lockup room and Kumar and the window.

She shakes her head as if that can't be real. "Michael," she interrupts, "tell me a te ot'er place. What's it like? Living anot'er time, anot'er body? Make me see it. My husband couldna."

"What was his name?" I ask. It's important. People connected to Teal are important. He didn't hurt her, maybe he cared for her.

"Olerud," she says. "Olerud Miesler."

"How'd he die?"

"Fighting along a te Russians, out on a dust," she says.

Jesus. Her husband died protecting her. I wasn't here, I can't resent him. I can even feel admiration, gratitude—*Goddamn it to hell.*

"Enow," she says. "Tell me what you see."

"Comes and goes," I say. "Usually, it's brief. Like a sharp kind of dream." I study her face, feeling the coiling of a mighty force held back, wound up....

And then...

Being with Teal, smelling and sucking in the tea, *my God. It's here.*

I start to describe to her the things I didn't realize I'd been seeing and dreaming, spilling it all. She's the perfect listener. She'll believe. She'll get it.

"All our life came from them," I say.

"I know," she says, nodding.

"There are millions of them spread over vast time, hundreds of millions of years—all different sorts and shapes. In the time that comes through strongest, most of the powerful ones, the ones in charge, come in two parts: a smaller rider and a big, stronger partner. I don't know who's smarter. They blend together, except when they're apart—which isn't often. They have tough shells."

"I know. Like lice." Her lips curl.

"More like crabs or lobsters," I say.

"We ha na lobsters here. How big are te old ones?"

"Maybe as big as this table," I say. "Very smart. Their world is beautiful. Under the ice, under upside-down mountains of seeping minerals, there are all sorts of creatures—hundreds of kinds of smaller shelly creatures, scuttling through gardens of animal flowers like anemones—long chains of glowing bulbs, like jellyfish, that light the way through their cities—clouds of little wriggling things like fish, also glowing, everything equipped with lights.... Glowing bacteria? But here, under the ice, fish didn't rise to the level of crustaceans...." Am I babbling? Get to the point. I shift gears. "Inside, where they think, they feel cozy—cozy and familiar. Not like bugs at all. I don't know what that means."

"T'ey wor kind?" she asks. "Not kill and be killed?"

"Maybe. I can't be sure. Seeing from inside—of course it feels familiar. A whole rich civilization, history going back millions of...whatever they used for time. Tidal surges, warm and cold spells. They could sense the rock getting colder. They could tell that radioactive decay was slowly fading in the moon's core. But the tides kept the oceans warm. And when the moon was knocked out of orbit…"

"Around Jupiter or Saturn?" Teal asks.

"Maybe Saturn. But Saturn was different back then. And there was more than one inhabited moon," I say. "Before the disaster, there were seven or eight." Pretty specific. Which voice told me that?

"Did te shelly t'ings break t'rough? Did t'ey travel?" Teal asks.

I think this over. Good question! They must have traveled to know about the other moons—right? Did they colonize them, as well? "I guess they'd have to have dug out through the ice. But a long, long time passed from the time they first built cities until they saw the stars."

"DJ and Olerud speak it te same," Teal says, lifting her face. Her eyes are pale, but she still tries to see. "Many ice-roof worlds. How far? How far back a time, do you t'ink?"

"Hard to know. Several billion years, at least—but even so, like I said, their world is familiar to me! It's as if I *could* know them, understand them, with just a little effort."

And a guide.

"We'd be friends," Teal says.

"Huh! I don't know about that. What if we told them we boil crabs alive in a kettle?"

Teal's disgust is precious. "Na me, na ever! Crush lice, maybe."

I move on. "And they're pretty strange—parasite or partner on a bigger—"

She interrupts. "Pairs. Olerud said t'at. But te ot'er moons… Wor all dead and smashed?"

I look around the gray cubby, my tension slowly easing. Alice was right, Kumar was right—Teal's my catalyst. Maybe it was Joe who told them, though how he'd know I have no idea. Maybe he could see it in us—but he'd have to have been clued in earlier. Joe's bright but he's no magician.

Maybe Joe's participation goes back to Kumar's or Mushran's first quest for the Drifter. Maybe Joe's been in on it since just after training at Hawthorne. Joe has always been my polestar, my goad, even my flail—but I've never understood him.

"No," I say. "They were alive before Earth cooled and had seas. They were the first life in the solar system," I add slowly, feeling part of myself, my human ego, wither under the implications. "Liquid water beneath deep ice. They were first."

"You get all t'at?" Teal asks.

I nod.

"My boy would a felt all t'at and more, as he got older. All their history."

"Maybe," I murmur. "Third gen... Whatever that means."

Teal draws her blind gaze down from the ceiling. "Too valuable a leave wit me," she whispers. "I lost Olerud, lost my sight, and t'en t'ey took my boy." She presses two fingers between her small breasts, barely visible beneath the folds of the tunic. "Mushran and Joe say he's going a Eart' now. Much safer away from Mars. What will happen a t'em? Will te bogglers on Eart' peer and study?"

"I don't know," I say. What in hell are bogglers? Scientists?

"Or... maybe t'ey'll be raised a go out a te old moons beyond."

"I don't know anything about it. I wish I did, wish it would put you at ease."

Then more sharply, reminding me of the old Teal, she says, "So many dead. Who wants what, who does a t'ing and why, nobody tells, nobody has the trut' or will part it wit' us."

My throat is too tight to even attempt to apologize. Besides, how is any of this my fault?

Joe and Kumar and DJ enter. Mushran is talking outside, maybe to Borden. "Ready for a rest?" Joe asks.

My vision is swimming. I want to lay my head down on the table, but I've kept my eyes on Teal. We're not going to be together much longer. I know that. I hate that.

"He is sa tired," Teal says. "He has been wrung out."

Joe helps me stand.

Teal is in the far light, tall, skinny, trying to look back, as her two tall friends lead her away. One has her own baby at her breast, and it's sucking and cooing.

Then... Can't see them at all. My whole body trembles.

"Good-bye, Michael!" I hear. "Get rest. See you soon."

I shove against Joe, frantic, losing it all, but he holds me. I slowly work my way back, but hate them all.

BUG DREAMS AND OTHER ODYSSEYS

They take me to a side chamber, outside and away from the annex. I lie on a small cot: dim lights, cool air. Jacobi and Ishida and Borden stay with me, but Teal is gone. Joe shows up for a minute, then Tak. I don't want any of them. So *fucking* tired.

"You did good," Joe says. "Take a break."

"Where's Teal?" I can almost see her next to me, like an afterimage. Did she turn glass? Is she going to be in my head all the time now? "Where are we going next?" I ask.

Jacobi touches my forehead. "He's got a fever," she says. Alice blurs into view. Her face swims in the shadows. "It's the tea, he's feeling it strong," she says. "Go to sleep, Venn. Sleep it off."

"I want to stay with Teal," I say.

"Not a choice," Borden says. "She's getting a rest, too."

"I need to stay close…"

"No one who stays will survive," Mushran says. He looks furtive, disappointed. I know that look. Chain of command. Bad orders.

I try to get up, but Jacobi and then Ishida hold me down. Ishida could hold down a gorilla. "You don't know that!" I shout.

"Teal isn't staying on Mars," Kumar says. "There will be ships enough to carry them back to Earth."

"All of them?" Jacobi asks, looking up at the others.

Kumar looks away.

"Why didn't you send them back with their babies?" I ask.

"We could have planned better," Kumar says. "But this is where we start again."

"How can I believe any of you?" I ask, woozy, studying them, looking for pressure points, places to put a knife—I want to kill them all, honest to God, I want to fucking gut them. Kumar is aloof, oblivious. In a fight he'd go down squealing like a shoat. Or maybe life doesn't mean anything to him, not if he can't be in charge, play the political power game. Maybe that's it—he's just a political drone.

Joe pulls up a chair beside Borden. She looks at Joe. He folds his arms and lets Kumar fumble his way through. They're arguing about something. I've missed part of it. In and out. I brush away Jacobi's hand. Alice is firmer. She takes my temperature. "Same as DJ's," she says.

"There is no assurance," Kumar is droning on. "To keep privilege and power, many on the division boards have deceived and been deceived."

"What about Mushran?" Joe asks. Mushran appears to have left. Disagreements, arguments...Like listening to my mom and dad yelling at each other in another room, while I lie in bed with the flu. "Perhaps he is still lying."

"We don't have any other options," Borden says. "We're told by people we trust that the ships are coming, and that Teal and some of the settlers will return to Earth—and that DJ and Venn will continue with us to Titan."

"Why not take us all to Titan?" I murmur.

"Stop it," Joe says. "We're Skyrines."

"I *am*?" I shout. "Who the fuck says?"

Joe shakes his head. "We go where we're told and do what we're told," he says.

"Told by *who*, goddammit?" I hate him when he feels he has to spell out the way things are to *me*, of all people.

"The President," Borden says, jaw tight. She still believes in chain of command, God bless her little pea-picking heart. Bad orders. I was right. They're all facing up to receiving bad orders.

"You don't know that!" I say.

"I'm told the President is now with our program," Kumar says.

"He's flexing whatever muscle he has with the divisions," Borden says. "Some commanders are refusing his orders. But... that's enough for me."

"And for me," Joe says, patting his knee and standing. "It's what we've been waiting for."

"Where are *you* going?" I ask him. "Earth or Titan?"

"Titan."

"Good!" I cry out. "I'll get it done there." I don't know what I'm talking about, clearly, but that's never stopped me. Didn't stop me from banging on my parents' bedroom door and shouting for them to be quiet, let me die in peace—swear to God. Then I fell over and puked on the carpet and my pajamas. "What about Teal?"

"Alice will accompany Teal and the others back to Earth," Joe says.

"Yeah," Alice says. "Lucky me."

"You'll die, right?"

"I hope not."

"They'll reunite Teal with her child," Borden says.

Joe is talking now. Wow, is he ever far away. "Jacobi's Ops team will finish here and six will go with Alice and the settlers, six will go with us. Litvinov is prepping his own team. I don't know how many of the Russians will come along to Titan."

"Fucking Titan!" I mumble. "Who's in charge of our sisters?"

"They're under my command," Borden says.

Somehow, I doubt that.

"They're with us," Joe says. "You think this place is a mess, I hear Titan is a fucking nightmare. Biggest goddamn weapons in the solar system, biggest battles, diving through methane seas to tunnel below thick ice to underlying oceans…ugly and old and cold. But somebody thinks it's worth claiming and saving, and maybe they're right. Maybe out there we can learn the truth."

"What about everyone we leave behind?"

Joe shakes his head. "I don't know how many will have to stay."

"I have asked for as many landers as they can spare," Kumar says.

"What about the Antags?"

"We assume their goal is to recover all the fragments."

"What will that get them?" I say. "We're human. The dust speaks to us. The Antags aren't human. That's how the tea works, isn't it?"

Kumar watches me, inclines his head, says nothing. I know more about this than any of them except DJ. Borden is smart enough not to claim expertise when I'm so obviously upset. Is she worried I might puke on her? I reach down and feel the tunic. Not pajamas. A tunic. Christ, am I confused. "I can't think now," I say, but nobody's paying attention, because I'm so clearly out of it. That pisses me off and I struggle. Ishida holds me down. I get fascinated with the way her arm works, lying across my chest. It's such a pretty arm, all shiny metal and composite.

"Maybe they'll allow the settlers to live," Kumar says. Did I hear him right? We're leaving settlers behind? "To provide them with assistance," he adds.

I heard it right. "Then shouldn't we kill the settlers ourselves, to keep them from helping the Antags?"

Joe can't answer, Kumar can't answer. The variables are too many. One step at a time, one problem at a time.

"Teal will be reunited with her baby," Borden says quietly. "We all want that."

The knot just gets tighter. My becoming valuable, for whatever reason, is the worst thing that could have happened to me. Or to them. I could just blow it all right now. I could become a prodigal goddamned monster, shooting tea dust from my fingers, spraying everybody until they're flocked with a thick coat of powdery green. I want to. Part of me really wants to self-destruct.

"What does Coyle say about this?" Borden asks, taking me by surprise.

The dead Captain Coyle is lost in the haze. "She hasn't checked in," I say. "She isn't real. She can't be."

"In any other time, under any other circumstances, I would agree," Kumar says. "I do not believe in survival after death. But it seems that turning glass elevates you to a quite different plane."

I look around the shadowy group. This is weirdly important to Kumar, to Borden. Joe doesn't commit. "You believe she's still here?" I ask. "I mean, floating around—but talking only to me and DJ?"

Long quiet. Sounds outside. People moving.

Kumar says, "Your experience is not unique."

Joe says, "Kazak saw Coyle, too. Really chafed that DJ was the only one who supported him. But before he died, Kazak was tuned in stronger than anyone. Mushran says it's not a plague. It's a fucking investment opportunity. If we can find and protect everyone who's tuned in, we might have a direct way into the old data. That's what Division Four's thinking—isn't it?"

Kumar maintains his steadfast expression. Borden nods once. Joe stretches. All this weirdness doesn't sit well with him. I've become a big part of the weirdness.

Kumar says, "If Antagonists attack with full force, this mine will become just like the Drifter. We have, I believe, less freedom of action if everyone is black glass and no one is free to interpret."

"Will the Ants attack?" Joe asks me, leaning in close. His nose bobs over my head.

"How the hell should I know?" I ask.

"A few hours ago DJ just sat by his sketches," Joe says. "He didn't draw, he just whispered over and over about big change coming, like what happened when they dropped the load on the Drifter. He felt that one before it happened, too. So did Kazak."

DJ senses it. He's right. I sense it, too. Coyle isn't being drowned out by my confusion—she's gotten lost in coming change.

"Yeah," I say. "Something big, anyway."

"Okay on that," Joe says with a deep sigh. "Here's what the last bitburst has to tell us. At least seven space frames are entering orbit, along with one or two bigger vessels. No guarantee what they might be."

"Spook or Box," Borden says.

Kumar looks languid, like a nap would be a good idea. Weird fucking reaction.

"Let's hope," Joe says. "As soon as the landers drop, we're pulling out."

I'm fazing. My head hurts.

"Hey!" Joe clamps his hand on my shoulder. "Still with us, Vinnie?"

"Fuck you," I say.

Joe pats my shoulder. "All right, then."

Borden looks disgusted. No letup, no certainty. She's made her pact, received her orders, and she'll follow through, but she doesn't trust Kumar and can't figure Joe. To her, I'm a crazy burden, neither ally nor asset. Teal and DJ and the Muskies are deep-sea mysteries. And nobody trusts Mushran.

"Your turn, ladies," Joe says to Jacobi and Ishida.

"Ma'am?" Jacobi asks Borden.

Given all Borden's learned and seen, and reflecting on the

implications of her orders, she can't trust herself, either, or her past views on reality. So we're all square. Every one of us is nuts.

"Just give us some time," Borden says to Jacobi.

I close my eyes.

That's a big mistake.

AND NOW A WORD FROM OUR SPONSORS

I'm usually smarter when I'm not thinking. My subconscious soup simmers all the time, even without the spice of Ice Moon Tea.

Now that I'm out of it, my inner Bug is eager to raise my level of education before we arrive in Saturn space. Proximity to Titan being important. Maybe crucial. I see and feel the broken bits slowly come together—the history of a massive undertaking, the best times of that old moon become clear, but out of sequence—

I take what I can get. And here it is, for what it's worth:

Back then, Saturn was a brilliant yellow-green ball, slightly bulging around the equator, while chains of small storms drew pastel whorls across her tightly banded surface. No rings, but at least fifty moons, and twelve were big. So how did the bugs see that, know that?

Hush. Close focus in time, more detail:

Our bug ancestors began their push by erecting a huge

tower on the seabed, beneath a great wide hollow in the over-arching ice shell. The builders were philosophers or thinkers. If you thought it, proposed it, you did it—no delegating back then. Strong minds implied strong backs.

Almost all of the "thoughts" and opinions appear to have come from the smaller, spidery bugs that rode and guided the bigger ones. They discovered through long, careful calculation (what did they count on? They had eleven sets of legs and I can't begin to figure the bits around the eyes and mouth—) that the fluctuating tides and currents and even heat came from a huge body some distance away. They didn't then know what a *planet* is. They'd never seen the stars. But they were intent on solving the problem of where the tides and frictional heat came from. The bugs were digging their way up through the icy crust to find out.

Over a couple of bug lifetimes, the tower rose from the ruined site of their oldest city—which had collapsed long ago in a cataclysmic quake or volcanic eruption. Volcanism on the old ice moon meant eruptions of slushy liquid water filled with gases like ammonia or methane or even cyanide. Up from the rocky core welled regular flows of compressed mixes of water and all these gases, highly saline flows that dissolved buildings and killed hundreds of thousands of fellow bugs....

But that was okay, apparently; the bug thinkers knew that the interior heat and mix of poisons helped explain their origins, how life began here in the first place. Death became a kind of deity to the thinking bugs, as much as they had a god—death and, for an increasing crowd of rarefied intellectuals, whatever caused the tides and friction. Whatever it was that kept them alive. Their god was something they thought they could find. I'm okay with that. I wish it were true for me.

The crustacean intellectuals, crawling hordes of engineers and architects turned builders, carved great chunks of ice and rock and stacked them precisely to rise almost fifty kilometers from where the old city had been, a sacred site for a sacred project. Nearly all of the crustacean cultures and subcultures were down with this, cooperative and cooperating. They seemed to have been more integrated and less argumentative than we are. Maybe more dangerously curious. What would they find as they punched upward with massive drills, manufactured with tremendous effort out of chunks of ancient nickel-iron in the ice moon's deep core? This is some time before the bugs started creating their crystalline records.

In this bit of history/memory, my most constant point of view is that of a bug who's going to be the third in line to poke through the hole they dig, rise from the liquid water that fills the hole—capped with a rapidly refreezing crust.

I REFUSE TO be completely subservient. Some of my own memories are rising now. As a kid, I watched documentaries on YouTube about Arctic seals biting through the thin ice to open breathing holes and places to pop up and look around. My inner Bug is nothing like receptive to these memories, but as judge of all that's emerging from our relationship, I decide it's a perfect metaphor.

Our bugs are going to wear the crustacean equivalent of pressure suits, big sealed tanks with portholes sized to accommodate their many eyes. The bigger bug will of course get the larger suit, but connections between the suits will continue the interchange both consider essential to life. Designing and making these connections has jump-started new segments of bug industry and communication....

Oh my goodness. The bigger bug is not an "it." The bigger bug is *female*. They're quite good friends, have known each other since they were krill, raised together in crèche, assigned to each other by a master midwife/matchmaker. Now they're partners. Husband and wife. Not sure what Jacobi or Ishida or even Borden would think of this.

Back to the history lesson. The drills have finished and been withdrawn. A kind of methane-acetylene bomb with a charge of pure oxygen is set off at the center of the borehole. The ice flies up into the space beyond. Liquid water floods the open hole, which becomes a giant crack that spreads about half a klick to either side, causing alarming vibrations in the tower and even partial collapse, and sending cascades of ice from the bottom of the ice shell, which kills dozens of bug couples in the viewing stands.

But we're not distracted. We're focused in a way that only a bug can be!

And then...

First bug couple is up and out. The larger support suit's crawling legs and tracks carry it a dozen meters across the darkness beyond, across the rugged and unknown top of their world. Jesus, are they excited—and terrified. Fear is amazingly similar for these bugs, very like fear as I experience it.

Fear and excitement.

Second bug couple is up. No instant death awaits, which some of the more conservative engineers had predicted.

And then...

We compare notes through constant clicking chatter, sonic rather than radio. We don't know anything about electromagnetism or radio waves. A great civilization, but physics is not our specialty. We do very well with chemistry, better than humans, maybe. As if being blind to the sort of things that enchanted Maxwell and Tesla and Marconi and Einstein gives us extra strength and sensitivity in other disciplines.

The sky is black. We don't call it the sky—we call it something like *roof.* (My tongue tries to shape the word—but they don't have tongues or teeth or lips...so I return to being a bug and don't try that again.)

Then our lead couple, our lead explorers, posit that perhaps a cloud of vapor has risen over the excavations—likely from the blast that opened the way. Makes sense, so we settle down and go dormant for an hour or so. We don't even send signals back through the pool down to our waiting comrades. Besides, the pool has frozen over again. We might not even be able to return. We've brought along a small drill just to communicate, but that may not be enough.

Hours pass. Finally, we appoint our leader couple as the pair who should rise and orient the suits, big and small, so that the male can see what *roof* looks like. Maybe it's another high shell of ice—a favorite hypothesis among our best philosophers down below. One shell after another, and only our own inhabitable, so why bother digging out?

Our leader couple looks up. We await his reaction. I can see that the fog has cleared, and the blackness beyond is relieved by...

But I must wait my turn.

Our leader couple is stunned into silence. Then he tells us we should all look up, if only to confirm what he is seeing.

We do.

After a long while, we come to agreement as to how to describe what we see, above the roof of our world. There is no other roof. Instead, there is a huge round blot of brilliance, radiating heavily in the infrared—our favorite mode of seeing. And all around it, like tiny creatures, much like those who surround us in the wilder regions of our inner sea: hordes of bright little specks.

But the specks are infinitely sharp, tiny.

"They must be holes in a greater roof, holes like the one we just dug," says our fourth couple, perhaps not the best and brightest, but most amusing and beloved. "Maybe they are shining lamps filled with little glowing creatures come out to welcome us."

They are something like "funny." A bug version of Vee-Def or DJ. We love them, love *him* (the little guy is our referent in these matters), but doubt that what he thinks is true. I'm working my brain overtime, and actively comparing notes with the sluggish but often more stable and even wiser brain of my big wife.

She comes up with a solution first. I love her for that. "I think those glows are other places made of ice, like our world," she says. "But there have been disasters. They've dug out to the surface, other explorers have broken through to the open, but their explosions were too powerful—and they are all on fire. They're burning!"

Perhaps not the most fortunate hypothesis. It is convincing enough that we scramble back to the frozen pool of water and frantically chip and dig down again. The cap finally breaks up and we dive through and fall, drifting down past what is left of the scaffolding and the drills, tumbling along the side of the tower of rock and ice, rolling, endlessly rolling until we are back among our companions, our friends, our supporters.

The funny couple doesn't survive. We will miss them.

Shit. My partner died, too. That means my host male will be dying soon as well. Makes me sad, very sad. Worse to lose that partner than to die myself.

Many sacrifices, much sadness—but also much discovery. Much to think upon.

We soon concluded that the lights in the outer blackness are not holes. They are burning spheres. Millions of them.

That was the first time.

We—that is, our doubled bug forebears—waited a very long time to try again.

JACOBI AND TAK stand over me. I've had my eyes open for some time, but only now do I see them.

"Wow!" Tak says. "You were way, way down. Feel better?"

"I lost her," I say. "They dug out, but I lost her."

"No time," Jacobi says. "We're moving out."

"Everybody?" I mumble.

Tak and Jacobi lift me from the cot. "They've cleaned our skintights," Jacobi says. "Pretty good job, as far as I can tell."

"Weapons?" I ask.

She says, "See if you can stand."

AD ASTRA OR ELSE

I'm doing better now. I know who and where I am, for a little while, maybe.

We're suited up and back on the Red. Litvinov's troops have lined up the vehicles to begin transporting settlers away from the mine. The settlers number about fifty. Most of the work in the mine must have been done by kobolds. DJ and Joe and the Russians organize the move. They pack as many settlers as they can into the first group of four vehicles—two Tonkas and two Trundles.

I've had no chance to say good-bye to Teal. Borden and Kumar and I stand with our Skyrine sisters. Captain Jacobi brushes my arm. Something about her attitude has changed. That worries me.

"Moving out?" she asks. I lift my thumb. I can't see her face behind the plate, bright with morning sun. "About time," she says. "Ishida asks if you're married or otherwise bespoken."

"Lifelong bachelor," I say.

"Figures. We're running a pool on whether you end up married to Borden, to your Muskie girl, or to Ishida."

She brushes my arm again.

"Terrific," I say.

"Gadget likes you."

"She'd burn me to a stump," I say.

Jacobi's face becomes visible as she turns. She's nervous watching the lines of settlers in their skintights. "We can hand over her instruction book if you want to study up."

"Thanks," I say.

Borden and Kumar approach from the Trundle. "One of those for us?" Jacobi asks.

"Three, actually," Borden says. "We're also taking Litvinov and ten Russians."

"Won't be enough for all the settlers," Jacobi says.

"Our mission takes precedence," Borden says.

Then Jacobi does something that astonishes me. She and Ishida flank Borden and stop her forward progress. Borden is surprised into silence.

"We won't lift until the settlers evac," Jacobi says. "All of them."

Borden stares her down. "Then you're going to die here," she says, voice tight.

"If necessary, Commander," Jacobi says. "I won't take the blame for killing Muskies."

"So says our lady," Ishida adds. The others gather to show support.

Kumar raises his hand. "This is not an issue. We have priority to return to Earth all who have a connection with the mines."

Borden looks astonished, and then really, really angry—like she wants to strangle Kumar. She comes plate to plate with him. "Why am I not kept in the loop?" she asks.

"To accomplish that," Kumar smoothly continues, "we have been provided ten landers—enough for all, I think. Might take an hour more, however. By which time Antags could be upon us with, as you say, righteous hurt."

Borden turns her back on us. She's feeling the thorny end of the shit stick and I don't know why. I suspect it's because Kumar just doesn't care.

"Maybe so," Jacobi says. "But we won't leave until they're off the Red. These people have suffered enough because of us . . . *sir.*"

Kumar studies her a few seconds, then acquiesces with a bow. "I will so instruct Litvinov," he says, and walks away. At this moment, I love our sisters with all my heart.

Jacobi's cheeks are pink with anger. "What's the deal with Joe Sanchez?" she asks, voice still tense. "Ishikawa thinks he's dead cool. Is Sanchez taken?"

I don't dignify that with a response.

"Don't go all GI on us, Venn," Jacobi says.

"No, ma'am," I say.

"Until we all get in the shit again and decide to fuck or fight, to us you're *still* a POG," Jacobi says.

"Yes, ma'am," I say. Sisterhood is powerful. Warm and fuzzy, spattered with blood and spit.

An hour later, still no sign of Antags or anyone else. All the settlers in suits have been loaded. They fill seven vehicles, including the Trundles, and twelve hang from the sides of the Tonkas. The round-faced Russian ballerina, Starshina Ulyanova, stands on the rear hatch step of the Chesty and waves for an accordion to be stretched from the nearest domicile. Not enough skintights for complete evac. Good planning all around.

SNKRZ.

I'm tired of feeling confused and shitty. I want to feel tight and angry, like coming off a good fight—like I can shift the stars with my rage, with the righteous indignation that stupid fuckers anywhere would dare challenge me and my brothers and sisters. True *grunt* rage, *hu-wa*! Best drug of all. Back when I last felt it, it turned my skull into a white-hot, chrome-plated death's head filled with sizzling brains—fearsome to behold. I'd like to feel that again. Having Jacobi rag me makes me think it might be possible. But not yet. Not unless we survive our lift from the Red and our big transport is ready for the long, long haul.

The round-faced *starshina* waves the vehicles off. The settlers are leaving first. We all wait quietly, if not patiently. I can imagine the quiet inside the mine—the second Void. Except for the kobolds. What are they doing to prepare? Because I know beyond a shadow of a doubt what our sisters have done. They've laid a network of spent matter charges, enough to collapse the mine, incinerate the Void, put full fucking stop to everything the Muskies have been doing. Expediency rules. They won't leave a thing for the Antags, and there's no way of knowing what *they'd* do, anyway. Maybe blow it up, too.

Two squads of Russians gather to either side of us as we watch the eastern skies. Together, we track the lancets of descending landers—eight sharp white needles spaced about two klicks away.

ANOTHER HOUR PASSES before the rolling stock returns and the vehicles line up to receive us. Two of the landers off to the east ascend on pillars of torch fire. Two more follow minutes after.

KUMAR AND BORDEN emerge from the hatch beside the accordion, DJ in tow. I wonder what he's feeling. I *know* what he's feeling, but I won't acknowledge it. This is a solemn moment. Something huge is about to happen down in the mine, something beyond logistics and spent matter and physics. Because we both know that spent matter can only poke this place in the eye and make it mad.

But when it gets mad, when it feels *afraid*…

Difficult to believe whoever's in command above Kumar is doing everything right. We're all expecting that before we go, the Antags or more sappers will arrive in force and there will be another fight. My emotions are narrowing. I've missed that sensation for so goddamned long.… The instincts it took a claw-nailed handful of DIs to beat into me over weeks and months at Hawthorne, Mauna Kea. We're all expecting to die, but we hope, we want, we *desire* with hot pink passion to fight and kill before we go.

The round-faced *starshina* waves her hand, all aboard.

"Ready, ladies?" Jacobi asks.

High overhead I see a fast-moving object brighter than the

nearby spot of Phobos. It slides quickly east to west, opposite the typical orbital track of our space frames. My plate enhances enough to show me an elongated, slightly blurry thing like a tied-up bundle of handkerchiefs. I point this out to Borden. "Is that our ride?" I ask.

She looks up. "I think so," she says.

"Spook?" I ask.

"Fastest thing in the solar system." But she doesn't look happy or secure.

The last group of Russians climb onto the frame of a Tonka.

"Sorry about the crap they're putting you through," I tell her.

She shakes her head, then straightens. "You're coming with us in the Chesty. Jacobi's team will join us. Kumar's orders."

"Yes, ma'am."

"Kumar is coming, too."

"Terrific," I say.

The settlers are nowhere to be seen, but the ships that lifted them off the Red have left black-rayed smudges on the basalt.

"Godspeed," Borden says to the vanished ships.

I instinctively look west. Over the low rise that marks the second Drifter, the second mine, and the reduced horizontal lines of the domiciles, four dust devils spin out their syncopated dance, twisted little pencils moved by invisible hands. I hope nobody will be left behind on the Red or down in the mine to experience what I sense in my hindbrain and deep in my gut. Nobody human.

We pack into the Chesty, into the tight spaces between

weapons and stores. Joe goes last. Ishikawa sits beside him. DJ sits beside me. "Amazing tea," he says. "I'm going to miss it."

The Chesty moves out. Ten minutes' ride to the last two landers.

Then it all blows.

The whole Chesty shimmies on its wheels. Something subsonic booms up into the chassis and through our flesh and bones. The boom rises to a roar and everything shakes and rattles as the shock wave passes under us. The Chesty heels over on its springs, lifts, and bounces back with a squealing jolt. The driver revs to full speed, ponderous at best, then spins us to face into the aftershocks. Those of us in the back crowd around the six small ports, all but our sisters, Jacobi's team.

They stay seated.

"Oh, good," Jacobi says, utterly deadpan. "It's beginning to work." She folds her hands and looks between her knees.

Kumar perches behind the Russian driver, looking through the windscreen. "Blessed Siva!" he says.

A cloud of dust towers over the mine. The domiciles are obscured—maybe they're already gone. I see the landers, our landers, sway like trees in a high wind. Three more ships are descending despite the activity off to the west. There are now five, enough to carry the rest of us.

"Out!" the driver shouts. "Move it!"

We seal our plates and abandon the Chesty, leaping and running toward the landers, Kumar straggling—having difficulty—until Borden and I lift him by his belt pack and sling him along between us. The sound is incredible. Definitely no need to look back. Pillar of salt.

The crew chiefs of each lander grab us at random and push

us toward the ladders. We climb like monkeys, all but Kumar, whose feet can't seem to stay on the rungs. Takes far too long. Takes forever. The landers are still swaying. From kilometers off, we hear the crust complaining: deep throaty screams made worse by the thin air. I look left in time to see the dust tower into a mushroom, then spread out. Around the mushroom's stalk, a crackle of basalt spreads from the low dome of the mine. The crust shatters like glass hit by invisible hammers and collapses, forming a vast, bowl-shaped pit, the edge too fucking close and coming closer. Yeah, Siva indeed—our wicked sisters did a real number down there.

I'm almost at the hatch, shoving at Kumar's butt. Then I make the mistake of looking back again. The color at the center of the pit is changing. Swift, dark, riverlike branches fan out to the expanding perimeter—

"Get the hell in!" the crew chief shouts, pulling me through the hatch and shoving me back into the cabin, which is crammed with people in skintights scrambling for their lives, maybe for their souls. Borden straps Kumar into a seat and looks at me, frightened out of her wits. I strap into my own seat.

"Two minutes!" the pilot shouts over comm.

There are people still climbing as we hear the other landers begin their motor ramp-ups to launch. And then we feel our own ship rise. The hatch hasn't closed. Alarms go off inside the cabin. We're launching and not everyone's in a couch, but the downward tug is just moderate—the pilot is hovering over the Red, up and away from the debris and collapse—

Maybe it all ends here.

"Sorry," Jacobi says from behind me. And again, "Sorry."

I can't see a thing. Hope to hell that Teal is up and away.

The hatch has closed. We have pressure. I open my eyes. Borden and Kumar are across the aisle. Our seats realign and the pods roll into position. The pilot issues safety instructions. I don't listen. I look back over the edge of my seat. Everybody made it, we're all strapped in, that's a miracle, isn't it? I make out Jacobi and a few of the sisters and a few of the Russians. I see DJ behind and to my right. He looks like he's napping and having a bad dream. Where's Joe? Where's Tak? Mushran? Presumably in another lander. We're climbing fast. The acceleration is probably at max. Leaving Mars isn't like leaving Earth. You can stand, if you are strong and fit—

And then, as if the shock is holding back my sensations and memories, I realize, I not only saw it—I *felt it*. The pit turned black as obsidian. All the surface for kilometers around turned deep dark glass, and then, like a second sky, a sky *below*, it twinkled with burning streaks and stars. The glassy, broken land filled with submerged and flashing lights.

"Twenty minutes to rendezvous," the pilot announces. He has a distinct southern accent. Virginia, I think. Maybe Virginia Beach. "What the hell just happened back there?" he asks.

Nobody answers.

I close my eyes and let the acceleration lull me. Not so bad now. We're off the Red, we're alive, things are working out. Better and better. Right?

PART TWO

BATMAN AND SILVER SURFER SAY . . .

I'm drifting again. For some reason, I relive the time when Joe and I were eighteen and crossed the border in Arizona, riding in a pickup down to Chihuahua with three other guys and a nineteen-year-old tomboy named Famke. That trip ended up kind of sweet and creepy. Guided by a crazy young Mexican kid, we crawled deep into a desert cave and found a curled-up mummy wearing a grass thong. Famke examined the body—she was studying premed—and said it was a girl and really old, maybe hundreds of years. The Mexican kid insisted she had been fifteen or younger when she died, probably in childbirth. Joe got a sick, guilty look and took a folded cardboard box from the back of the truck, taping it together and mumbling something about her being lonely all these years, and now, she was back with her kind, with young people; she needed to go home with us. He insisted on removing her from the cave and bringing her back. He didn't want her to be lonely anymore. We'd drunk so much beer, he thought he was saving her from the dark and the dust.

He filled the top of the cardboard box with dried brush.

We made it back despite stupidity and too much beer, crossing the border with the cardboard box in the back of our van, saying to ICE it was filled with stuffed and mounted frogs we were planning to give as gifts when we got home. Two inspectors cracked the box's crisscrossed lid, barely peered inside, and waved us through.

Back in Chula Vista, we went our separate ways, except for me and Joe. Famke flew off to work in Africa. The other guys melted into the southland. Joe kept the mummy in his parents' garage until his mom opened the box one morning, pulled out the brush, and screamed. His dad called the cops. No charges were filed. Nobody could figure out how many laws we'd broken, or what to charge us with, and besides, by then, we'd already joined the Skyrines. The authorities ended up putting the mummy in a museum in San Diego. Strange days.

I slide from kid-flick memories into deeper sleep. It seems to go on longer than the few minutes left before our rendezvous. Some part of the kid flick is still with me, because I see piles of old comic books spread out on a narrow little cot in a room with a crazy, leaning roof—an attic bedroom not much bigger than a closet and filled with shelves bent under loads of books and boxed comics, an old tablet with a cracked screen, another tablet with a keyboard that projects from the front onto a desk, so I can write stuff—not that I write much. A few essays. Once I tried to write a comic and draw it as well, but didn't get very far. I remember I loved *Silver Surfer.* The freedom, the audacity, that chrome-shiny body. Kind of like T-1000 on a surfboard.

I never liked *Silver Surfer.* I never had an attic bedroom. I'm trying to wake up and not succeeding.

This isn't about you. They're shutting me down slowly, and I just want to move around a little before I'm done.

I see the Silver Surfer float along the aisle of the lander, and he's conversing seriously with Batman. Jesus, I do not think they would ever get along. Alternate universes. Two different kinds of bad attitude. One cosmic, the other…

I tell myself over and over, I never read *Silver Surfer.* I never had an attic room. Never wanted to write comics. So *who* loved him, and who could imagine him hanging out with Batman?

It's Coyle. Coyle is dreaming inside my head. She's decided to share.

"Stop it," I say. "Please."

You and your fucking train—and Jesus, that mummy! *I want out. I don't know how to get out! I don't know what I am.*

"You're a ghost," I say.

I'm not dead. You know I'm not.

"I don't know anything."

I've been sucked in and I'm being stored away. Like all the others, only slower. Something seems to think I'm useful like this. Still active.

I can feel my lips moving. I'm mumbling, but I can't wake up. "They're all glass now."

It's not glass.

"What the hell is it? Silicon?"

Not that, either. If the crystals are threatened, they reach out and absorb. That's how they learn about threats—by absorbing the things that threaten them. I threatened them. Now, I'm getting stiff. Solid.

"DJ says all of Mars could turn glass. Then you'd have lots of company."

I've already got *company. You wouldn't believe how much company.*

"Skyrines?"

Yeah. Some Voors, some of my team. Others, Russians and Muskies, that didn't finish before they were blown up in the Drifter. They've already been recorded. Stored. I try to avoid them.

"Right." I start to shiver. If I shiver enough, maybe someone will wake me.

Coyle goes on: *You saw me get absorbed. You thought I was dead. So did DJ. I still don't know what happens after, except... before I'm done, I can still talk to you.*

"If you call this talking," I say.

Shut up and listen. This place I'm in, if it is a place, is filled with big stuff and little stuff. I think a lot of it is old. I mean, really *old—billions of years or more. With my help, maybe you can access some of it. That's what it wants. But I need you, as well.*

I just want her to go away. I want it all to go away so I can be as sane as I was before.

"I'm already there," I say to this craziness. "Ancient bug history."

Not just that. Really important stuff. With my help, you might be able to understand. Interpret. But right now... I can't help. I'm locked out. There's a kind of firewall that stops me from looking around and searching. Keeps me from being active.

"Meaning what?" I ask.

Batman and the Silver Surfer have parted ways and are now just floating. I see them despite the fact that my eyes are closed. But then, my eyes have been closed all along.

I think this place needs a user to get it to open up. Someone alive. Really alive. Somebody with a need to know that deserves access privileges.

"Is it a kind of library? Why don't you check out a book or two?"

I am *a book, shithead! There's only so much I can do. I'm becoming a record, and records are tightly controlled.*

"They don't let books run the library, huh?"

I refresh or something every little while, and I'm allowed a kind of exercise—meeting up with similar records—and that feels good, but... Oh, crap. I'm in the cage again. Time out. No more for now.

I finally manage to crack my eyelids. Blurry, Joe and DJ hang over me.

"You okay?" Joe asks. "We couldn't wake you."

DJ smiles. "He's okay," he says.

Ship attachment noises ring out around us.

"We're transferring," Joe says.

"What's all this about turning glass and old records?" I ask DJ.

DJ makes his "it hurts to think" face. "It's pretty huge," he says. "I don't know how huge. When I hook in through one of the ones who turned glass, I just..." Again the pained expression. He shakes his head. "Let's go over that later," he says.

"No, now," I say.

The ship lurches. Our Skyrines and the Russians grab couches and stanchions. Jacobi flows smoothly past, followed by Ishida. Borden is waiting in the alcove opposite, beside the stowed pod. Crew Chief follows the last of our group. "We've docked," he says. "You got three minutes. I want you out of here as fast as possible. I will not stay connected to Spook for any longer than I have to."

"Got it," I say, then focus back on DJ. Borden listens closely.

"The tea hooks us in," DJ says. "Nobody's figured out how. But we're guests. We don't yet have full privileges."

"Coyle said the same thing," I say.

"Sir, that's *not* Captain Coyle," DJ says. "Everyone who turns glass shows up sooner or later. I don't know if we can trust anything they say, because the records have their own motives. They need to help us to stay flexible. They need to be useful to a potential user."

Joe shows his puzzle face.

"I can see the bugs, some of their history, their living back then, because the records want that," DJ says softly. "But I don't know what's true and what's propaganda—understand? The records cover *everything*. That's all I got."

"Yeah," I say. "But where are they? In the glass?"

DJ spreads his hands, nods, points his nose left, then right. "Kind of like that," he says.

I pull up from the couch. "Maybe Walker Harris knows," I say.

"Who's he?" DJ says.

"Came to visit me at Madigan. Could be a Guru."

"Amazing!" DJ says, totally credulous. "What do they look like?"

"A guy. Let's go," I say.

It's DJ's turn to stall. "Did you dream about Silver Surfer and Batman?" he asks.

We both twitch.

"Yeah, just now," I say.

"I've dreamed that so many times," DJ says. "Bat and Surf keep arguing, never resolve anything. Is that Coyle?"

"I think so."

"Well, she doesn't like me as much as you, but she's stuck with us, right?"

"I heard it different," I say.

"Ice Moon Tea, the records, whatever you want to call it, makes Coyle repeat that dream. I wonder she doesn't get bored."

"She's definitely irritated," I say. "That sounds like emotion, doesn't it?"

DJ thinks this over. "Yeah," he says. "But maybe that was her ground state when she was alive."

"We have to leave," Borden says, listening, taking notes in her head. I'm still undecided about Borden but this part I definitely do not like.

"Come on!" Crew Chief shouts, waving his arm. There's a frantic note in his voice. Spook ship actually frightens him. "We've only got a few minutes!"

We pass up the aisle and through the hatch into the accordion. Windows in the accordion's long stretch show us a shiny, curvy, intricate white framework wrapped around long clusters of glowing spheres like Japanese paper lanterns—and surrounding everything, those shrouds, the bright outer skirts, pleated panels rippling like silk in a slow breeze. Doesn't look practical, barely looks real.

Kumar and Mushran and Litvinov meet us on the other side. "We get privilege of Star Gown," Litvinov says. Russian name for Spook. "Three weeks to Titan—"

"Excellent!" Kumar says.

"Not so excellent. Departing Earth, Star Gown was attacked," Litvinov says. "Three weeks may be nine weeks, or months, if she is not at full speed. There is damage to seeds, to weapons, and damage to two drives."

Kumar looks perturbed. With a shake of his head, as if dismissing this doubtful news, he moves ahead to the hatch opening into the bigger ship. All of us compete to twist and find a better viewing angle.

Jacobi shoves her hand out. "Shit—there, and there," she says. We see gray streaking the shrouds and, farther aft, curled and torn struts and vanes. Forward, on a long, twisted boom that once separated cargo from forward living quarters, shattered spheres bunch like smashed eggs in a carton. "Looks bad," Jacobi says.

We pull ourselves along ropes that suddenly acquire wills of their own, stiffening and then coiling, rudely tugging the last of the lander's passengers into the Spook's shadowy gray interior. I swing up beside Borden as we move into a pitch-black chamber. Sounds big in here. Long echoes from the squeak and whistle and snap of the ropes. Then the lights come on, and everything turns White. Even harder to see how big the space is. Distant bays, cubes, trestles hung with rounded transporters. Spook is *big*.

"Can this ship still get us out there?" I ask Borden.

She squints at all the whiteness. Everything here is spotless and clean, despite the outer damage. "We're here. The settlers have made it to their frames. Everybody on the landers is safe."

"I'm turning you over to CWO Mueller," the lander's crew chief says behind us. We had forgotten he was still there. He makes a face at what he's seen. "Then I'm taking off."

"Mueller isn't here yet," Borden mutters.

"She will be." Crew Chief makes another face, as if he's glad to avoid the encounter, then tosses a quick salute, takes the rope, and grapples back to the hatch. The hatch hisses and snicks shut. Pressure pokes our ears—more echoing clangs and far-off, metallic scraping that seem to come from all around. The landers that delivered us are away. We're on our own.

Kumar hands his way back, sweating profusely. "Pilots say the ship is capable," he tells us, "but threats gather, and to reach full speed this close to Mars will be difficult."

Borden asks, "Where in hell is Mueller?"

The ropes slack and we transfer to grips along a series of parallel rails. We line up between the rails like a line of expectant gymnasts.

"Here she is," Borden says.

The Spook's crew chief swings down from a hatch overhead, arms and legs spread like a swimmer at the end of a deep dive, just before surfacing. She's forty-something with a Persian-cat face and looks like a former beauty queen who's spent too many years under the Texas sun—pretty in a rough fashion but hard. She wears a slender white crown that curls around her ears and seems to be listening to someone or something unpleasant. With a brisk nod, she removes the crown, lifts her pointed chin, and focuses her full attention on us.

"I'm CWO 7 Mueller," she says. "Beulah Mueller. Grunts call me Bueller. I'm go bitch on *Lady of Yue*, so listen up!"

She's a formidable presence. We listen.

"We have an incoming Box that doesn't want us to leave, and a squadron of disgruntled corvettes are about one-twenty K from us. They've been chasing us since NEO, they caught us once halfway to Mars—causing the damage you've just seen. We probably can't afford another run-in."

"Losses?" Kumar asks.

"All our gunnery mates, three out of four glider pilots. Fifty-six dead."

This news shakes Borden. "If we get to Titan, can we even *begin* our mission?" she asks.

"We can try, Commander," Bueller says. "Let's worry about that after we finish Spook prep. Is this all of you?"

"All," Litvinov confirms. Borden sadly agrees.

"We asked for a hundred and forty. I count thirty-one," Bueller says. "Waste of a big ship!" She grabs a pair of handles and swings in ahead of Kumar. The bars lurch and haul us forward. "First phase is coming up. Anyone here rated for big weapons? Bolts and long-range disruptors?"

Ishida, Jacobi, one of the *efreitors*, and Ulyanova raise their hands.

"Good. Talk to me in a few minutes. Right now, all of you strip and we'll get you right with Jesus."

The rails carry us forward to a more constrained space, walls dark with streamers of purple. I see little sparks in my vision. All of us going transvac experience cosmic rays now and then. But these sparks leave neon trails. They don't look like cosmic rays. More like optical migraines. Just a hint of what's to come.

Bueller watches as we shed our skintights, this time without the help of gravity, a one-handed maneuver—other hand on a handle—that some accomplish with speed and grace, but which takes me longer.

"I want to see you *naked*, Venn!" Bueller shouts.

"Yes, ma'am."

Bueller's voice becomes painful. Worse, I find it difficult to look at her—I keep wanting to look away. There's something off about her outline, her image. Is it me? The purple streaks and neon sparks? A weirdly opticked crew chief. She just doesn't look real. The rest seem to agree. No one will look at her directly without a squint or shake of the head. Joe is off to my left. I catch his eye. He knows something we don't. Christ, now I'm feeling like dried bonito—downright flaked.

The shed skintights drift off to nobody seems to care where in the dark chamber. The rails drag us along, bare feet dangling, through a rectangular opening in the far bulkhead and into a space fully as large as an aircraft hangar. Here one rail takes half of us to the right, the rest to the left. Bueller hangs back and hovers, tapping heads to indicate right, left. The grunts do not appreciate the familiarity, but clearly, Go Bitch doesn't give a damn. We're all she's getting and she's not happy.

Filling the center of the great white chamber is a steel wheel about thirty meters wide and two meters thick across, its inner rim studded with black bumps. The wheel is the first of three that form a tunnel or gantlet. I do not like this. Nobody around me likes this.

"We have to go through those?" Jacobi asks.

"Yeah," Bueller says.

"Why?"

"Purge!"

"What kind of purge?" Ishida asks.

"Quantum," Borden murmurs, but I'm the only one who hears her.

Ishida rubs her temple. "Like castor oil, ma'am?"

Bueller looks clown-sad. "Don't you read our briefings?"

"We've been busy, Chief," Jacobi says.

"It ain't about your fucking bowels," Bueller says. "Downsun, you've been hanging with bad company since before you were born. Pasts that never were, futures that will never be. They slow you down. Those wheels will start the process of getting you clean."

"Sounds like a tent revival," I say.

"Think of it as a cosmic car wash. There'll be another at waypoint—if we make it, which is getting less and less likely, goddammit! MOVE!"

Bueller swims around us, effortless as a sea lion in an ocean swell. One by one, in two lanes, she guides us through what could otherwise be subway tollgates, closer and closer to the great studded wheels. The tollgate lanes end at two steel autopsy tables. Each is sprung from behind by a heavy piston. Five meters from the first wheel, Bueller taps me and Kumar and tells us to lie flat against the slabs. Not autopsy tables—more like human pinball paddles.

Kumar looks at me with those mild, calm eyes. "I'm told it's not unpleasant," he says.

"You first," I say. He rewards me with the merest grimace.

Behind us, Bueller taps Ishida and Jacobi next, then two Russians. Our sisters exchange finger-hooks and sharp dares and line up. The Russians clump, waiting to see what happens to us. Bueller swims back and jostles and jabs. This makes the

Russians unhappy. Go Bitch doesn't give a fuck. Neither does Litvinov. The Russian colonel looks terminally depressed.

Kumar and I try to lie flat against the tables. Simultaneously, they hiss and not-so-gently shove us through the first wheel with just a half twist of spin. Kumar gives a little shriek, I clutch my balls, and both of us fly neatly through all three wheels. My hair stands on end. I don't have much hair and what there is is short. My fingertips tingle, but most curious of all, my innards try to decide whether they're properly arranged. I swear, it's like a fucking math wiz wants to shuck my guts as a topological experiment—particularly my colon. Maybe I'll just turn inside out. Won't make a difference, even inside out, humans are still just donuts.

The wheels ratchet three bumps counterclockwise and wait for the next pair. I let go of my balls. My muscles relax. My bowels stay tight and inside. I'm suddenly right with Jesus, clean and sparkly—renewed. Kumar's source was correct—as weird as this is, the total sensation, once the purge is finished, is not unpleasant. I feel like a thunderstorm has blessed me with cool air and a lungful of charged ions. Maybe that's it. Maybe we're all being ionized. I've run into tech sergeants and engineers—including DJ—all Tesla freaks willing to swear that everything the Gurus provided had already been invented by their hero. Some insisted the Gurus weren't real, that the government was just dosing out bits and pieces of the stuff Tesla did back in the twentieth century. I'm so invigorated I'm giving their crazy theories a new look.

Bueller gets us all through without a hitch. As we clutch ropes and bars beyond the wheels, staring owlishly, deciding whether or not we have complaints, wide circular lids at both ends of the chamber open and we see what waits beyond—fore and aft. It's a longitudinal view down the hull of the Spook, from a position about fifty meters out from the centerline.

"*Fuck*," Borden says with a frightened reverence. That's the second time I've heard her utter this grunt standard. But I agree. No other possible reaction.

Let's take the description in layers.

Judging from what we saw earlier, the fore end of the Spook is dominated by a wide gray bell, more of a shallow bowl, about sixty meters in diameter. From the convex center of the bowl juts the bullet-shaped bridge or command center, the ship's prow. The bell's concave side protects the bridge, command center, and crew areas from radiation or other weirdness aft. Classic.

Looking aft, however, there's little or nothing classic or familiar about the Spook. First comes a slender run of steel-gray pipes. The pipes surround and support glassy blue modules, like grapes stuck between soda straws. In line aft of the straws and grapes comes a procession of space frames filled with payload or cargo, arranged in fasces like cylinders in a revolver. Each chamber in the cylinders reveals the rounded bronze or gray tip of a seed—what I assume will become, on Titan, a weapon or vehicle or some other piece of equipment. They look like bees waiting to crawl out of a hive. Just aft of straws and grapes, and just before the space frames, the designers chose to mount defensive weapons, extensible pods that rib and groove the transparent outer hull.

"Damage," Borden observes. Many of the pods are blackened, dark—or gone. Bueller makes a little grunt, but adds nothing.

The three long "skirts" begin aft of the payload, about a

third of the ship's length back from the bridge. When we first saw them, they rippled and flowed, kind of pearly, but now they're stiffer and singed with streaks of gray—not as pretty but still impressive. They surround and partly obscure a stack of pale gray disks, each about sixty meters wide and separated by trusses like coins in a magician's hand. Even damaged, this central complex shimmers with a foggy uncertainty that makes my eyes cross. Like Bueller, none of it looks entirely real. Maybe it isn't. The trusses and coins run aft another fifty meters beyond the skirts' hemline to the Spook's tail—flaring black cones that I assume are engine nozzles, ribbed with red and black vanes that might shed heat. All of this, the Spook's business end, is wrapped in a fine hairnet of intersecting struts and beams.

Seen almost in its entirety, the ship is weirdly beautiful, like a blown-glass jellyfish leading a parade of steel and enamel fruits. Doesn't look remotely human-made. None of this does, really.

Bueller's sun-chapped lips pull her ruddy cheeks into a hard grin. "That's enough," the crew chief says. "We're transvac in fifteen minutes. We need you properly stoned."

"Stoned?" Ishida asks, one eye wide.

"*Stowed*," Bueller says. Her grin flattens. Comically somber, she waves us on.

"She's nuts," Ishida says, not quite out of the crew chief's hearing.

"These are traditionally odd people," Kumar says. "They have adapted to an odd ship. But *Lady of Yue* has been traveling to Saturn and back for five years with never an incident."

Jacobi lifts an eyebrow. "Except now. Ship looks pretty banged up. How much can she take?"

"She is *very* strong," Kumar says. "I have been told—"

"You've never been on a ship like this, have you?" Borden asks him.

We pause to admire the broken protocol.

"There has never *been* another ship like this," Kumar finally says, voice low.

"Guru theory?" Ishida asks.

"Not precisely," Kumar says. "Wait Staff was instructed to approach humans who had particular ideas, to fund them and give them laboratories in which to work. We did. This is one of the results."

"I knew it!" DJ says. "It's Tesla shit, right?"

"All human, huh?" Jacobi says, in no way agreeing with DJ. "But guided by Gurus. And Socrates's boy slave understood geometry from birth."

Again, learned sister.

"We eat first?" Ishikawa asks.

"No time!" Bueller calls from the front of our line. "We assign soccer balls. Big Vamoose in fifteen minutes. Short sleep. *Then* food."

"Soccer balls?" a Russian asks behind me.

"Big Vamoose?" another Russian asks, frowning.

I slip my hand out flat, showing motion at speed. He still looks puzzled.

"What happens in the second purge?" Jacobi asks.

Borden decides this line of thinking is not productive. She calls down the line to Litvinov, "Anyone see Mushran?"

The Russian colonel is making sure his troops are organized and prepped and distracted. He points forward. "Went before," he suggests. "Ship is big and very clean!" he adds cheerily. "Never stay in such fine hotel." His troops appear unconvinced.

Bueller warns us against touching or even brushing each other for the next few minutes, so we keep apart—not that there's been much hugging. What *does* happen at midpoint? Maybe I'm too encrusted with unresolved bits, a deep dark sinner who won't make it. Maybe I'll be bleached out of existence. I might have some of Coyle's sins hanging on me as well. But my inner voices have chosen to be quiet—no Bug, no Coyle. I'm all alone in here. Feels almost normal.

I turn left and look up through a clear panel into more structure. We all look. Beyond intricate shadowy architecture we get a glimpse of the brownish limb of Mars, slowly rolling.

"Bye-bye, Red," Jacobi says.

I keep staring, like maybe Mars can answer something for me before we leave. Above the limb, I see a star. The star goes black. The space around the star goes even blacker. Then, something huge cuts a shadowy wedge out of Mars. The wedge seems to double, sharpen, and form an arrowhead.

Jacobi and the others have turned away, waiting to be led to their places for the next ride. Try as hard as I can, I can't make sense of what's happening out there, and after the confusion of our intro to the Spook and all the other shit we've been through, my instincts are numb.

The wedge digs deeper into Mars, blocking most of what I can see. Then I see it's part of a cube, a huge cube—and its corners are pushing out and twisting around, shaping pyramids, which in profile look like arrowheads. Between the pyramidal corners and the main body of the cube, sparkling spiderwebs are being drawn by the thousands.

It's the ship we saw in orbit before departing from Earth.

It's Box.

I tap Bueller on the shoulder to distract her from herding the rest of us aft to our soccer balls. As she slowly spins about, a high whistle pierces the air, and *Lady of Yue* shudders around us, then begins an awful wailing sound, like a woman who's just lost all of her children.

The skirts, the sails that flow aft of the cargo and crew areas, are spreading wide, revealing more damage as they expand—but also sending out their own spider-silk sparkles. The sparkles fan to shape a nimbus, then flow farther aft, where they cage a welding-torch-blue glow. Fascinating to watch, painful, hypnotic. Leaves burning afterimages on the backs of my eyeballs.

"Don't look!" Bueller shouts, then grabs my shoulder and shoves me toward the others. There's a weird sensation, like the ship is expanding longitudinally, like we'll soon be squeezed out and left behind, surrounded by vacuum. "Grab hold! We're moving *now*."

I feel myself drifting aft, my grip on the rail insufficient to keep me in place against the growing acceleration. Borden and Ishida are sliding along right next to me, along with Ulyanova and two more Russians. Below me I see Jacobi and Ishikawa and DJ. I can't see Joe or Kumar.

Then—we're a tangle of limbs, bodies, heads colliding against the far bulkheads. Cables and equipment sway and swing above us. Bueller still tries to pull herself forward, but she's finally pried loose and joins us in the tangle, right on top of Borden.

Everything around us reflects that far, sapphire-blue arc light. Through the forward frame, I can make out that Mars is gone. But not the black cube. That shadow is following, then trying to flank *Lady of Yue* even as we untangle, cursing and climbing free. Bueller rises over the mass and looks around, eyes flinty—then points to Ishida, Jacobi, the *efreitor*, and Ulyanova.

"Outboard to the weapons," she says. "We have four. We need five."

"Venn," Jacobi says. I try to remind her about my not being rated, but she shrugs it off. "Just bigger point and shoot," she says. "Right? Follow Ishida and you can't go wrong."

Joe watches us from a recess, where he's shielding Kumar. He tips a salute at me. I mouth something rude, but he's already turned and is dislodging Kumar from a nest of snaking cables.

At Bueller's command, more rails and cables descend, and, behind Jacobi, we all grab hold, to be yanked outboard so hard I wonder that my shoulder stays in its socket.

"Keep your eyes forward!" Bueller calls as we move through the framework, toward the weapons pods on their translucent booms, now retracted snug against the outer hull. I count twenty pods—fifteen that were apparently ruptured during the previous encounter, no doubt venting their contents—their gunners—into space. Five are still intact.

We climb in. Ishida takes the pod closest to mine. Jacobi teams up beside Ulyanova. The *efreitor* seems happy to be working alone.

Bueller stands by the root hub.

I've fitted my nearly naked body into the bucket seat and watch the laces strap me in. A half helmet swings up from the rear of the pod and cradles the back of my skull. Something buzzes along my spine. Guidance? Nerve induction? I look over at Ishida, but can't see much—the brightness of the pod's surface obscures her details.

The pods extend and we are now surrounded by stars, with *Lady of Yue* below. Box is trailing behind the arc light, but still closing the distance.

"We caught them by surprise when we left NEO. Box has been in a hurry ever since," Bueller says through comm. "She's larger and faster, but rising upsun, chasing us, she still hasn't had time to shed all her sins."

How does Bueller know that?

And what the hell does it mean?

"We still have the advantage," Bueller says, but her voice drops a note.

"Box already found you once and clobbered you," Jacobi says. She sounds right next to me.

"We need five minutes!" Bueller says. "Those sparkles running to the corners of the cube are drive tension distributors. Cut them with your bolts or disruptors and you'll slow her down, and that'll give us just what we need...five minutes, maybe, but not a second more."

I fit my hands into the trigger gloves. I'm in charge of a bolt weapon. I know how they work, in smaller form, on a planet's surface—but this seems natural enough. My fingers feel the guidance and trigger post and I test it, also natural enough. Another buzz along my spine, this time reaching out to my fingers. The pod swings on its pedestal, and I see, along the gleaming inner surface, a set of reticules and crosshairs move into place. They converge on a corner of Box, then outline several of the tension sparkles, whatever the hell those are.

What if I still have no fucking idea what I'm doing?

Ishida speaks in my left ear. "Three of us will carve out the far corner, with its interior exposed—see those lines?"

"I see the far corner."

"You will trim the near corner."

"Harder to see those lines," I tell her. "Have you done this before?"

"Never in space," Ishida says. "Follow instinct. Hit what you can, but make it count."

"If the pyramids ride any higher, if they extend any farther, you can't help but see the tension lines," Bueller says over comm.

"Yeah," I say, starting to feel really ill. Something is dragging us along through the stars like a cat drags a rat. I assume it's our own ship. We still haven't finished getting straight with Jesus, right? Worse, we're newbies manning weapons that are totally vulnerable to being blown wide open, like glass bottles in a shooting gallery.

Then Ishida and Jacobi loose their bolts. I follow those pulsing white dots, watch them carve the far pyramid's tension lines, watch that sharp black corner of the cube shiver and twist on its extended post....

And then I focus on the lines just visible below my own assigned pyramid, linking it with the main mass of Box.

The reticules align.

Box sends out its own bolts, a firefly mass curving around from the far side, presumably the business end, and traveling twice as fast out to our ship, where they nick another smoking groove in a skirt, then climb up to sizzle one of the pods—

The lone *efreitor* is surrounded by a ball of plasma. His pod ruptures and bits of him fly out into the darkness, streaming behind like a tiny comet's tail. We keep firing,

Bueller keeps shouting in our ears. We keep cutting spider-web tension lines.

Then all at once, *Lady of Yue* really cuts loose, and in our present state, the stars take a horrible spin—and we are no longer effective as gunners or as human beings. I spatter the inside of the pod with the contents of my mostly empty stomach—mixed with blood. My eyes feel as if they're going to fall out on my cheeks.

But Ishida and Jacobi exchange calm comments, battle discussion—in Japanese. Ulyanova chimes in in Russian. Somehow the tone alone helps me keep it together—that, and another buzz along my spine. We've had a definite effect. The corner pyramids are retracting and Box seems to be wobbling. Maybe even getting smaller.

I think Box is falling back—miracle.

The pods retract. Bueller opens them and extracts us one by one, ignoring the smoking ruin of the *efreitor*'s pod—gathering us up in her arms, wiping us down with her sleeves, then grabbing our damp collars and tugging and shoving us inboard using feet, hands, legs, arms, herding us. Her own face is streaked with tears and spattered with vomit. Maybe ours, maybe hers.

"Did it work?" Jacobi asks, slurring her words.

"Don't ask," Bueller says. "Maybe." She huffs and tugs. Ishida gives me a thumbs-up. I have no idea what the hell just happened, or what we did—whether it was real or just a nightmare. But through the structure, looking out to where Mars had once been, and Box had hovered, I see nothing—

Just a gray smear of stars.

"Move it!" Bueller shouts. "We got four minutes to get you packed away."

"We're fucking puppets," Jacobi says. "We don't understand any of this!"

Borden helps Bueller marshal us toward the centerline. Jacobi is still fomenting. "The Gurus are so goddamned frightened they're sending us out here and just pulling strings. How the fuck did that ever happen? Does anybody know what's going on?"

"Wait until you see Titan," Bueller says grimly.

Something comes back to me, something Kumar said. *That's what the Gurus like. They like it interesting.*

Makes me want to puke all over again.

THE BIG VAMOOSE

More rails slide from above. Bueller is a dozen meters ahead. She tells us to grab and go. The rails take us aft through the soda straws and blue spheres—Bueller's so-called soccer balls. They still look like grapes to me. Borden is next handle over. Jacobi and Ishida are to my left. All gawk in wonder or worry. As we're transported aft, we pass the first few triplets of blue spheres. They're dark, with stripes faintly barber-poling across their surfaces—out of order?

Finally we arrive at spheres that glisten pure blue, no stripes. Bueller swims backward, assessing our nearly naked forms with a practiced eye. She tells us to pay attention and assigns each a number. "Name and rank don't mean shit. Size, mass, composition are important. We're balancing our balls." Not even a grin.

Numbers light up on the corresponding spheres, and our rods and handles pull us up next to our assignments, so awesomely efficient it threatens to bring tears to my eyes. I wonder if this is how the secretary's heroic son got out to Titan a few years ago. Conveyed in brilliant style, using such sophisticated might and know-how—only to get himself killed. Maybe eaten by one of those insects in the Spook's tail, or something weirder down on Titan.

Crew Chief quickly opens a plastic box and removes stacks of gray circles, like doilies or lace yarmulkes, each sealed in gel in an envelope of transparent plastic. "Here's the good stuff," Bueller says. "I guarantee pleasant dreams."

The envelopes gleam and squish as she passes them out, one apiece.

"Part one of your brain boost, weeks of training—makes you all good citizens. Don't mess with these beauties. Follow instructions to the letter or you'll be shit down the chute, useless to me or anyone else."

Jacobi and Ishida examine their packages with curled lips. "Could have used one of these earlier, right?" Jacobi asks me.

Borden and Joe and Tak and the Russians hold theirs gingerly.

Two minutes left.

"They're called caps," Bueller says. "Used to be an acronym, I forget for what."

"Cranial Amplified Programming," Borden says.

"Yes, ma'am. Now you know why I forgot. You don't need to shave your heads, just pull the caps out of their wrappers, place them over the center of your crown, and they'll settle in and glue down. Leave them there until they fall off. They don't put anything inside your skull but training and info, and that'll take twelve hours to set up and become useful."

"Not for these two," Borden says, pointing to me and DJ. "We need their heads clear." She takes Bueller aside and they have words. The commander has doubts DJ and I are up for this much stimulation. I hear something about her not knowing all that they put me through back at Madigan. Wouldn't want to trigger *instaurations*. Maybe she said *installations*. Either way, what the hell are they?

"*Everybody*, ma'am," Bueller insists with a concerned expression, brooking no dissent, even from rank. "We're really short and we need expert drivers. If they don't get it, they won't have the proper training, and they won't have touch ID. The machines won't recognize them, they won't be able to coordinate with the team—they could all die down there!"

Grunts love to watch command argue. Makes us feel warm and cozy. Bueller's winning, but Borden isn't happy. She backs off, head lowered, like she wants to butt someone, anyone.

"Me, too?" Ishida asks, touching her metal cranium.

"Yeah," Bueller says. She delicately examines Ishida's head, finger hovering, and studies the line between metal and flesh. "Plenty of room. You'll be fine," she says.

"*Arigato*," Ishida says.

"What's in them?" Tak asks.

"Reflex learning, part one. Key ideas. Words and phrases that will speed your getting acquainted with seed product down on the Wax."

"Product..." Ishida says.

"Weapons and vehicles," Bueller says. "Seeds begin to suck up processed materials as soon as your glider connects with the reserves stockpiled on the base platform. If the base or the platform still exists. We'll know that in a couple of hours, after we get there. We can't see it from orbit. Understood?"

"Vehicles and big weapons get assembled in place," Tak

says, as if this makes all the sense in the world. Joe watches us from forward, where he's sitting between Borden and Kumar.

"Starting with those seeds," Jacobi says.

"Right," Bueller says.

"Wax?" DJ asks.

"Whole damn moon is covered with waxy residues, along with poisons, corrosive bases, and saline cesspools. Worse than you'd encounter in your worst nightmare. There's even traces of something like sarin gas, and if *that* seeps into your gear..."

Better and better. Bug is back and thinks it's all very cozy. Saline solution ripe with metals? Mother's milk to ancient life. Lightning and electricity? Once there were entire ecosystems that dined only on electrons and scavenged their dead to replace membranes. We're all wimps compared to the great old ones.

Thirty seconds.

Borden, Jacobi, Ishida, Ishikawa, Kumar, and I share a number. That means we'll cohabit a grape. We crawl inside, Borden last. The big blue sphere is heavily padded with thin, sun-yellow lamps hiding between the cushions. I see the swirly pattern, like being inside a soccer ball. The hatch closes. Ishida mutters and Jacobi looks around, anticipating the next slam. From our point of view, new tech has never implied comfort.

"Resuming now," Bueller says.

Second-phase acceleration begins. It's much gentler than the first. We shift to one side of the ball and bump the cushions. No straps, no drama. All there is to it. We're cargo, packed and ignorant but so far comfortable enough. Warm and comfortable.

"This is Big Vamoose?" Jacobi asks.

The pressure grows in that same direction. Ishida closes her eyes, claps her hands, mutters. Maybe she's praying again.

We're floating inside a soccer ball, wearing yarmulkes, hitching a ride on a Chinese warrior lady with long, burned skirts—about to fly off to rescue an entire moon. I'm still recovering from watching our bolts trim Box, from feeling *Lady of Yue* mess with Jesus and everything else about reality. I still can't believe any of it. But then, I didn't believe I was going to Mars the first time, either.

Jacobi spread-eagles and bumps into Borden's leg. Borden withdraws, tightening her space. Ishikawa's taking it all in stride—no strain, no sweat. Kumar tucks his doilied head, folds his legs and arms into a lotus, and rolls to a point of stable rest.

Finally, Crew Chief's voice reaches us inside the sphere. "Guidance reports Box still tracking at a million klicks, so close your eyes. That's what I do. Close your eyes and count backward from ten."

I get to five before my fingers tingle. I feel a weird crawling and tightening on my head. The cap, I assume. I sure hope my quantum junk has been scrubbed.

Then…

I black out.

Don't feel a thing.

COBWEBS

Darkness, close and warm. Air smells stale, like I've been here awhile. I remember where we are. A moment of concern, not quite panic, as I think the lights will come on and I'll be surrounded by desiccated mummies.

But the ball brightens and everyone's fine. Borden thrashes, as does Ishida, who might hurt someone if she's not careful—but she quickly regains motor control and looks embarrassed. "*Gomenasai*," she says.

"*De nada*," Ishikawa says, rubbing her shoulder.

I feel reasonably chipper. My scalp itches. I look around. There's something silvery and dusty on our heads, like a net of gossamer threads. I pat my scalp. The others refuse to pay attention, so I thump my crown and say, "Cobwebs, ladies."

They reach up, hesitate in unison—kind of comical, like they don't want to find a spider. Then they pat the gossamer and make disgusted faces.

"What the fuck is this?" Jacobi asks, inspecting a clump of threads.

"Laying eggs," I say.

"Fuck you!" Ishida says, and keeps plucking and balling up the stuff that comes out of her short hair. "It's that goddamned cap."

Kumar wakes next, legs still tucked into a lotus. He reaches across to Jacobi's temple and pinches up a thread. Jacobi's reaction is swift; she grabs his hand, ready to crush fingers, snap wrist, break arm—

Kumar freezes. Privilege does not precede him everywhere. He says, "Pardon me. Do you feel any difference?"

"No." Jacobi shoves his hand aside.

He flexes his fingers. "Nor do I, yet."

Borden wakes last. Seeing the others, her hand goes to her scalp. Her expression is priceless. "Jesus Christ!" she says. "Is this it?"

"Part one, the crew chief said," Kumar observes.

"I demand a raise," Ishida says.

The lights brighten. The hole in the soccer ball slides open. Bueller peers in. "I'm cracking my little eggs," she says. "Chicks are bright and fluffy. It's been two weeks. We're about halfway. Come on out and get some food."

"Not hungry," Ishida says.

"Me, neither," Jacobi says.

"Mandatory," Crew Chief says. "You've learned a lot in the last few days and we want to set it firm. Believe me, you won't want to miss *Lady of Yue* at full sail."

Ishida, Jacobi, and Borden finish removing their gossamer. Ishida collects the threads, wads them up, and leaves a small, dusty clump about an inch wide suspended in the middle of the ball. We push out through the hole. More smart ropes offer themselves and we move forward between the white metal beams. All very efficient. No bouncing, no collisions, just straightforward transport beyond the spheres toward the big bell.

The outer hull of the ship has darkened to a deep, cloudy-sky gray.

Ishida glides past me. "Maybe we'll ride centipede together," she says. I can see it. A great big machine, bronze-colored and round-headed, big slit-port for an eye, with a thick, muscular body and a long crawling tail—machine or monster? Now residing as a seed in cargo stores.

SNKRZ.

Jacobi guides herself toward Ishida. "Gadget, how's the equipment?"

"Smooth and shiny," Ishida says. "I feel innocent."

"Me, too," Jacobi says, looking unsure of herself, and burps.

Ishida lifts her real eyebrow. "Sir, your being innocent worries me."

For the moment, I also feel pretty good. *That* worries me. Nobody hauls grunts in comfort. There's got to be misery. And here it is. My turn for a bilious belch.

Jacobi looks green. "Not again," she says.

"What?" Kumar asks. He looks surprised, then turns a lovely olive. His stomach twitches. We're all popping sweat, trailing a mist of salty drops.

More rope lines appear from the other side of the long vineyard. We're joined by Ishikawa, then by a bare handful of Russians, but many of the ropes are empty—no Litvinov, no Mushran, no Joe and DJ. These Russians don't speak English. Not having skintights and angels puts us at a disadvantage. We're as dumb as we look.

Crew Chief meets us at the apex of the rope ride, holding on to a steel ring mounted around a big circular opening. "Jump off and wait here," she says. "We've got crew quarters beyond. Should fit you all in."

"Crew get a good sleep?" I ask, trying to avoid another heave.

"Nobody sleeps but passengers," she says. "*Lady of Yue* is a cranky girl."

"Who's driving?" Jacobi asks.

"Two rabbis," Crew Chief says.

"Rabbis?" Ishida asks.

"That's what we call them. They keep the ship right with the law."

I look aft and finally see Joe and DJ and Litvinov and more Russians, including Ulyanova. A gentle breeze wafts forward. Crew Chief tells us to release the circular rail and go with the flow. We tumble with the currents. I feel like a wet dandelion seed with a sour tummy.

DJ moves up beside me, spreads his arms, flaps, and twists. "You'll believe an asshole can fly," he says.

"Keep tight!" Bueller says.

The opening takes us into a tube about five meters wide and maybe fifty long. Halfway along, the tube turns clear as glass and we end up in an outboard bubble just aft of the weapons pods.

Lady of Yue's skirts no longer ripple. They've moved forward a hundred meters, where they shroud the soda-straw vineyard and the cargo stores beyond like a stiff cape, with the gray bell as a great round hat. The whole Spook seems to have grown to maybe two thousand meters from stem to stern.

"Where the hell are we?" Joe asks, pasty and damp, behind me and DJ. Bits of cap still fleck his scalp.

There's activity on the other side of the bell. Something large and pale and curved rises over the rim of the bell, then moves aft below the skirts like a hoop half-hidden by hanging laundry.

"Here come the garters," Bueller says. "Aren't they perrr-ty?"

The natural light this far out in the system is gray and indistinct. It's going to be even darker out by Saturn. The stars, with so little competition, shine sharper and brighter than ever. We're a hell of a ways from Earth, from Mars, from the sun. It's lonely and empty out here.

What's the reverse of claustrophobia—agoraphobia?

"*Lady of Yue* has three garters in nine sections. In part, they strengthen the holds and stability vanes aft during the next phase of flight. We'll get to Saturn space, from where we are now, inside of three days. This is the hard part, ladies."

We watch the garters join section by section—what we can see of them. Jacobi huddles with her squad. Our Skyrine sisters cock their heads, listening girl to girl. The guys might as well not be here.

Bueller says, "Matter down close to the sun acquires bad habits and old sin. Matter that knows sin is held back, but matter that is cleansed becomes young and fast. We have to get this far out from the sun to shed the last of it. That shit really starts to fall away when we hook up the garters."

The Russians are stony. The last thing any warrior needs is a feeling that our strength is tied to evil ways and fucked-up souls. We know what we've done and where we'll likely go because of it. Only God has promised to understand. It scares me that out here, maybe we've passed outside His boundaries. I hate this fucking *Lady of Yue*, hate all ships that carry us into harm's way—I really do.

"Of course, it's all temporary," Bueller says. Again, her weird, Persian-cat look. "When we return downsun, matter reverts like a sailor on liberty. Now it's time for pudding. After you eat, one more little nap. We'll wake you in Saturn space about three hours from Titan."

COOK'S TOUR

We get our pudding cups in the small cafeteria, really more of a coffee shop. The cups contain brown goo that tastes like chocolate or coffee or toffee or all three, pretty okay and makes us feel stronger. Crew Chief waits patiently.

Ishida asks Bueller why we aren't given a chance to inspect the cargo aft—the big insect-looking things. "Does cap training kick in when we see them, or when they're finished?"

"Won't mean a thing to you right now," Bueller says. "They're seeds. They get finished on Titan. Saves a lot of mass."

Our tummies are full. Drowse hits us as we return to the vineyard and our soccer balls.

"How long since you've been back to Earth?" Jacobi asks Crew Chief, eyelids drooping.

"Too long," Bueller says. There's a wistful something in the way she says it. She closes the hole to our ball. The interior gets dark.

"She can't go home," Ishida says. "Too many times out and back."

"Too many times stripped and reloaded," Jacobi says.

We sleep. We sleep in hopes all our sins will be gone when we wake up. Goddamn, what a sleep. If it's all the same to you, General Patton, I'd rather shovel shit in Louisiana.

PART THREE

TITAN

Again, we feel pretty good when Bueller pops the soccer balls and we spill out. This time, there's an undeniable extra layer of youth and freshness, a new enthusiasm that comes from whatever's happened since the garters were applied. Yet nothing about Crew Chief has changed. If anything, her outlines seem fuzzier. I look around. None of us are exactly crystal. Big Vamoose must have affected our vision.

I hope.

Bueller takes us back to the outboard bubble. *Lady of Yue* is a Sally Rand kind of gal, slipping her white feathers over the best parts, showing less than you want to see, less than you need to see, but enough to keep curiosity fresh. I vow that's the last time I'll think kindly of this massive, silk-skirted bitch—but in fact I can't feel too down on anything because of that damned *freshness*. Maybe there is a long habit of sin way back in the old neighborhood, where so many terrible things have happened. Somebody once called that Karma. I don't ask Kumar about Karma. Too alliterative.

Fuck, I'm cheerful.

Borden and Kumar and Litvinov form a little triangle in the passage forward, as if blocking the crew chief from exiting without more explanation. But she's wrung out, and all that's left to explain is that we're on our last reserves. *Lady of Yue* is going to deliver us with all we're likely to ever get to accomplish our mission—whatever that might be. We're lucky to be alive.

"Take it slow," Bueller says. "Take a moment to find yourself again. Sorry to say that we've made you a very lumpy bed, my friends." The Persian-cat look is gone. She seems so damned out of focus I want to rub my eyes.

She peers forward and we rotate to see Kumar preceding a pair of small, skeletally thin figures in dark gray coveralls cinched around their waists—ugly but practical outfits, comfortable in zero-g. Both have prominent gray caps on their scalps—thicker than what we were given. They look permanent.

Kumar says, "Our pilots want to pass along a last bit of information, and wish us luck."

"These are the rabbis," Bueller explains in an undertone. "We call them that because of their relation to the law, to deep physics, and those caps. They get new ones every trip. Their caps don't fall off, and they don't take them off until they get new ones." She sucks in a deep breath at the audacity of what's happening. "Rabbis don't *ever* meet with passengers. Socialize, I mean. This is special, so be nice."

Both of our pilots have short, kinky black hair, flattened noses, and rich umber skin. Except for their thinness, they might be Pacific Islanders, descendants of the first humans to navigate by the stars. It's a strange meeting, leaders of a doomed crew to an equally doomed expeditionary force.

The pilots take us back to the observation bubble. They want to join us in viewing our destination. At first, they say very little. They speak with their golden-brown eyes, and they point.

Lady of Yue is descending toward Titan, which right now is between Saturn and the distant sun. For the first time, we see all of Titan eclipsing the sun, a moody golden scythe cradling a dark brown ball, backlit by stars and other moons—and by Saturn. The full glory of Saturn and its rings holds our attention for a good long time. Everyone is transfixed.

Almost everyone.

I track Joe's attention because Joe won't let the pretty stuff get in the way. Both he and Litvinov survey *Lady of Yue* fore and aft to get a better picture of the damage. It's bad. Two of the main cargo frames and two of the balance vanes beyond are marked with gray gouges and slashes. Hard to know whether anything in the frames can be salvaged, but the vanes do not look useful. Three of the six skirts are stiff and dark and one has a peculiar tear running its length, edges still sparking, which I might be able to understand if I knew just what they were made of in the first place—

Then Litvinov and Joe turn. The pilots are actually going to speak to us. Bueller is astonished.

The older pilot has streaks of gray around his temples and the skin of his face looks like soft leather. We settle in, grow quiet, and turn toward him like kids on a bus trip. It takes real presence to make Skyrines settle in so intently.

"We would like to bring better news," he says in a wispy

voice. He has a strong, out-of-kilter gravitas—we can see him, we assume he's there, but the light he reflects seems incomplete, and when we look sideways, he doesn't quite stick to the background. "We've traveled here for seven seasons. First season, we had stations around the southern hemisphere, and Antags had stations around the northern. We were stretched too thin to fight. More of an exploratory season, learning how to survive, trying to figure the best way to carve down and access the seas—because that's what both Antags and humans wanted to do."

"The Ants told you that?" Ishida asks.

The older pilot smiles. "No, dear," he says, like a patient grandfather. He doesn't look that old, but the grayness of his reflected light gives that impression. "We sent out surveillance machines, both crewed and automated. Most didn't come back. That was the only killing going on that season, until the very end.

"Then we learned the Antags were digging deep. They'd broken through to a polar sea and were sinking big machines and fanning them out through the canyons and around the ridges, up to the shelving slopes and crustal caps, as far as they could reach. They made it down first, but we were right on their heels, and we began a two-pronged push on the surface to close up their ventrances—cryo-volcanic fissures and blowholes. We were delicate, because we wanted to preserve as much as we could. We used methane jets to carpet bomb the northern polar regions with conventional explosives, then sent our best big machines on long marches overland. We thought we'd surround and seal off and just vent-hop until we'd closed all of them. Didn't work.

"Our first-stage product wasn't that efficient. The Antagonists were better at converting raw materials. Their machines grew faster and became bigger than our machines. They chewed us up on the surface, and we never made it into the deep oceans. First season came to an abrupt end just as we were able to defend and finish our own ventrance. A very brave force descended during the short pause to see what they could see. We had to abandon them."

I can feel Coyle listening, agreeing. *I was there.* Bad season, worst season of all—highest percentage of casualties. She stuck around for the second delivery of soldiers and seeds, new product, new designs—after taking in the lessons of the first season.

"Season two was different," the pilot says. "We lasted, though still with many casualties. We cleared more vents, finished our exploratory journeys from the southern poles to the equator—even claimed vents north of the equator, old Antagonist entrances—surrounded them, sunk in and defeated them, kept the enemy from digging out—thousands of their machines were destroyed or lost. We lost dozens. Finally, a good season for us, terrible for them.

"But the Antagonists had learned. Season three was the most important of all. That's when we came upon the saline jungles. Some called them cities. They were old and seemed deserted, but our Wait Staff advisors communicated with the Gurus, and they were very interested."

Mushran regards our dubious expressions with a dignified nod. The pilot defers to him, while Kumar moves around our little group as if conducting a diagnostic survey. He seems concerned about too much knowledge being added all at once. Knowledge can change the mix.

"We thought this was more archaeology than battle, which

was fine by me," Mushran says. "I like to learn and live. The saline jungles were intricate mazes made of compacted salts and waxes and plastics, hard as granite. Traveling between their branches was like seeing coral reefs from a worm's point of view. They stretched for hundreds of kilometers, rising to touch the crust like pillars—mostly around the equatorial regions, where the tides were strongest, where the aurora sang bright, and purple currents flickered like lightning. Really. Just like that. Continuous and unbelievably beautiful."

"You were on Titan?" Jacobi asks him.

"Along with Captain Coyle," Mushran says.

We regard Mushran with more respect. This does not affect him in the least. "When we first explored the saline jungles, we thought some parts might still be alive—but there was no life. They were barren, populated only by electric currents and ionized, oxygen-free membranes, like cell walls but many kilometers across. Nothing like triple worms or spider castles."

"What are those?" Jacobi asks.

"You'll see them. Still, the jungles seemed dynamic—the way the purple discharges and exchanges moved. Some of our observers were especially interested. They formed a cadre within the battalion and called the purple flows inside the cities 'I/O,' without explanation. We thought they meant the Jovian moon. But later we learned they meant *Input-Output*. The saline cities might be dead, but they were still active—still very much in use."

"By who?" I ask.

"We did not know," Mushran says. "About the time of the sixth season, we heard rumors about the old mines on Mars. Our I/O experts were again interested. And when they heard that Antags were dropping comets to destroy the Martian mines, the old fragments of moon, our experts quickly returned to orbit. We were told to abandon the saline jungles and fall back to our fortified deep-ocean stations. Many of us returned through our few open vents to the surface and caught gliders back to *Lady of Yue*, which returned us to Earth. Some of our experts were already anticipating what happened in season seven. Kumarji referred to these new activities as a 'war on information.' But none of us knew whose information was being targeted. That's when our stations began to get seriously pasted. And that's also when we saw evidence that Antags were attacking not just us. They were going after each other."

"We can't know what we're supposed to do here," Jacobi says. "Who are we defending? What's left to defend?"

The others murmur and nod agreement.

"What's our mission, Commander?" Jacobi asks Borden.

"We have no combat orders," Borden says. "Division Four tells us to deliver Corporal Johnson and Master Sergeant Venn to Titan, get them as close to the saline jungles as possible—and wait for results." She looks exhausted and folds her arms.

The older pilot picks up the narrative. "Our last orbital season, we saw that Titan was being repeatedly bombarded by comets."

"Antag?" Litvinov asks.

"We presume," the pilot says. "Nearly hyperbolic orbits. The maps made for the previous season are useless. River networks, plains, and highland landmasses have been extensively reworked. Eleven out of twelve installations have fallen silent, presumably destroyed with all personnel. However, cap training—instructions for operating your equipment and weapons systems—is up-to-date. As for the strategic situation, and whether there are still Antagonists—nobody knows."

Without farewells, the pilots depart. We're quiet for a time. Then Joe taps Tak, DJ, and me, taking us aside, and pulls us in close. "Captain Coyle served on Titan years before she was sent to Mars," he says. "She expressed her opinions and got busted down. When they sent her back to Earth, she promptly re-upped, went full MARSOC at Camp Lejeune, and rose to major in record time. Then she talked back some more and got demoted again, but they still gave her tough assignments. They gave her Mars. Anyway, Borden thinks you two might have a special connection with Coyle that could help us down there."

"That would have been *years* ago," DJ says.

"Even so, that's a big reason you were plucked out of Madigan. Kumar and Mushran and Division Four believe in ghosts."

"Do *you*, sir?" I ask.

Joe's look is veiled. "Prove me wrong," he says. Tak stands by looking rock steady. Bless Tak Fujimori.

STATS

Titan grows hour by hour. Bug and I like it in the bubble. Well—Bug doesn't actually express an opinion, but I speak for it.

Borden and Kumar persuaded the other Skyrines to leave me alone. Borden wants me close to Titan. In full sun, the old moon looks like a big dusty orange shot a little out of focus. Dim at the edges (it's not very bright out here), brownish in places. Foggy. Most of the details we see are the frilly, tortured edges of high methane clouds. Methane. Swamp gas. *Right*. There are methane oceans down there and methane rivers. Liquid methane falls as rain in drops bigger than marbles, slow and steady, washing down in rivulets from the waxy, sandy, icy land. Titan is orange and brown and frilly and mysterious.

Operations have come to a strategic halt. Ishida and Jacobi think we're on the ragged edge of completely pulling out. They anticipate, they hope, that the entire mission could be aborted. Borden and Kumar know better. They say nothing.

Litvinov is hiding somewhere with his troops. This waiting isn't good for any of us. Hanging loose on *Lady of Yue* is really weirding us out.

Despite the survey that says half our seeds are damaged beyond recovery, I think we're dropping soon. DJ agrees. Joe agrees.

No word from Captain Coyle.

Borden asked me a few hours ago if I felt a stir, like I was closer to something important. I don't. Maybe we are, but I can't force it. DJ and I don't compare notes. Mostly we avoid each other.

———

Joe disobeys Borden's strong suggestions and visits me in the bubble. We don't speak, just watch as the ship enters Titan's long shadow. Saturn-shine partly fills the moody darkness. There's lightning in the high methane clouds, dozens of silent flashes like giants trying to light cigars. Did I say Titan was *big*? Bigger than Earth's moon, over half the diameter of Mars. Everything is poison down there. Atmosphere consists mostly of nitrogen. And it's *old* nitrogen, maybe from the far reaches of the Oort cloud, that somehow drifted down long after Titan was formed. Titan's nitrogen differs from that in the gaseous nebula that helped shape Saturn itself, which...

More useless crap? I don't know. Bug likes it. Bug is compelled to acquaint itself with how much things have changed since his day. They've changed a lot.

To me, all by myself, listening to nobody and watching only with my own eyes, Saturn is a big piece of art glass dropped "swish" through a banded platinum hoop. Bug sees it different. He remembers Saturn as green with no ring. Something big happened a long time ago. Isn't that what this is all about?

Did Bug come from around here? The rings are new, Bug decides. But yeah. This system is where home *was*, probably a moon just a little smaller than Titan. Then something big happened. I think it could have been another planet or a wandering dark sun. It shoved some moons out and pushed others into Saturn itself, changing its color and maybe helping create the fickle beauty of the rings. What I read back at Madigan, though, tells me the rings are fragile and maybe they just come and go. Bug doesn't express an opinion. Neither does anyone else.

In brief, however, this is where we all began. Yada yada. One can only hear about the birds and the bees so long before it gets boring. Any thoughts, Captain Coyle, any guidance? Nothing. That's okay, I can put that aside, because suddenly there's a shitload of data pouring into our helms from *Lady of Yue*, supplementing cap learning. I drift in the bubble with Joe beside me, taking it all in.

The supplement is gentle at first, taking us back to basics—more detailed stuff about Saturn and its moons. There's Iapetus, famous for being a yin-yang moon, white on one side, black on the other. Iapetus's white is deposited water ice, its black is spray-painted by dust kicked up from impacts on another moon, Phoebe. Bug seems to remember Iapetus, but remembers it as neither so black nor so white. There's Enceladus, which is pretty small but has a lake of water under one region. Bug doesn't know anything about Enceladus. Or Rhea and Tethys and Dione and lots of much smaller moons.

Then the *Lady*'s data turns harshly practical, adding more

layers over what the caps have already infused. As a battlefield, Titan is unbelievably difficult. Most of the water in the surface layers is mineral ice—like rock or sandy grit. Lava on Titan is water mixed with ammonia, rising from Titan's seven inner oceans through deep vents—cryo-volcanoes. All but two of the oceans are salty in the extreme, and not just table salt. There's ionic sulfur and potassium—a devil's brew that at times generates amazing electrical currents, which some of our machines—especially the excavators—are designed to use to advantage.

Basically, Titan is a giant wet cell battery. No one in his right mind would choose it for fighting ground. Our basic protections need to be stronger than anything made for Earth or Mars. To that end, there's one new plus: Water, along with hydrocarbons scooped up from the surface, can be woven into a superstrong fiber. Don't ask how. The structural diagrams make my head hurt. Did you know that concrete contains water even after it sets? I didn't.

Then—basics again, like a break between bad news.

Titan's brown color comes from complex hydrocarbons called tholins. There are lots of different gases down there, many of them poisonous, some flammable (if you have a lighter filled with oxygen!), but mostly there's nitrogen. Because there's lots of lightning and other electrical discharge between the methane clouds, billions of tons of tars and waxes and precursors to more complex chemistry are made and scattered over the surface or swept into the basins of the methane seas. These organic compounds will provide many of the raw materials used by our weapon and vehicle seeds to double and even triple their present mass.

Follows more harsh. We've been fighting down there for

six years. *Lady of Yue* fills us in on what those battles were like, how they were fought and with what. First impression: big and scary. Second impression: worse.

Joe's eyes close and he curls up. I feel the same way.

But there are some things *Lady of Yue* and cap learning can't teach us. Having been hit by quite a few comets in the last year or so, as the pilots told us, Titan's topology has been massively altered. It's possible even the number of inner seas has changed, not to mention the outer methane lakes. Titan now rocks to a different music.

It's clear Borden and Kumar and maybe even Joe are of the opinion that the Gurus know what's really down there. Question remains, why is it so dangerous that they'd jeopardize the entire war?

Final bit of info: We'll be descending in twenty-eight hours, a ship's day—if the landers can be pried from the twisted frames, if the seeds can be salvaged, if there's still any good reason for us to drop. The grunt's delight is that matters of life and death are rarely his responsibility until he's deep in the shit.

LAST CALL

Two of the five gliders respond positively and check out to Bueller's satisfaction. With our reduced force, all we need is one to put us down on the Wax and complete the mission. We'll get just one chance. *Lady of Yue* will station-keep for as long as she can.

Bueller escorts us down a tight, cold aft corridor to inspect the best glider. It's a genuine aircraft, not the pop-up-and-down landers used on Mars. The fuselage is almost eighty meters long, bulbous and heavy at the nose, oval in profile at the middle, where the wide delta wings are currently upswung, casual and awkward. About five meters behind the blunt nose circle twelve intakes, each two meters wide. Farther back, behind the wings, the glider's middle tapers to a more slender V, followed by three jet exhaust nacelles spreading wide the profile. The whole thing finishes with a screw-twisty triangle of ailerons.

As we watch, the glider's fuselage opens long hatches to allow stowage of seventeen parcels, varying in size between five and twenty meters. These are so-called seeds from *Lady of Yue*'s aft bay. They look like presents for a grim Christmas, long and lumpy, concealed by black plastic wrap cinched down by red strapping. Stowage in the glider is accomplished by slender and flexible mechanical arms, watched over by a skinny, naked crewman enclosed in another bubble on the end of a boom—the only crew member we've seen so far. His outline is exceptionally fuzzy, for which I am grateful. He pays us no attention whatsoever.

"These are your rudimentary seed packages," Bueller says. "Some will combine in place to form more complicated structures, like excavators or centipedes. Others will take more time and grow out to full size by themselves, mostly the vehicles supporting big weapons—zapguns, ionics, penetrators. Once placed in their cradles beside the station, all the seeds will dip from the station storage tanks, and they'll also start pulling in gases and liquids from the local atmosphere, plus solid raw materials arranged for them just outside the installation's perimeter. I'm being told that the station itself may be recycled if those supplies are not sufficient, so you'll want to get in and get prepped quickly.

"Seeds are hungry," she says. "Don't fuck with them. Don't get between them and raw material reserves. Don't mess with *anything* growing. Half-finished product has been known to absorb whatever it touches. Stay the hell away from developing product."

We all nod. Respect your weapons. Nothing new. Then why am I trying to swallow my Adam's apple?

The ship's now-rigid skirts form a pale backdrop around *Lady of Yue*'s damaged midsection. I try again to assess the ship's overall condition. Doesn't look great. Optimism always leads to disappointment. Pessimism is wiser anytime we're about to land in the shit. And that is surely where we're heading. Maybe this was a suicide mission from the start.

Bueller has let us absorb long enough. "Time to load," she says.

DOWN TO A DISTANT SEA

Our cleaned and repaired skintights are handed back and we clamber gingerly down the dim passage into the glider's main cabin, equipped to carry fifty. We're only thirty.

Bueller hands out another stack of caps and taps her head. "Ready?" she asks. "Part two. We save the best for last." We shuck the doilies and inspect them. Damp and fibrous, as before. Again we paste them over our crowns. Ishida's cap folds in half away from the metal side, and settles down on softly fuzzy hair and flesh. She looks at me, looking at her. "I'll be fine," she says. "What about you? How many haunted heads can you handle?"

Jacobi grimaces.

We push ourselves back in the glider's narrow couches. Bueller checks us over, nodding at each fitting. DJ's cap squirms on his crown and he reaches for it. Bueller slaps his hand.

"Bon voyage," Bueller says as she returns to the hatch. "Wish I was dropping with you. I surely do. Suck smog and come back soon." She withdraws. The hatches seal. Behind us, muffled groans, clangs, sounds of machinery and fluids.

Cap works faster than last time. There's an odd taste in my mouth, my entire body. "Hey!" I say out loud. I now see and understand, very clearly, that the liquid oxygen necessary to burn a portion of Titan's atmosphere is being pumped into the aircraft at the last, after the seeds are stowed. Our so-called glider is more of an ice-sucking jet designed to enter atmo, inhale combustibles, light them off, then power along for a few hundred klicks and coast to a tightly controlled landing.

More visuals. On our way down, and maybe even on our way back up—if we ever get that far—we'll become ramjets, packing in nitrogen to increase pressure in the fuel mix. The combustibles either freeze or condense on the chamber walls, and the precious slush is skimmed by the outer whisks of the turbines toward the combustion chamber, where the engines inject oxygen and light the mix. Whoosh. I thought the idea of using oxygen in a Zippo to light your cigarette was funny.

It's how we get down there.

Once down, we're destined to crawl, dig, excavate...and walk. Okay, that's good, I get that. Walking is good. Big, bulky diving suits, thick legs, sometimes with tractor treads for feet, sometimes with huge grippy boots...

And the goddamnedest, most primordial-looking machines we've yet seen. As big as destroyers, bronze and silver, with a dozen segments and lateral tree lines of ornately fringed legs for carving and crawling and digging—for burrowing deep through ice and rock into the interior oceans of Titan, and for tangling with, and surviving, other monsters. These machines come with their own problems and weaknesses, natcherly, and no certainty there'll be enough material down there to allow them to grow to full size or reach full armament. In which case, we might have to scavenge the surface of Titan and hunt for machine corpses before we can dive deep. More delays before we fight. But also, delays before we die.

If we fight at all. If there are Antags down there, or our own people hot on our trail. My head hurts. At this stage I seem to be mostly asleep. I certainly can't move, which is fine because I'm locked into my couch. A coolness runs all up and down my memories. The cap is pulling away the pain, flooding me with more words, more impressions curious and harsh, informative and discouraging, all necessary to my in-depth training. Not thinking, really, and not worrying, just taking it all in like a sponge—not so bad. Even the bad news feels pretty good. Got a thing you want to think about? Hey, here's something *better.* The concepts build in reverse like bricks falling out of a tornado to make a building. Boy do I prefer listening to angels in our helms. We can be bitch-friendly with our angels. We can complain about them, give them rude names, hijack their stupid certainties to help cement squad morale. Not *this*. We are becoming the caps.

My muscles twitch. My fingers curl as if wrapping around controls. The last of my diminishing flare of curiosity illuminates a distant question: Where do these caps get their reflex knowledge, the muscle training and innate instincts? Maybe I don't want to know. Maybe cap knowledge is distilled from dead Skyrines.

The cap floods my curiosity and drowns it with more concepts, pictures, diagrams, like a magician forcing cards. Coyle remains silent. Bug remains silent. Maybe they're learning right alongside the little homunculus that is me, the tightly curled-up kid trying to pretend he's watching cartoons before going off to a school he hates, a Central Valley concrete blockhouse filled with kids too crazy to ever get into the Skyrines. It was there I learned that civilian kids are the worst. To Army brats. Maybe they thought I was the creepiest kid in the school. Maybe their moms told them about my mom, or my dads. My real father was stationed at Fort Ord for a year but we didn't live on base. Until they divorced, my mom spent her mornings in a cannabis haze, but she tried to be good to me. She kept herself just a little whacked-out from the hour I left for school until 6:30 p.m., when she could start drinking—but she really wanted us to live a normal life.

Not so easy.

Before I met Joe, I tended to jump without looking, because nothing could be worse than staying right where I was. I wasn't cruel or sadistic like some of the truly fucked-up kids I knew—the ones who strung mice on nylon lines and watched them dangle and squirm. Jesus, not like *those* little monsters.

Okay. I'm going away now.

Or not.

Something is trying very hard to put my conscious mind up out of the way, on a shelf, to get on with cap and reflex learning. I don't resist. It's all cool. I'll have time to examine personal questions, try to resolve old philosophical issues, like, Why become a Skyrine? Why volunteer to fight? In part, to seek adventure. But also because war for all the shit is neater and cleaner and sweeter than civilian life.

All right, that's a lie. That's delusional. Help me out, Bug! What was life like in the really olden times? Were there cool bugs and cruel bugs, good and evil bugs, dumb and smart bugs, bugs pious and bugs blasphemous? Were you all smart and nobody dumb? Why can't I hook into those truths, Bug? I'm thinking you're—

Shut the fuck up.

Ah, at last! Coyle steps back in. She seems to take me down from the shelf and shake me like an old T-shirt.

Listen. This is important shit. We're going to where we might actually learn something.

"Yeah?" I mutter. "Like what?"

Like where I am.

If you don't know where you are, you don't know who you are, right? Here are the eternals: The shit remains the shit, the fight is always confused and messed up, and in the end—

Goddamn, Venn, hang on. Something really weird is coming. I think you're in for it.

Coyle was worried about something. I've been waiting for whatever that might be, but I'm still surprised when it arrives. My brain locks up. Thinking stops. Topped out. Too damned full. At the same moment, maybe, comes a sharp jerk. I feel our axis of motion changing. I confuse that with cap visuals of seeds sprouting, growing, like carnival balloons plumping out, becoming monstrous, making crew and warrior spaces, getting ready to take us in. Then that all mixes with motion and coolness and calmness.

Synesthesia, big word. Mom liked to read dictionaries. She and my dad and several stepdads—she chose them soon after he left, one after another, very much alike—would read pages to each other from an old paper dictionary or a volume from the *Encyclopedia Americana*, after dinner, in bed, and smoke Old Tobey, as she called it, and laugh at the big words.

I think I'm in my bedroom, nine, ten, eleven years old,

trying to sleep but listening to their muffled voices telling me all about Titan's atmospheric pressure and natural caches of raw material and how to find them, how to get your machine to self-repair if damaged—take a dip in a methane lake or where volcanic water streams down through carved-out, wax-lined valleys, down to where the plastic trees pop and—

Mom says, on the other side of my bedroom wall, beyond the stick-and-wallboard and chalky Army paint job, "Your machine will know you because of your touch. Touch ID is key to security and operational efficiency."

Mom? Is that really you?

Pulls me up short for a moment, along with another hard jerk, bump, double bump, and a

Roar.

Now my eyes are open. I peer through a port. Blackness outside turns orange, brown, then muddy yellow. We're getting closer and closer to the answers. But first we're going to have to dive or dig. Bugs dig up, we'll dig down. Maybe we'll meet halfway. But the bugs have been dead for billions of years, right? Deader than Captain Coyle.

Man, I really need to *wake up.*

And this time, unfortunately, I do.

INSTAURATION ONE:
MADIGAN MADRIGAL REDUX

I'm wrapped in sheets, twisted into a cocoon soaked with sweat. I open my eyes and see a gray ceiling, roll against the tug of the sheets, and see a wide sliding door and beyond that a familiar room. *Too* familiar.

I unwind from the sheets and stand by the side of the bed. I feel myself, soft ribs beneath gray underwear, thigh muscles, sinews between my legs, balls okay, cock okay....

Hair on my arms and legs, around my junk, hair on my chest, fuzz on my head. To my right is the narrow door to the bathroom, where the light above the shatterproof mirror has been left on—as always.

I blink away a smear of sleep.

The battery-powered electric razor rests precariously on the counter beside the sink. I leave it there, about to fall off every time I use it, as a kind of protest. Maybe I can bankrupt them with busted razors. No outlets anywhere, in case

I want to try to electrocute myself. I wouldn't, but they've been careful not to provide temptations or opportunities.

I bend down and feel under the foam mattress. The sap is still there. I haven't taken it out, haven't yet been rescued by…

Who?

I lean my head on the bed. The rumpled sheets and blankets look like a topo map of mountains. All rearranged, tangled, no good now.

Shit. Of course none of it was real. I had no idea how weird they could get. How far back does it go? How much do I remember about Mars? I remember meeting Teal, being rescued by her in her buggy. I remember the Voors. I remember Captain Coyle and her Special Ops team. Not all a dream. But everything since being locked in at Madigan is now in question. The whirly-eyed inquisitor finally got to me, finally pushed me into the madhouse. I can almost remember his name…which of course I learned in the dream.

Kafka?

Kmart?

DAYS PASS. NOBODY visits. Food arrives as usual, but tastes bland, pasty. I read, but the paperbacks don't mean much. I can't remember the last page. I can't even remember the cover of the book, unless I turn it over and stare at it, and then, it doesn't seem to matter. Elmore Leonard? Louis L'Amour? Daniel Defoe?

The bell rings at the window. Takes me forever to get out of the chair and answer. I'm toasted. They've finally broken me. Brilliant piece of work. Just lead me out to the end of my rope—somewhere out near Saturn—and jerk me back and that fucking does it. I'm one sad little white lab rat. See my twitchy nose, my beady pink eyes?

The bell rings again. I pack some energy down into my legs and stand to get to the window. The face behind the glass is not the whirly-eyed inquisitor, it's the other guy. The one who claims he's Wait Staff. (But didn't the inquisitor claim that, too? What was his fucking name again, Kafka or Kaffeine? Total toast!)

The face asks, "How are you feeling today, Master Sergeant Venn?"

"Not so good, Doc." I stick my tongue out and say ahhh. He smiles. This guy looks like a mannequin, the way he dresses, so fashionably lost and feckless, someone's idea of a middle-aged nerd.

"Have you been sleeping well enough?"

"Too well, Doc. Take me out of the oven, please? I'll tell you anything you want to hear. Really."

"We don't expect that, Master Sergeant. We are most concerned about your welfare."

"Then let me go. Let me walk on the beach. You can surround me with MPs, I don't care. I just want to feel sand between my toes and smell the salt water. See the sunset. I need to know I'm back on Earth for real, not somewheres..."

My voice breaks. I can't finish.

"I am most sorry, Master Sergeant. Perhaps soon. But first, I have to report that we have conducted an investigation into your longtime friend, Lieutenant Colonel Joseph Sanchez."

"What about him?"

"It seems he is not all he appears to be. Certainly not all he told you he was. Why do you trust him, Master Sergeant?"

"Fuck you!" I try to shout, but it's a raspy croak. I step away from the window and turn my back. Why so angry?

"He was ever your *instigator*, was he not?" I hear behind me. "He was the one always leading you into trouble."

I try to go to the bedroom and close the door, but the door won't close. I want to go into the bathroom but my legs won't carry me there. I stand by the bed and think about pulling out the sap and just whaling away at my head.

The voice goes on, calm but concerned. "He encouraged you to enlist in the Marines, and then to join the Skyrines. He accompanied you through basic and vacuum school and much of special training thereafter. He was with you at Hawthorne and Mauna Kea, but he was not with you at—"

"Just shut up," I say.

"While you were training with your drop squad and various chiefs at Socotra. He rejoined you before your first drop on Mars. Did he seem different to you at that time?"

He didn't. Maybe he did. I don't remember.

"Did he tell you what he had been doing while he was away?"

He did. He didn't.

"Thereafter, did he not always seem to have special knowledge about the unpleasant situations you were subjected to during your actions? And was he not always there before you, able to locate you and extract you, even during the most extreme circumstances?"

I return to the living room to face the guy in the window. Is he the same guy in the window I remember from the last time? Doesn't matter. "I know about you," I say. "You're not Wait Staff. Your name doesn't show up on the lists."

He ignores that. "Joe Sanchez is a very special individual, is he not?"

"He's my bud," I say.

"Then why has he betrayed you so many times?"

"I don't know what the fuck you're talking about." Suddenly I'm calm and collected and cool. I'm as frosty as a fudge bar in Fargo in February. Vee-Def said that once.

"Are you really anything without Joseph Sanchez? Are you even a complete human being, Master Sergeant Venn?"

"What's your point, you horse-fucking little dweeb?"

The guy smiles not in cruelty or triumph but in pity. Like he knows he's about to change my life and not for the better and he almost regrets it.

"Joe Sanchez has been stringing you along since before you were arrested, Master Sergeant. He has used you to advantage, and will use you again."

"How?" I shout. "I'm stuck here! Bring him to me! Put us together in a room with you and some Louisville Sluggers, I'll knock the Guru shit out of you—"

The guy behind the glass takes a peculiar, isomorphic side glance that smacks of a special effect gone wrong.

"That's it!" I say in triumph. "That's what Kafka said to me. He said you couldn't be Wait Staff. You have to be a Guru!"

"I *am* a Guru," the guy says, and then, briefly, I see him without the overlay. He *looks* like he could be a fucking Guru, but I've never seen one, so how can I be sure? He's not exactly a mammal, he's certainly not a bug, and he's definitely not an Antag. Also, he's not ugly. He looks efficient and smaller than I would have thought. The figure behind the glass keeps talking. Where's his mouth? Somewhere above the bump that might be a jaw, below the wide ridge that holds a shiny gray bar that might be his eyes. Gort eyes. RoboCop eyes. Shit. I still don't see his mouth. Just little motions above the jaw. Maybe he's a straw-sucker.

"You should ask Joseph Sanchez the following questions," he says.

For a while after that, I don't hear anything. I stand there trying to focus on the window, on the deepening darkness beyond the glass.

Sound returns.

"Ask Joseph Sanchez—"

"Yeah, ask him *what*, Goddammit?"

"Ask him about Corporal Grover Sudbury. Ask where he went with the corporal after your comrades exacted their punishment, and what they both did there."

"Sudbury vanished," I say.

"Everyone has their role, Master Sergeant," the voice says behind the window. "The relationship between Sudbury and Joseph Sanchez is popular, Master Sergeant. Far too popular to waste."

GOOD MORNING, MOON

Someone taps my helm with a padded metal finger. "Venn. Wake up." It's Ishida. She's persistent. I wake up—again. She's taken the seat next to mine. Borden is across the aisle talking earnestly to Kumar and Mushran. The glider vibrates, roars—again with that huge, MGM lion's roar—and we roll clockwise, then counterclockwise. The nose lifts, the tail vibrates, something big groans, and the whole airframe shudders.

"Rough ride," Ishida says with half a frown.

"I wasn't sleeping," I insist, but my words are mushy.

I look forward and see Ishikawa, Jacobi—Joe. Beyond them, Litvinov and the backs of the Russians. Their helms are distinctive. When did we put on our skintights? I lift my hand, check the seal with the glove. Same ones made for Mars, but newer—cleaned and pressed. I do not remember any of that. Are we off *Lady of Yue*?

Apparently. Yeah. We're on the glider, aren't we.

I clench the couch arms. Coming awake or out of my

trance or whatever, to *this*, does not feel good. I'm clearly a danger to everybody, blacking out like that.

"Did we all make it?" I ask.

"We're not down yet," Ishida says. "Look." She motions for me to close my plate. I do, and blink down a display. The glider feeds our angels a decent external 270, plus data in sidebars and two ratcheting crawls. I turn my head and the external goes with me. The glider is surrounded by swift brownish haze—methane clouds. A film keeps trying to stick to one or more of the cameras but gets swiped every few seconds. We're sloping into a valley of ten thousand smokes, but it's not fire that makes the smoke—it's freezing methane and a lot of other stuff, all described on the lower crawl. The turbines must be sucking in fine water-sand and that explains the surging and roaring. But we haven't crashed. We're still descending.

Everything gets brighter. The haze begins to clear and we see lower decks of brown and yellow clouds, a small sun cutting through a serrated break—the most surreal and beautiful sunrise I've seen. A flat deck of cirruslike clouds above the glider burns golden yellow.

We're down to five klicks from the rugged surface. Rising gray plumes of sandy water ice spew from black, shiny cracks that have to be dozens of meters wide and many hundreds of meters long. Below those cracks...down through them...what? Inner oceans? Deep in the cracks something green or silver-gray churns and bubbles. Ice lava, the crawl says. Ammoniated, highly saline water that just won't freeze solid and shoves up in a methane-steaming, ammonia-vapor slurry.

Planes, trains, and automobiles all the way. That's my life. But now we've gone as far as we're going to go, end of the line, right? Journeys end in warriors meeting. Which warriors?

Are Antags still down there?

Any of *us* left?

I'm working to ignore the blackout and what I experienced. Going back to Madigan. Fuck that shit. I should have been section 8'ed as soon as I got back to Earth.

Time-release terror.

"Huh?" I flip open my plate and look around. Nobody's spoken in the noisy cabin. It's Coyle. She gets me every time she pops in like that. She's clear, crisp, like inside my suit with me. Almost solid. Ishida has become engrossed in her helm display and pays me no attention. DJ, across the aisle, has kept his plate open and is studiously peering at nothing. He's out of it, too. We're both mainlining a strong signal.

Doesn't explain the—

Borden called them instaurations. They must be time-release psych capsules implanted back at Madigan to knock you down in case you get out of their control. I heard of that sort of stuff during Special Ops training. How to control a team that's gone rogue—implanted suggestion. Drives rogue agents to question everything. Commit suicide. Ups the ante if you disobey orders or defect.

"You think that's it?" I have to work hard to think my words back at Coyle rather than say them aloud.

Maybe. I'm not you, I don't feel all of you.

"You sound stronger here. Are you stronger?" I lean my head back in an agony of conflict. Trust isn't part of my tool-kit now, because everything's up for grabs.

Shut up and just keep the objective in view. There's something down below that shitty layer of gunk that's brought us this far.

"How do you know any of this?"

Because I'm part of it. I don't like it, but I am. We're going to where it's all coming together—where everything is held tight. So far, I'm not fixed into that memory. Until that finishes, I'm still flexible. I can make decisions and not just answer questions. But that's going to end soon. I don't like what might be replacing me. Doesn't feel right, but I can't see it clearly. Big Kahuna? Another bug? I don't like any of this.

Sounds like Coyle is dropping back into babble. I'm caught up in my own problems. I have a choice. Either I give in and let the *instauration*, the Madigan poison, spread, or I pretend it never happened, don't tell anybody—don't look Kumar or Joe in the eyes for the next few hours. Keep trying to stay part of this team, which, God help me, I'm actually thinking of with that weird combat affection called unit cohesion, spirit of the corps. Jacobi's juju is working on me as well as the sisters and the Russians.

I'm full of spirit, all right. Spirits, more like it. Haunted head, indeed. This is what, number four? I can't juggle that many balls.

I concentrate on the view. We're flying between low hills, turbines roaring on both sides, glider rocking like a carnival ride, then swooping up and down. I drop my eyes below the rim of the helm and the image from the outer sensors follows. Below—through rising silvery mist, swirling and blowing away at unseen nitrogen winds—

The debris of battle. My God, so much broken, blown-up shit!

I hear the occasional gasp or oath from the others, buried in the continuous roar. Ishida beside me is speaking Japanese, probably a prayer. Her sweet voice is musical counterpoint to what I'm seeing, what we're all seeing.

In jumbled mounds every few hundred meters across a flat brown prairie lie what look like thousands of stomped-down, bronze-colored centipedes, but *huge*—hundreds of meters long. Even crushed, they appear thick and strong, robust around the head and long in the middle. They're too damned big—big as ocean liners and cracked open, smashed, their lumpy, glistening interiors open to the corrosive mist. Around and inside them, nothing moves. They're squashed, they're dead. We're flying into a landscape littered with dead monsters. Some of them are ours. Some are not. The biggest of the big, the most powerful, now just wreckage on the Wax.

"Four minutes to station," Borden says over glider comm. "There's not going to be an accordion. Have to move fast. We'll find heavy combat gear on the other side, but for this transit, these suits will have to do, and that means we've got all of five minutes to get inside and get cleaned off."

I pull open my plate. Joe hunkers, waiting. I watch him suspiciously. Does he know shit I should know, should have been told a long time ago? Why would I even care what happened to Corporal Grover Sudbury? He was a rapist, a scumsucking shithead. I don't want to think about him, and maybe that's the point. I'm out of Guru control. They have me rubber-band screwed to a fine knot, about to snap, primed to step out into the poisonous cold and open my plate. Put an end to the guilt, the fighting—the confusion.

DJ leans back and reaches through the seats to tap my shoulder. "Stick close," he says. "It's going to get weirder, but

I'll be there with you." He looks serious. DJ rarely manages to look completely serious.

"Slim comfort, DJ," I say.

"It's *bad*, sir. You hear what I hear? Captain Coyle has been here. She says to tuck prunes and hang on to your fudge."

Behind us, listening, Ishida splutters a giggle and reaches a gloved hand to cover her mouth like a Japanese schoolgirl. Damn, that touches me. Somewhere inside, our Winter Soldier remembers being shy. If she can keep that core alive after all that's happened to her, I can sure as shit maintain. I notice she's found a pen and scrawled something on her skintight. I saw it on her previous skintight but didn't pay attention. She's written "Senketsu" above where her blaze might go. I don't know what that means. On her own suit, Ishikawa has written "Junketsu." I'm about to ask, but Borden tells us to seal and check suck.

Alarms in the cabin.

Glider hard-bumps and slows to an abrupt, lurching halt.

TITAN F.O.B.

The installation is a gray, snow-spattered hockey puck about fifty meters high and maybe twenty times that across. We did not get a good look before the glider nuzzled up to one side.

We unstrap and bunch in the narrow aisle. Borden pushes up mid-aisle and props her hands against the bulkhead. "Half-charge weapons. We'll move out in squad order, three teams," she says. "Jacobi's team first, Litvinov and Russians next, Sanchez and Johnson, Fujimori and Venn, take the rear." She gives me a stern look. Joe moves up beside me. Tak pushes through the aisle to stand beside DJ. DJ doesn't relish being POG any more than I do. "Two on point for each team," Borden continues. "All but points keep weapons belted. Damage to the station must be avoided at all cost."

The lock passes us outside a squad at a time. We don't wait for the others. It's every one of us across the crusty Wax and gritty ice-sand to a big black canopy that offers some protection against the weather, like a tent flap.

In the ten meters between the glider lock and the station, our arms and legs become coated with a fine, spreading layer of liquid methane that instantly starts to steam. We're warm enough to boil methane. That means our suits are losing heat fast. Sandy ice-grit lands as well and turns to mixed slush that curtains off and refreezes, weighing us down like hanging chains. That distracts us momentarily from the sensation that we're being squeezed by a big, cold hand. Titan's atmosphere is almost half-again denser than Earth's, and our skintights are designed to hold suck, not keep shit out.

Borden tries to alert the station that we need the outer lock opened. I see her lips move behind her bedewed faceplate. No response. Either nobody is there, or comm is fucked. She makes hand gestures and somehow communicates to us that there's a way in—maybe she knows the code.

My world-line is just a vector arrowing through a rugged trail of bad places relieved only by weird sanctuaries where you have to know the secret word or carry a fucking master coin. And it's not just me. That's human space in a nutshell. That's all we've conquered in the vac—stretched-out orbital threads between little BBs on which we depend for our lives. Most of the universe hates us so intensely it spreads itself so vast we can't even think of going there. Down where I am, it's cycles of hell spiraling in ever-shrinking circles. Inside, outside. Vac or poison outside, me inside. Tubes and coffins, more tubes, more coffins. Eternal returns of day and night.

Is it day or night? Day, I think. We landed at sunrise. The glider could have slid around to the other terminator, but Titan's pretty big—that would have taken a couple of hours.

Borden finds a big checkerboard. "Venn, get up here."

I join her and Joe and Litvinov.

"Make yourself useful. Coyle should know the sequence."

"She's not very reliable," I say, but then I reach up and slap my gloved hand on the squares in a staccato sequence. What are our chances? Good, it appears.

The big outer hatch yawns wide in the great curved side of the hockey puck, really big—way over our heads. Dreamy blue light beyond. Looks like a cheap nightclub, but it's easily large enough to hold us all. I'm as surprised as anybody. DJ pats my shoulder, but this still isn't enough to make our commander happy.

We gather within the hatch. Comm is dead, probably screwed by the clouds of ice dust and sand, but the cold nitrogen is dense enough, and sheltered from precip and wind we can hear each other pretty well.

"Glider is about to unload seed cargo!" Borden shouts. "The seeds will activate outside the main hatch. We'll want to keep well out of their way. Early on, they don't recognize people."

"Don't get between product and material!" DJ calls out in Bueller's Texas accent.

The last swirls of ice dust and vapor make it hard to see even inside. The bluish light cuts through some of the haze, but it's still not bright. We trudge across the hangar with a weird, high-stepping gait, plucking the soles of our steaming boots from dark muck and slick crap. Water has laid down a rugged gray sheet spackled with sticky-looking black gobs. Who gets hangar patrol and cleans up? Maybe nobody's left alive in the station. That would be a kindness—dying rather than being stuck here.

My nose twitches. Something stinks in my skintight. Something acrid. Maybe I'm imagining it. Sweat is kind of acrid, plus the stinks we all make—fear, hormones, pheromones, even hydrogen sulfide and methane. But this smells like *ammonia.* I do not want to smell bitter almonds next. That would be it for all of us.

"Move it!" other voices shout. My nose was right. Our suits aren't holding suck in the cold. The seals are hardening, cracking, corroding. Real incentive to get deeper into the station.

Since nothing welcomes us, Borden walks over to the far wall and the outline of a smaller door. She lines me up and I slap at another checkerboard while the others bunch up like schoolkids after recess, stamping our boots, feeling deep cold seize wrists and ankles—suit heaters can't begin to keep up—and why not? How fucked was the planning? Why did we have only Mars-rated skintights? We're off the grid.

The smaller door opens. Sun-yellow warmth blasts the ice dust to slush and rain and we all crowd into the brightness, dripping and soaking and no doubt stinking of everything rich and strange.

I look back over the jostling, steaming crowd, through the door into the hangar behind us, and see big, dark silhouettes of things rolling in. Offloaded seeds, bronze or black and shiny, making deep rumbles. They're growing fucking hair! Jesus, they're actually sprouting thick slick fibers that writhe like Medusa's snakes. If they follow us inside, we'll become part of their balanced breakfast.

The smaller door slams down.

I hold my breath until I see the seeds are not joining us. For a moment, we stand without words, silent and stinking, until the ceiling sprouts spray heads and we're sluiced three times, three complete spray-downs, so forceful we're shoved against each other like pins in a bowling alley.

When we're clean, the inner station opens another door and allows us to proceed. The next chamber is also yellow. A crudely lettered sign has been slapped onto the door between. It reads, "Don/Doff."

"What the hell does that mean?" DJ asks.

"Put them on, take them off," Tak says.

The first thing we do is shuck our skintights, already frayed and blistering, and on Borden's orders, toss them into a disposal bin along with helms, angels, everything. Out with the old. Almost naked. There are thirty of us in the station. We haven't seen anyone else. Are we alone? Nervous, anxious, pacing, we mill and slap shoulders and ribs to stay warm. Despite everything, I feel a sudden need to get my hands on those big weapons. I want to get to work—*need* to get to work! Because of Bueller's cap I know nice things, encouraging things about centipedes and excavators and nymphs and crushers and stampers, about deep scrawlers and excalators. I know how to work them. I can see them! I can almost reach out and touch them.

Borden pulls us up short. "First up is the latest fashion," she says. Her voice is high, reedy. She's pepped on relief and exhaustion and maybe on the last of the cap training. "Appropriate apparel for the occasion. Without heavy-duty suits, we won't survive if there's even a minor breach, and we won't be able to work outside." She points down. "Or below."

"Found 'em!" Tak shouts. One wall of the chamber is covered by big steel crates labeled "Anti-Corrosion Pressure Skins, Style K(int)." There are ten crates, each claiming to contain twenty suits, but six of the crates are empty. Tak and Ishida and Jacobi open the next two crates. Inside hang thicker, bulkier suits, still wrapped in shiny plastic. Tak tears a hole in one and opens a diagnostic panel on the helm beneath, checks the readout, then moves on to a second and a third and gives a high sign. "These look good," he says.

Jacobi flicks at a scrap of silvery fabric attached to the inside of a crate lid. "What's this?" she asks. It's a brief message scrawled in Japanese and Russian. "What's it say?"

"It says, 'Don't wear them,' " Ishida translates.

Starshina Ulyanova reads the Russian. "Same," she agrees. "Both in one hand—one people writing."

"Yeah," Ishida says. "Probably Japanese."

"What's the ink?" Jacobi asks.

"Could be blood," Tak says. He reaches down and picks at the message with his fingernail. A flake falls away. He looks up at me. We stand back.

"What the fuck's wrong with the suits?" Ishikawa asks. "They look new."

The air inside the station is clean and breathable but frigid. We're turning blue. The old skintights—even if we could recover them—would likely be full of holes by now.

"Check the other crates," Borden says. A thorough search of the crates reveals no other notes and no other choices. "We need these," the commander concludes. "Get them on and let's assemble a search team. We'll carry sidearms, nothing bigger."

We "don" the bulky gray suits. Circlets of heavy plastic and metal wrap arms and legs and thorax. A full suit-up involves letting auto-clasps grab and tighten each band, which takes about ten seconds, keep your fingers out of the way. The helms are bulky, faceplates narrow and thick. But Titan gravity is lighter than on Mars. The suits feel only slightly heavier than our old skintights.

Mushran adjusts his helm with help from Tak. We swing the plates shut briefly to read what the new angels are saying. Not much. A small blinking display reads, "Adjustment under way. Please be patient." Sure. Never a choice.

Taps are in abundance on one side of the chamber. Hundreds of warriors at once could take in gasps and sips and energy before going outside, before riding those big weapons into battle on the Wax. We suckle for a few minutes, looking at each other from the corners of our eyes.

"About seventy hours' worth," Joe tells Borden. He reads the reserve for these essentials—maybe one more dip, then the reserves go empty. Unless we lose a lot of the team. We pluck loose. Time to reconnoiter. The Russians huddle with Litvinov. Jacobi's team surrounds her. They confer for less than a minute. Litvinov and Jacobi step aside to whisper with each other. Then Jacobi approaches Borden and Kumar.

"Where's Mushran?" she asks.

Kumar shrugs. "Gone ahead, perhaps," he says.

"Stupid!" Borden says with considerable heat. She's sick of Kumar and Mushran, I don't doubt.

"I do not disagree," Kumar says. "He has never listened well, nor followed others willingly."

"Fucking honch," Jacobi says.

Borden says, "Before we fan out, time for details. They're not good." In her most cautious and low-key voice, she tells us, "*Lady of Yue*'s arrival survey shows that we're down to just this one station. The others don't answer and *Lady of Yue* couldn't see them from orbit."

"No welcome wagon," Jacobi observes. "Anyone left?"

"The station's only signals are automatic, and those sporadic," Borden says.

"We're going swimming, right?" DJ asks. "Into the fissures—the volcanoes?"

Borden won't let him get ahead of her. "Our orders are to secure the station and check out the product taking shape, or any other equipment we find, reopen the vent if necessary, then, attempt to access the inner sea."

"I'm prime for that!" Ishikawa says, flexing her fingers. Teen eager to take the family car out for a spin.

Borden is unimpressed. "We don't have a large enough team to do it all. I'm making the decision that we take control of whatever product has already been shaped and proceed below. There may still be a deep-sea installation under the crust and no more than a few hundred klicks from here. We don't know what it looks like, what it contains, or what the inhabitants have accomplished. But that's our destination, unless *Lady of Yue* says otherwise."

"No reports?" Ishida asks. "We don't know what's happening down there?"

"None that reached Division Four," Kumar says.

"Secret even from Wait Staff?" Tak asks.

"Secret from me," says Kumar. "I do not know about Mushran."

Mushran has reappeared without being noticed, a singular talent. He is still adjusting his suit, wincing. All of us are uncomfortable. The Russians are stretching, exchanging unhappy glances. Mushran looks up and around, eyes darting at the activity, like he knows something we don't but it's not yet time to share.

"You went away," Jacobi says. "Where to?"

Mushran nods reasonably. "About a hundred meters up

and in, there is a kind of control center, damaged but repaired. There are bodies."

The Russians get up. Litvinov shakes his head; there's really nothing to translate, nothing to explain, that isn't already obvious. Borden tells Joe to look into Mushran's claim. We recover our sidearms and charge up the bolt pistols. The guns seem puny. I'm hungry for product—for our bigger, badder weapons and transporters. We head for the next chamber over, following the path Mushran must have taken, and see that it was converted at some point into a makeshift armory. The armory occupies one of four chambers that radiate inward from the lock antechamber. Only damaged and broken sidearms—bolt rifles and pistols—remain. There are also three piles of spent matter cartridges, all depleted. It's dark and quiet. Station is operating on severely reduced power, just barely enough light to see and getting chillier. Our suits are doing a fine job keeping out the cold, but we've left our plates open until we get used to the narrow view. Plus the damned things are starting to pinch. I flex to get the joints to break in faster. The pinchings move around and sharpen.

"I don't trust Kumar or Mushran, and I still don't know what to make of Borden," Joe says.

"She seems square to me," DJ says.

"She's befuddled," Joe says.

"Aren't we all," Tak says.

Joe scowls. "I'm not convinced she's up to command, double that with Kumar and Mushran hanging over us."

" 'You go to war with the army you have,' " DJ quotes sententiously, " 'not the army you want.' "

"Don't fucking jinx us!" Tak warns. He's serious. DJ knows better.

"Sorry," he says.

"Anyway," Joe continues, "Litvinov seems to have a grip. What about Jacobi?"

I think maybe now I should tell him about the time bomb in my head. How it focuses on him. How that makes him a threat to whoever planted it, and how that makes me wonder what the hell role he played in all of this. But I don't.

"Jacobi's strong," I say. "Moody, but she's got her shit together."

Tak says to Joe, "*You've* been moody since Kazak died."

"Moody?" Joe snorts. "I'm crazier than DJ."

"Good to know," DJ says. "Wouldn't want to excel at anything in this outfit."

"But I'm not going to let the crazy loose until I learn why everything we were told is a lie," Joe says. "And why that became obvious to Kumar and Mushran only a year and a half ago, about the same time Antagonists started dropping comets on Mars—and here, too, apparently."

"Ancient history," DJ says. "But I don't hear much from Coyle, and hardly anything from the others—" At this his face goes ashen. "Got to say, they all scare the shit out of me. They're human, but *not*, know what I mean?"

"I fucking do not know what you mean," Joe says. "Thank God."

We pass a bank of cylindrical elevators and equipment lifts filled with debris, pipes, cables. We find the stairs. The steps are bigger than we're used to, with odd grooves up the middle of each riser.

"Tail draggers," Joe says.

"Antags?" DJ asks.

"You guys tell me," Joe says. "This station has been occupied by both sides at one time or another, so Mushran says. Three combat operations to control and secure. We won the last one, supposedly." He nudges the grooves with his boots. "Antags must have turned glass at some point, right? So you'd channel them, too?"

DJ and I shake our heads. No Antag ghosts. I don't know whether that would be an interesting experience or not, but right now, this damned suit is really doing a number on my joints and stomach and I don't need any further distractions.

We walk up both sides of the staircase, which curves slowly around a long, inner bulkhead, up about twenty meters—a decent climb. My knees are binding now, and it isn't the climb. Feels like tacks are being driven into my elbows and ankles.

A wide, deeply cold hallway leads to a dark circular space. The broad, shadowy floor beyond sinks through several levels to form a kind of arena. Mechanical arms and racks of stacked disks hang motionless from the ceiling.

"Drones?" Tak asks.

"Vent probes," Joe says. "Probably broken, or they wouldn't still be here."

We look as we pass. Not a clue. There's a lot more debris at the center of the arena, and the steps have been slagged—melted and cracked, the cracks sealed with a lighter gray putty. On the far side, big plates of transparent plastic have been shoved over two wide openings, held in place by foam sealant.

"These suits fucking *hurt*," DJ says, shaking out his arms, then kicking one leg so hard he almost loses his balance. Mine is pinching more now, too. The pinches are even sharper, really painful. I'd like nothing better than to "doff" the fucker and see what's going on inside. But we're across the chamber and join Tak to look at what lies beyond those big, jerry-rigged plates. Tak takes point as we kick at the debris, trying to make sense of how much damage and why.

Joe walks up to the plates. "Jesus, come look," he says. We gather in front of a mostly transparent panel overlooking a slow-motion, boiling caldron about a klick wide and filled with rising mist and broken machines. "Our vent," Joe says. "Lots of battle damage. It's dark down there, in the center, but you can still see."

We press close to the plastic. What lies beyond is spectacular and discouraging. The station was constructed around this fissure, this volcanic vent, like a thick wall around a half-frozen lake. Titan's dark brown night sky casts a faint glow over the complex. Methane snow drifts down through the cold, clear nitrogen, hits the slushy liquid, and instantly puffs away...to rise into the brown sky, refreeze, and drop again. The continuous cycle of snow partly obscures a churning, circulating graveyard of diggers, submarine-like transports, big, broad-shouldered mechanical centipedes—hard to know how much buoyant crap is out there, passing in twisted review before our unhappy eyes.

"Looks abandoned," Tak says.

"That it does." Joe looks at me. "Any more clues from Captain Coyle?"

"Nothing," I say.

"Bug?"

I make an effort to raise Bug. I almost get something—a warning? A memory? A brief suspicion of knowledge, quickly extinguished. "Sorry," I say.

"Great." Joe turns and swings out his glove. "Over there.

Mushran was right." There are bodies on the opposite end of the viewing gallery. I count four.

We stand over them.

"Human," DJ says. "Not combat casualties."

"What, then?" Tak asks. He winces as he kneels. "Group suicide?"

The four lie half-in, half-out of pressure suits like ours, spaced apart from each other as if caught up in their own private agonies—naked jumbles of contorted, mummified limbs. Two men, two women. The men hold knives in skeletal hands. The women seem to be trying to extricate their legs from the bottom halves of their suits. Dried blood covers the floor. Almost no smell.

DJ says, " 'Don't wear them,' right? Written in blood?"

Joe whistles between his teeth. "Keep tight," he says. "Don't guess. Know."

"Yeah," DJ says.

"Ow," Tak says, then grabs his stomach. Joe is next. The sharp pain for me is in my right calf, like a dagger shoving through.

"That's it," I say. "The suits are bad."

We try to help each other out of the suits. Tak is difficult. It's like he's glued in. When we remove his neck plate and helm, the neck support pad takes an upper layer of skin, leaving raw, oozing pink. He's in agony but doesn't say a word. We pick the knives off the floor and start hacking and carving at the tough material, each working on the other, pulling aside automatic clasps, lifting and removing rounded plates. Joe raises up his own neck piece. Little bloody wires push inside, still wriggling toward each other—still trying to grow together.

"What the hell!" Joe says in a mildly peeved tone. He grabs a wire and pulls. Beads of blood follow.

The gloves are the hardest. Wires have worked around all my fingers, and one is still plunging through my thumb. I take it at the root, in the wrist of the glove, and pluck it out with a sick moan. Joe is making the same noise as he cuts and then tugs wires from his thigh, his hip, his arms.

Tak is free first and stands breathing hard before the transparent plates. He's managed to skip and roll his way into the middle of the bodies. One of the females congratulates us with a wrinkled grimace, as if still watching through her dark, shrunken eyes.

We stand naked again in the cold, drops of blood falling in quick-freezing spatters. The wounds are painful, intimately horrible, but I don't think any one of us is going to die. Barely in time.

"What now?" DJ asks.

"Tell the others," Joe says to Tak.

"Right." And Tak is off at a run.

"We're staying?" DJ asks.

"We're looking for more suits and someplace to get warm," Joe says. "We can't do anything back there. Why didn't Mushran say something?"

"Because he has a death wish," I say.

"Fucking A," DJ says.

A quick, hopping survey of the arena chamber overlooking the fissure tells us nothing, gives no clues as to where other equipment might be. Our feet turn blue and go numb.

Tak returns with Borden, Litvinov, and Jacobi. Ishikawa trails. All but Tak still wear the suits. Borden looks at us with mixed pity and sympathy. "We're going to need to find you more suits," she says in a small, not-quite-resigned-to-this voice.

"Fuck that!" Joe shouts. His words echo. He points to the bodies, the pools of blood—the red drips from his own flesh. "Mushran saw this, he knows about these fuckers—he must know!"

"I'm sure he did," Borden says. "When he saw Tak, he looked shocked—then angry. He asked him what the hell he had done."

Litvinov adds, "Bastard said, 'It's only little pain.' "

"Shall we ash him?" Tak asks. Tak never threatens lightly.

"Back off that shit! We don't have a choice," Borden emphasizes.

DJ says, "I'm not wearing a fucking iron maiden."

"Screw you, screw all of you!" Joe shouts, his voice hoarse. He lapses into a fit of coughing. We're turning grayish blue. All the blood is retreating to our core.

"We *need* these suits," Borden says. She looks down on the bodies and the blood. "I don't know what happened here. Panic. Poor leadership."

"Goddamned right, poor leadership!" Joe says through his coughing. He sags to a squat, then falls over on one hand. We're getting too weak to resist the inevitable.

Five of Litvinov's soldiers join us. They carry four of the bulky suits, still enclosed in sealed plastic bags. They hold them up beside us, sizing. Their faces look ghostly, resigned.

Tak's look as he takes a deep breath, lowers a big gray pressure suit to the floor, and strips away the plastic is classic Tak. Pure American Bushido. DJ is next. He squats on a bag and inspects his feet. Signs of frostbite.

"No options," Borden says.

"And when it's over," I ask, "will they ever come off?"

"I don't know," Borden says.

"These must be new," I say. "Coyle didn't say a thing."

"She's a fucking ghost!" Borden says with a rare bright spark of anger. Nobody at Division Four or on *Lady of Yue* warned our commander about these difficulties, either. "Why should she care?"

We open the bags. Warrior and armor, all one. And then I remember what Coyle said, long, long ago.

She *did* warn me. I just wasn't paying attention.

FISSURE KINGS

Except for the corpses, the station is deserted, a barely functional shell of what it had been before Titan got its face rearranged in the last prolonged assault. Miracle it survived at all. But no miracle for us. In outline, the hockey puck is not much more than a thick wall around the inner vent. The onetime stadium roof over the vent has collapsed, letting in the elements—mostly methane snow.

Now that we're back in our suits and suffering the unexpected and literal breaking in, Borden and Litvinov escort us back to the armory, where, under the watchful and nervous gaze of our comrades—plus Kumar and Mushran—the outer walls are shifting and bulging, with alarming snaps and groans, to allow us access to developing product.

The walls begin to smoke and shiver.

"Eating station!" Litvinov says, and he may be right. We seal our plates. The air is frosting, the water freezing out.

Three huge, round, bronze-colored heads dissolve and

shove through the station's outer wall like fish rising from a milky pool. The wall puckers and seals around them. Ports pull open in each head, inviting some of us inside—and cap training alerts us who goes into what vehicle, whose ID will match with the product, who's trained for which segment of our mission. Depending on the size and complexity of the weapon or transport, there will be one, two, or three drivers, and room for at most five suited warriors—I can see that, feel that.

The slow-building ecstasy of enthusiasm finally arrives. I get it. These guys are good, great, brilliant—whoever designed caps, product, station! We're being primed to do our bits without complaint. It's even better than the first after-drop rush when we stand up on Mars. Pain is sweet. We welcome each jab and stab, each strung wire through our muscles, around our bones. Prepped and pumped, in pairs or triples, we break from the tight-packed herd into which we've instinctively clumped and, new boots gripping the slippery, icy floor, climb into the ports in the round bronze heads.

The first of the heads, fully crewed, withdraws with puffs of vapor, leaving behind a glassy sheen of freezing liquid and a smoking, dripping hole through which another head suddenly presents. This one's ours. I'm with Joe and Tak. DJ is going with Borden. Borden looks at me with her usual concern—I'm her charge, her ward, right? But we're operating according to the instructions of a higher authority. We're not much more than automatons riding the giant machines. Grunt zombies. Quite different from the drama on Mars. And I'm down with that.

Judging by the size of the round head, Joe and Tak and I are being assigned to a big one. Buddies, all former mates.

Outstanding. But then Starshina Irina Ulyanova, the round-faced ballerina, moves in after Joe and before me, followed by Ishida, then by Jacobi, and *that*'s our full complement. Not a problem. We're nothing if not flexible. I move to the middle and take a moment to study the inside of the head. We're in a big, broad-shouldered bronze centipede—do centipedes have shoulders?—very like the ones whose crushed remains litter the ground outside or slush around in the vent. With the portal closed, we occupy a cabin about five meters wide and ten deep extending back to the thorax. It's dark and warm, like being inside a heated gourd. Web cap training tells me the freshness of the product is responsible for that—heat of manufacture. We'll cool down once we plunge into the vent or dig through the crust—both are possible with this machine. It calls itself an Offensive Scout, Advance Response, or OSCAR. It can swim or dig or just crawl over most surfaces. Pretty universal. Other types are more specialized.

Tan ribbons fall from the curving bulkheads and shake out into vertical hammocks, with pads and clamps arranged to lock on to our suits. Ulyanova is the first to lie back in one of the ribbon hammocks. Lights above her switch on and match color with a small, bright light over her faceplate, green for green. The clamps lock to her midriff. The pads suck down on her pressure suit. She settles back and relaxes, then tries to look back at us, but her suit is stiff—we're all stiff. No rubbernecking.

The rest of us follow her example. Our lights match, too. All good. I'm happy drool and grins. Shit, this is fine, so fine—even as something smooth and cool worms up my penis.

Ishida places her arms and legs into a bay to our right. Her hammock adjusts accordingly and she sits up. I can't see her face, can barely hear her voice in the whir and growl of the centipede, our Oscar, preparing to move out. Tak's and Joe's hammocks slide forward right behind Ishida. I'm carried center and aft. We're now in our assigned stations, even though we're not yet clear what we're about to do.

Within minutes, we feel a lurch aft and a wide transparency slides open forward of the driver. Oscar's face now has a big rectangular eye. Plastic? Metal? I'm betting on a tough, cold-resistant plastic. Wonderful how we use language to mask ignorance. Cap learning carries almost no info on the engineering behind these monsters.

Then, following a cheerful burst of digital notes, we can hear everyone through comm. I content myself by looking forward between Joe and Ishida. Tak is at my two o'clock. We're on the move. Through a wavering shroud of methane snow, Oscar crawls up and over the edge of the hockey puck. It's easy to see how busy our delivered seeds have been. The outer walls of the station on this side are so corroded and marked they've nearly been eaten away. The hangar where the glider delivered us is already gone. A crawling phalanx of three more fresh machines scours the top of the station, trailing from their stumpy, jointed tails those awful, questing, chewing snake-tresses—

Tresses busy slapping, cutting, lifting, and then simply *absorbing* the station. Maybe the product will absorb the corpses as well. Grunts into machines. Total combat efficiency. Wouldn't brass love that?

Way back in my head is a velvety blackness, like a curtain

in a darkened theater, and it's slowly drawing aside. There's nothing onstage yet, but soon . . . ?

I'm distracted as my helm offers a much wider view. Direct retinal imagery. I darken the plate interior and become a disembodied pair of eyes moving ponderously through the slush, advancing on outthrust claw-clamp feet to peer over the inner rim of the station . . . down into the vent. The vent's inner lake swirls like a gigantic, half-frozen toilet bowl of combat shit slowly being flushed. Hey, I'm in a good mood. I'm laughing in my big thick helm, even as painful and intrusive bits of the suit—*my* suit, my friend!—absorb my sweet flesh the way product eats the station. I'm down with that. I'm down with pain, poison, and frozen death. Happy to serve!

We hear Borden's voice, transmitted by sound through the saline solution, echoing and chirping. As usual, she brings good news. "Last transmission from *Lady of Yue*," she says. "Big hurt is in the system—a Box and seven other ships. They'll be in orbit around Titan in ten hours. Box can deliver hundreds more seeds, enough to overwhelm any Antag residues—or us. They aren't transmitting to *Lady of Yue* and they do not appear to be here to help."

"Fifteen to thirty klicks descent through the crust before we swim the deep ocean," Joe says. "Catch up on your reading—this is going to take a while."

"Payload is ready for delivery, right?" Jacobi asks. She means me and maybe DJ. I'd be flattered, but I'm still distracted—severely so. I feel the awful loss of control of my own thoughts, like I'm being funneled down another pipe. Another poison capsule is breaking open in my head, the second trap—the second *instauration* is on its way.

A suave, mellow voice asks, "What's it like, Skyrine? After all these years. Look back upon your long and astonishing list of experiences, and tell us in your own words...."

The velvet curtain opens wide, the stage fills.

I fall onto it.

NO NO NO FUCK NO

I'm standing on a huge platform, small and alone, before a dark, unseen audience of millions, maybe billions. I'm completely naked and flooded in light. I look down on my nakedness and see that my arms and legs are chewed and wrinkled, red and brown and leathery. I'm alive but uglified. The audience sighs with a far-off storm of sympathy. They love my ugliness. Fighting has made me into a fucking Elephant Man. Thank you for your service! War is so...so...evocative! My wrecked body arouses in that unseen crowd deep emotions they can't otherwise imagine having, right? Emotions they don't *want* to have, not in real life, but that's entertainment, isn't it? *Horrorshow*, as the Russians say.

Time to do my bit for the cause.

Somewhere above me the suave Voice lists in boring detail the actions in which I've participated, the war zones I've visited. Some I don't remember or have never heard of—places on Earth and everywhere far and wide. There's been war on Earth? Then we fucking screwed up, didn't we? I don't need this. I just want to return to the action, to wherever it was I just came from, to finish fighting beside my fellow Skyrines and learn whether we're all going to live or die. I don't want to be debriefed or celebrated or encourage folks to buy bonds. That's true fucking old-school.

Business well over a billion years old.

And so—

I dig deep and find Coyle, beg of her, defer to her, she's been listening close—

Enough. No need to be a ghost before you're dead!

She seems more faded than the last time, but she somehow finds the means, the inner roots of this delusion—reveals them to me—and together, we put the poison back in the capsule, shut down this fucking engram, this *instauration* or whatever it is.

Attaboy, Venn. We're so close! I know there's something in here that will help you... A little more time for me to move around, and I'll find it.

UNDER PRESSURE

What?"

The curtain closes. Gone in a flash. I open my eyes. I'm back in my hammock, listening to my fellow crew members as the giant bronze centipede probes the half-frozen water of the vent lake. No wonder I have a hard time distinguishing dream from reality. Time to get down to the real business at hand. I look left and right and see through a thick haze five other transports. Six in all. Arrows and symbols tell me Borden is taking point. She's with Kumar and Mushran—a lot of honch in one vehicle. Maybe she'll dive so deep the whole damned vehicle crushes. Bye-bye, brass. Bye-bye, whirly-eyed Wait Staff. Cap training prissily informs me this is not a good attitude. Maybe not. But Borden's craft is definitely descending first. And what a craft! If ours is like a centipede, hers is a tank-tractor earthworm about ten meters across the beam, its eight segments equipped with rippling treads on *three* sides! And the first five segments are studded with robust grasping arms. The arms and grapplers and other Swiss Army knife extensions will grasp and cut and weld and do all manner of crazy shit. Borden's earthworm can dig faster and swim deeper than any machine in our phalanx, our flotilla, whatever the hell we are. She's not just taking point, she's presenting a serrated edge.

I don't actually *see* this. I remember it. I even know how to drive that talented bastard, should I need to. I receive another burst of pain-free pleasure as reward for accessing cap training. Your grunt *can* learn new tricks.

"Why does everything have to look like insects?" Ishida asks.

"Bugs made us," Tak says.

"I do not believe that," Ishida says. "Never have, never will."

"What, then?"

"Angels," she says primly. "Spirits. *Kami* and *yokai*."

"Yokes? What?" Tak frowns as he peers ahead.

"*Yokai*," Ishida repeats.

"That's like fairies," Jacobi says from up front.

"We are made by fairies?" Ulyanova ventures, first words she's spoken since we sealed and departed in the Oscar.

Ishida sighs. "Not fairies, *yokai*." I see someone has again scrawled *Senketsu* on one shoulder of her suit. Not ink. Blood, I suspect.

Oscar crawls over the floating wreckage, shoving big pieces aside, while we listen to hollow thumps against our outer hull. We're trying to reach an open space in the slush where we can descend without getting hung up. Temp outside is fluctuating wildly. Inside, our suits pinch and adjust some more. I feel something slide up my rectum. Terrific. My guts twist like a tub of worms. But then, almost immediately, the other pains subside. My guts settle. Anesthetic enema? Small mercies.

Oscar propels itself with big cilia, arm-sized rubber strips rippling in sequence, scooping and shoving fluid behind, speeding up or slowing down to steer right or left. Buoyancy tanks in our tail and below the cabin fill with liquid. If Joe and Jacobi want to rise, the tanks boil some of the liquid into steam. Sluices eject the resulting thick salts and gaseous ammonia. When they cool, they suck in liquid again and we sink.... Makes a little singing sound behind us, like a chorus of crickets and birds, along with the deep chuffing of the cilia and the faint squeaking of the joints.

Ishida resumes. "I wonder what the spirits of this place are thinking," she says. "*Yokai* do not enjoy intruders."

"They don't like humans much at all, do they?" Jacobi asks. "Ladies with long black hair and no eyes, right?"

"Not a *yokai*," Ishida says softly.

"Well, let's hope they don't mind us taking a dip right... *here*," Joe says. "Hold your noses."

I suck in my breath as our forward view suddenly goes dark. Tiny sprinkles of the dimmest gray light blur and blink around us. We feel more impacting chunks of wreckage. There's a body. Did I see it or just imagine it? A frozen face in the darkness. Now it's gone. Nobody else saw it, or nobody will admit it. How long can a corpse float in this corrosive stuff?

"Releasing minnows," Jacobi says.

"Tracking," Joe says.

Little silvery lights brighten and flow ahead, five-centimeter drones that swim and corkscrew through the slush. They vanish quickly into the dark, but draw traces on the dive screen and in our plates. The minnows return what they are sensing tens and then hundreds of meters ahead. They're our scouts and pickets.

Polymerized, membranous currents of almost pure water are flowing down here, held together by the powerful electrical fields. In our helms, they show as sinuous auroras rippling and waving deep into the fissure. We just passed through one—electric, icehouse cold.

"Strong current flow," Tak says.

"Don't rub your toes on the carpet," Joe warns. "Whole ocean down here is like a giant battery. Lightning on the surface sparks *up* to the clouds. Cooks the hydrocarbons along the way."

We're all tied together, exercising cap-infused skills necessary to take charge of this beast, guide it, expand its sensory range—

Hours pass. I don't mind. Everything is fine. I can't feel any more poison capsules. Maybe I'm done with them—or maybe they've already done their work on me.

We finish our long dive between the rough, massive walls, then level off at twenty-three klicks and keep station under an immense icy dome. Minnows tell us there's nothing below but slushy ice, more current membranes—and then the deep, deep Titanian sea. No sensation of pressure. Nothing in the ears. The Oscar is intact and our suits are doing their work. We're pretty broad targets in the IR, I think. Cap training does not contradict that opinion.

Some machine, that's our Oscar, our centipede, and some

crew, sinking into almost unknown waters to see what we can see. I laugh in my helmet.

Keep it together, Venn!

I can barely hear or feel the captain. It's like she's slowly turning glass all over again.

OLD AND COLD

All of our sensors are tuned on the world beneath the crust. The deep saline sea that winds its way around Titan, around the equator and extending fingers north and south, with isolated lakes both saline and fresh, as if springs from far below access pure ice down in the mantle. The clarity of the sea around us is remarkable. The current flows seem to attract all the debris from the water and channel it deeper, to spread out across the seabed. Titan's seas are constantly being purged. Based on what I learned in the textbooks at Madigan, that doesn't make any sense. Such a process would have to be guided and controlled—implying at least a living ecosystem, if not a civilization.

But Jacobi's feed to our helms is undeniable. We're swimming through crystal-clear waters, way below freezing, with occasional cloudy globs of ammoniated, debris-laden slush being drawn toward the current flows—disintegrating and descending in long charged plumes as they glide past like UV rainbows.

We pass under a low-hanging arch of crustal material. The Oscar switches on its brights and scans the surface of the arch. Another icy dome, shot through with veins of black gunk. Where it's most purely ice, it sparkles with a million reflections, a galaxy of glints. Farther along, we encounter a breccia of ice and clumped boulders held in place by a thick mortar of brown, gray, and black tar. Our lights warm the mix and rocks fall away.

"This could get hairy," Joe says.

The falls reveal fresh underlying material—and frighten big worms or insects—fifty or sixty meters long! They escape from the sudden brilliance, burrowing deeper into the matrix.

"Jesus!" Jacobi says. "Sure those aren't Antag weapons?"

"Pretty sure," Joe says. "Alive?" he asks me.

"Yeah," I say.

"Your bugs?"

"Much younger."

"They're not talking to you?"

"No."

"Maybe our cousins?" He gives me a sour grin.

A few of the worms are large enough to kick out more boulders. We dodge two such rockfalls, then get a glimpse of huge mandibles on a wide, plated head—mandibles that pinch in from five sides, a pentagon of grasping, cutting jaws. These creatures are at least ten meters long, their serpentine bodies covered with bristles.

Borden communicates from the lead vehicle. "Serious question, Johnson, Venn—are these things intelligent? The ancestors of your bugs?" she asks.

"I've never seen anything like them," DJ says. "But that isn't exactly an answer."

As we glide along a cleft exposed in the archway, we see more of the bristling worms. They dance in our lights as if in some sort of ecstatic ritual, then gather along their lengths and link clasping bristles to form triads. Each bristle tip has a minuscule claw—small by comparison to the bulk, but maybe as big as a human hand. The bristles cling together like Velcro, then let go, and the triads break free to burrow up into the breccia. As quickly as they appeared, all the bristling worms are gone.

"Easy come, easy go," Jacobi says.

"Like in sand or aquariums," Ishida says. "Acorn worms. Priapulids."

"I'll bet you've eaten them with rice," Joe says. "Maybe they're out for revenge."

"No, sir!" Ishida sounds alarmed.

The crystal waters and the ice above again look empty and pristine. A wavy purple flow comes close to our Oscar on the left wing of the formation, so we move off—the entire squadron banking and retreating like birds in a flock. The cilia hum along our hull—hum with intermittent slapping sounds. Maybe they're not in complete sync. Maybe they're getting old. How long does a machine last down here? Longer than our Mars skintights, I hope.

The bottom of the ocean rises beneath us, low gray hills studded with boulders as big as Half Dome.

"Everybody stoked?" Joe asks. "All cheery-bye?"

"Tol'ably so," Tak says.

"Don't be," Joe says. "Don't let the tech use you. Stay sharp and independent. Remember—everybody else who came down here is dead."

"We don't know that," Jacobi says.

Ulyanova makes a little sigh.

We all saw the wreckage around the station. And the condition of the station itself. Did everybody just give up? Antags and humans at the same time? Before the Antags could find or confirm, or destroy, what Captain Coyle believes is at the heart of…

Watch yourself, Venn.

This time, I can almost see Coyle. She's standing in a long hallway between rows of black columns. She's found a relevant cache of records and is trying to communicate what she's found to me. *We're here. This place is incredibly deep and strong. I've been checking out newer history. And you're in. The library accepts you as a legitimate user.*

"What history?" I ask softly.

Coyle says, *Our shelly friends broke through their crust, then retreated, but centuries later, they did more than that. Much more. They sent spaceships. Some of the ships reached Titan and other moons. Others went much farther—all the way to the Kuiper belt, even the Oort cloud. Huge places out there. Sun-planets!*

"How long ago?"

Got to slow down. Got to rest. I'm not going to be a guide much longer. I'm becoming part of the archive. I just looked at myself—shit! All of me. My DNA, my memory, scars and breaks—everything. It's all being preserved, fixed. No words to describe how that feels.

Then—fuzzy quiet.

"DJ!" I say.

"Yeah. They're fading," he murmurs. "Something else is coming."

"We're going to meet our makers?" Ishida asks.

"Are they still alive down here?" Jacobi asks. "Is that why we're here?"

"Electrical strong to port," Joe warns. "Ocean's opaque ahead."

In our helms, we see our cloud of minnows zipping forward from our phalanx, spreading, darting little waves of lights, and a purplish glow off to our left, signifying the superflow of salty ions that could melt our Oscar if we intersect the boundary. Like touching a giant power cable. What keeps the current from smearing out through the water? Salt gradients. There's a fresh thermocline separating that flow and our own like an insulating blanket. Oh, we're bathed in ions—but nothing the Oscar can't handle. Whereas over there, in the purple, deadly potential is being shunted from the depths to the crust, and carrying curtains of debris along with it.

"Could melt through and make another vent," Ulyanova says. Smart sister. Smart Russian sister. With a round face and a ballerina body, not that I can see any of that through the suit.

"Uh-huh," Jacobi says. "Just keep us out of the purple."

The Oscar hums and vibrates. I'm still trying to orient and remember what I read in the textbooks back at Madigan—trying to encourage the web cap training to fill in details—but things have changed a lot down here since our caps were programmed. There are wide gaps in our education.

Then, instead of Coyle all casual in a Karnak of black columns, I see pale brilliance. Quiet, bright silvery spaces. I close my eyes. The silvery void is infinitely dense, filled with infinitely thin lines and figures—like pressing knuckles into your eyes in a dark room. Geometric eyelid movies—only *bright*. I have my eyes closed and it's *still* bright. Will I ever be able to sleep again?

The silver wants something. It expects something—a response. But what's the question? It's flowing through my mind. It's practiced on the record of Coyle, I presume, but it still stomps around like a bull. Christ, I feel like a man about to be drawn and quartered, my hands and feet tied to snorting horses, and there's an idiot-faced fuckhead with a hammer, about to stroke down on—

Inquire.

Not a voice. Not even a word, but immediate, coming from all around and shivering my head like a gong. I jerk up so hard in my suit that everything hurts, joints, feet, hands, neck—all the wires tugging as my muscles tense. If I don't stop jerking I'll be sliced into bloody pieces!

Again:

Inquire.

"Yeah! Yes. Right here. Don't go away." I keep my voice low, but that doesn't stop the others from hearing. They're busy. I have no idea what they're thinking, what Joe or Jacobi is concluding about my little whispers in their helms. I know they can't hear what I'm hearing. Maybe DJ can. Maybe he's hearing the same thing.

"I'm listening. What are you? Who are you?"

Again the holographic presence, not words, not sound:

You have an ancient port of entry.

I don't know what to say. In confusion, I open my eyes to the helm display of the saline sea, our flashing minnows, outlines of the other machines powering ahead, leveling off.

"Deep station in about thirty klicks," Joe says. His voice sounds loud, overwhelming, but not any more real than the presence. "Something's still there," he adds. "It's not putting out a beacon, and it doesn't answer."

We're leveling off at three hundred meters beneath the crust. All of our sensors combine to show we're cruising above deep canyons between long, razorback ridges.... Curving mountains running parallel, separated by a klick or less and meeting at right angles with other ridges, like the pocketing squares on a roulette wheel. There are no bottoms to those squares. Nothing the minnows or sensors can measure. The geology here is a total mystery. Is it artificial? If so, made by who or what? Made *when*?

After all I've been through, it's still a shock to realize that what we're seeing echoes with other parts of my understanding, what I've learned from Bug and Coyle—confirms that our connection is real. I'm not imagining anything. Coyle, my inner Bug, the silvery void...

If I accept that I'm not crazy, and this is why I was rescued from Madigan—why I was picked up and kept there in the first place—knowing that makes it a little easier. I swallow hard. My throat is filled with needles. DJ and I are here to make a tight, strong connection with something old and important.

The silver space fragments. Everything shivers, reassembles. Something else is here with me. Something new but familiar to my inner Bug.

Ripples form in the brightness.

Inquire.

"Yeah," I say.

"What's up, Vinnie?" Joe asks.

"Keep it down, sir," DJ says. "He's working."

"Got it."

Do you have a guide?

"Maybe," I say. "I can understand you, whatever you are."

With a guide, you can learn how to access the archive, if you are a qualified user.

"I had a guide," I say. "She turned glass on Mars. She's been warning—she's been telling me about you…I think."

Eyes open. I'm twitching all over. The Oscar slides around a massive mineral growth, glowing faintly in the ocean darkness—all the other weapons report in, chiming and chitting at each other, maintaining formation but veering starboard to get around that thing that connects the ocean floor to the crust above.

Joe fans out the sensors. We can all see the result in our helm displays. I have to poke with my eyes through the silver, but I'm learning how to do that.

We're in the middle of a mineral jungle—a deep forest of crystal pillars, each dozens of kilometers high.

"The mother lode!" DJ says.

We slowly move into the jungle. DJ begins to whistle. The tune sounds familiar, but I've never heard it before. Still, it brings on an oddly familiar mental state of congruence and connection. The brightness is becoming tangible. I can feel it wrapping my skin, flooding my mind. It's bright and silvery, and while I can feel it, so far it conveys no information, no meaning other than its own strength and reality.

Again my thoughts are overlaid by vibrating, wavering lines, infinite geometry—and again, I feel and hear Coyle. Her voice is distinct. It ripples the silvery space. The connection between this silvery space and distant archives—on Mars and elsewhere—becomes manifest.

I'm still here, Venn. I've got a short reprieve, I think.

I'm still your guide, for the time being. Go ahead. Can you understand?

"Jesus! Captain. Yes."

We don't have much time. It's ready. Ask it something.

"But what the hell is it? *What*'s ready?"

Inquire.

"I don't know what to ask!"

Ask it about poppa momma shit and where we come from and where we go, and why the Gurus and Antags don't want us down here. Ask it about moons. You won't like what it has to say. I'm dead, but I've had a chance before I settle in to poke around—and I don't like it one fucking bit. But you got to ask.

Ask now.

Coyle is thinning rapidly, thinning and fading.

"What's happening to Captain Coyle?" I ask.

Your guide is becoming memory, which is atonement. We recognize your guide's music, and we recognize your music. Because you have the proper music, you can be a user.

Inquire.

"Why don't the Gurus want us down here? Or in the Drifter, in the mines?"

Choose one question.

Make it a good one, Venn! This place is freakish particular.

"Why is everybody trying to keep us away from *you*, whatever you are?"

You have been lied to.

Inquire.

"By who?"

Across billions of years, we who acquired this memory have encountered forces of decadence and corruption. These forces succeed by persuasion and temptation. They must maintain your ignorance or they will fail. We can relieve your ignorance. Because of that, we are a threat to them.

Inquire.

"You okay, Venn?" Jacobi asks.

I'm not. Inquire! Shit. I don't like where this is going, because it's confirming what I already sense, maybe even *know*, and that's not good. I don't want to learn any more. Besides, Coyle has thinned to a wisp.

The vibrating silver turns insistent, brilliant red. No wasting time down here. Painful!

Something pounds on the outside of the Oscar. The giant bronze centipede rocks and shivers. Joe and Ulyanova and Jacobi are fighting to keep the machine under control.

Flowing out over the deep-ocean mountains, around the column of salts and minerals, our minnows report a steady stream of icy daggers, each six or seven meters long, like huge icicles, driven by frilly, ionized currents: a blizzard of electrified torpedoes sweeping in at dozens of knots.

"Incoming!" Jacobi says. "Hold fast!"

The minnows scatter to get a wider perspective. We still can't actually see—it's dark and the ocean here is almost opaque—but the minnows are working the whole spectrum, plus sound, which is incredibly precise in the cold. We can hear what's happening for thousands of klicks, even the echoes off the ridges and roulette pockets—

"Twelve big machines at three klicks, rising from behind a low ridge," Tak says. "They're about where the station is supposed to be. They look aggressive, and they're *huge*."

"They're not ours!" Jacobi says. Her voice is small and deadly calm.

The new machines, sensing us, suddenly fan out and descend to hide in the corner of two intersecting ridges. We can't see them. We can't see anything.

"We're exposed," Tak says.

"I know that," Joe says tightly. I understand him well enough to know he's either following orders from Borden and Kumar, or he has something on his mind. Maybe both. Asking him right now will only distract him. He'll tell me when he's ready.

Or when *I'm* ready.

"Ice torpedoes holding," Ishida says.

"Slowing," Joe says.

"Why don't they just take us out?" Ishida asks.

The ice torpedoes keep station in a cloud around us, barring our progress—but not coming any closer. My head throbs with the red field. I don't know what it is or why it's happening now. Maybe I'm having a stroke. Maybe all the shit in my head has finally blown me up inside.

Slowly, though, it's starting to convey information. Lots of it. Confused, historic, and strategic...if I could understand Bug strategy!

"Slow down," I say through gritted teeth.

"Nobody's moving," Joe says.

"Venn—what do we do now?" Jacobi asks.

I wish I knew.

Ishida has been assigned to our weapons. I click down the list in my head, feeling a sudden dread that we might actually use them—and that isn't what the red space is telling me is appropriate or necessary. We have place-keeping mines, remoras that attach and deliver spent matter charges, torpedoes bigger than minnows but working the same principles. And that's pitiful. Whatever's out there is equipped with weapons way beyond the ones in our arsenal. They've harnessed Titan's electric flows. They've been here longer, they're survivors, and they're way more powerful.

But they're not moving in for a kill.

"What are they?" Ulyanova asks.

Joe strains to look back at me. "You're our ace in the hole, Vinnie. You and DJ."

The red space turns silvery again, and in that infinitely dense collection of waiting information, another figure appears. Not human.

"Coyle," I say. "Goddammit, Coyle, what is this? Where are you?"

Handing off, Venn. I'm settling in to fixed memory. That means I'm finally going to die... except when people remember. You'll remember me, won't you? You'll pray for me?

I remember DJ's attending Coyle as she turned glass, and my throat tightens. "Always," I say.

It'll be hard to work with your new partner, but she's still alive. She's a user. And she's smarter than me, with more experience.

"She—? Descendant of the Bugs?" I ask.

Same as you. Good-bye, Venn. Take care of our troops. And best of luck.

I reach out and feel around with whatever senses once connected us, but I can no longer detect the essential part of Coyle. The hard-core, almost cynical devotion to duty, the bitter sense of humor and doubts about my innate abilities... the devotion to life, despite a career of dealing death. Captain Coyle is gone.

No. She's here. She's just not *active.* I *can* see her. *All* of her, spread out like a silvery blueprint before me, naked and complete—everything that turned glass back on Mars, stored, transmitted, has been fixed in the archive, faithfully and truthfully preserved. Feeling no passion, no pain, but eternal—timeless and totally revealed.

"Jesus Christ, Captain," I say. "You're fucking *beautiful*...."

But of no use to me now.

"Who's talking to you, Venn?" Jacobi asks.

"Coyle's fixed," DJ says.

A new outline sparkles in my mind. The archive has other plans. It wants me to move on. I have the awful feeling that Coyle tried to save the most difficult for last. *She?* I'm not yet seeing anything solid or embodied, more like the shape of a mind, and very likely that's what this new presence sees when it looks my way. How the hell do we communicate, if that's even an option?

Then—

It's a reality.

The new voice is startlingly sweet, like birdsong in a forest. It rises and drops, and then finds a kind of level range, and I know it for the first time—like Coyle, female, but very different. I'm about to confront the new user, but between us rises again that master steward of the ancient memory stores, the thing whose existence has scared the living fuck out of the Gurus and the Wait Staff.

Inquire.

"What do we say to each other?" I ask. "How do we do this?"

"What are they, Vinnie?" Joe asks. He sounds remarkably scared. "Bug descendants? Natives of Titan?"

"I don't know," I say. "Captain Coyle isn't in the picture anymore."

You have the music. You are suitable as users.

I think this through quickly. I feel like an idiot. I feel as if my lips are moving as I try to read a book.

"You're mumbling again," Jacobi says, irritated.

I open my eyes. Ishida is watching me. The silvery void wraps across her concerned face.

"Steady keeping. Ice torpedoes still wait to crush us." This is Ulyanova.

My focus shifts. I stare into the infinite silver at the resplendent, uncertain outline of the other user, the mind that is also here, and by golly, there is a certain *something*, an awareness that we are related, maybe more distantly than a snail or a cockroach, but still...

Inquire.

Like playing a TV game show. I sat next to my grandmother on that old-dog-stinky, Afghan-covered couch in Fresno while she watched her favorite game shows, and she knew the rules, the routines. I need to be as smart as my grandma.

I try to stay away from the new user and focus the silver on the master steward. Don't want to say something stupid or be rude.

"Are we both descended from those who made you?" I ask.

Yes.

Inquire.

"Another mind?" I ask. "Something else affected by the tea? DJ!" I say.

"With you, bro," he says. His voice has changed. "This is a joint and a half, ain't it?"

"Can you see the other one? The other user?"

"Yeah."

"What do you think?"

"I think I should resign my commission."

DJ is a noncom.

"Tell me!"

"Well, this much is obvious," DJ says. "It's not Coyle, it's not a bug… and it's not human."

"You guys are driving me nuts!" Joe shouts. "Give me some actionable!"

After all Joe has done to and for me, I feel a weird moment of justification.

"Those folks out there, they don't want to kill us," DJ says with a deep sigh. "Not anymore. We need each other."

"What the fuck does that mean?" Jacobi asks sharply. She looks stretched and exhausted. We're twelve klicks beneath the icy crust of Titan, within sensor range of a grove of massive, crystalline pillars that rise from the cross-ridged floor of the saline sea to the frozen roof. The ice torpedoes are poised between us and a flotilla of huge weapons—overwhelming force.

I break through the silver and look steadily at Jacobi. "Captain Coyle has handed me over to something else," I say to her. "Someone new."

She gives me a conspiratorial squint. "What sort of someone?"

"Still trying to find out," I say.

Inquire.

“What do we do now?” I ask the steward.

Use the sense your music gives you. Speak to your partner.

“We need to surrender,” DJ says softly.

“Is DJ nuts?” Joe calls back. “Vinnie—is he nuts?”

“I don’t know!” I say. “Maybe they want to take us someplace safe. Someplace where we can meet and talk.”

I still can’t see the other clearly. Maybe she doesn’t want to be seen clearly. Maybe there’s not that much trust despite our common music and the master steward.

Inquire.

“Where do they want to take us?” I ask. I feel the archive lightly brush parts of my mind.

Use the sense the music gives you.

Great. I’m sitting on top of the most massive data store in the local universe, and it’s a stickler; *I’m* the user. I make the decisions. I could spend the next million years working through inquiries about limitations and rules, but all I got in my head is an image of that Antag helm on Mars, cupping a broken bird-head with four eyes and a raspy tongue.

And based on what I’m learning, remembering *that*, remembering all the dead and the dying and all the blood on my hands, all the friends and fellow soldiers now gone and all the blood on *their* hands, and all the bird-heads we’ve broken back there on Mars and Titan and everywhere else…

Nearly all *female*…

And then I get it. I understand. I know who’s out there, who’s driving those weapons. We’re both descended from the bugs.

And we’ve both been deceived.

That’s *huge.*

I simply want to break down and cry.

I rise above my confusion and try to figure out my strategy. What do I believe? What's the truth, and how liable are we to counterintelligence, cointelpro, whatever the fuck you call it? I'm not a very good juggler. Maybe this is one ball that's primed to explode.

Inquire.

"What went wrong? How did this happen? Who are the Gurus and what do they want to do to us, for us?"

The others hear me. They're stunned into murmurs and prayers. Jacobi is trying to stifle sobs. Skyrines have sharp and sometimes predictive senses. Some of us already know the shock that's coming. I feel sure that Joe knows. Has known for some time. Like Kumar and Mushran and even Borden. Division Four. Traitors all.

One inquiry at a time.

"Yeah—why are the Gurus doing this and telling us these things?" This seems to be simple enough, related enough to deserve an answer.

For billions of years, they and their kind have sold war to the outer stars.

I'm not sure I understand what that means. "Our war, you mean? Sold it how? How do you know this?"

One inquiry at a time.

"How do you know this?"

Long ago, they convinced us to fight with our brothers.

It lets me experience more directly what it's saying—I see data feeds and communications radiating from our solar system. We're being televised. We're being recorded and spread around the galaxy....

"It's a business for them? We're entertainment?"

They transmit your fighting and dying, your wars and pain, out to far worlds. It fits an old pattern that to these forces, advanced into decadence and boredom, your people and troubles, your murder and pain, are amusing.

Inquire.

"Bugs fought for them?"

Many did. Those wars destroyed four moons. The final archive that preserves that history is this one.

Inquire.

Damn right. There's a big question here. "Where did the moon come from that hit Mars and sprayed Earth?"

At the last, in desperation, one moon from this system was flung inward toward the sun, toward the young inner worlds. It failed to arrive as planned, and struck the fourth planet.

And helped start life on Earth—all by mistake.

Inquire.

"You thought you were losing?"

Yes. We were losing.

Inquire.

"Did you lose?"

That was long, long ago, and the builders of the archive have long since passed on.

A painful subject, I sense, even to an objective archive. "They're dead?"

Passed on.

I can still conjure up a clear picture of Bug. Ugly and covered in baroque carapaces, a united pair of creatures—brains and brawn. This image, the statistical portrait of an entire culture, has until now served as a representation of what the green dust awoke in the Drifter. Somehow I've drawn reassurance from its example—however strange and distant. But

I never thought of Bug as a warrior. An explorer, a thinker, a strangely friendly presence—but never as a hero, and certainly not a tragic hero.

"What's happening in there, Vinnie?" Joe calls out.

The steward of the archive is withdrawing, no longer serving as an interface, an interpreter. It wants me to move on.

I hear the birdsong again. It's starting to make sense. I get impressions on a broad spectrum. Background details, snippets of directed voice—psychological coloring. The new presence might be on one of those massive ships or weapons out there. Wherever she is, she's a user. She's alive. And that means she can ask *me* questions and make accusations.

I don't want to understand. I want to shut down. I'd almost rather die than complete this fucking quest. But I'm not going to die, not right away. Not in time to avoid the truth.

I begin to understand almost all of the pretty song that is the other voice:

> We [are told] we share inheritance. Difficult to accept. We [see] you. You arrive ready to fight. We [see] your vehicles and have [stopped them from becoming threats]. [Who are you], why have you come here?

I sense the urgency. We're surrounded. They're extremely wary, but desperate—like us—and achingly curious. There has been so much pain and loss. They don't know our origins or our intentions, but they still have hope. I sense that they have fought against their own kind. They've suffered great hardship to reach and survive on Titan and tap into the archive. They, too, were touched by the ancient memory of

Bug. Likely they, too, had comrades who turned glass. I wonder if Coyle met any of their dead, and if so, why she didn't tell me.

Because I am still alive. Because honor and duty still matter to me. To us. And that's messing with me big-time. But I also have a duty to this mission, to the people who thought I should be here, that DJ should be here. That we could learn and help them understand the mysteries and deceptions.

Expose the big lie.

So I bear down and focus on the other user. I don't use words—so little time. Instead, I show this new presence the Drifter, the crystal pillar, the green dust smeared on our skins. I show DJ in an ecstatic mood, rejoicing at the ancient connection.

I try to convey the experience of Captain Coyle.

And I show the new presence Bug.

Back in turn arrive visions of a precisely parallel experience. The colors and outlines are difficult—I have to focus on one of four separate views that otherwise cross and confuse. The four images come from four eyes. Some of their kind were once smeared with green dust. Their genetic music is the same as ours—the dust worked on them as well.

We are also alike in being aggressors. We're like cocks set against each other in a ring. If we are victims, we are willing enough—ideally suited for entertaining distant worlds.

I cannot escape the truth of who it is I am talking to, *what* it is that confronts us across the deep saline sea, through the ionized membranes, from within those larger and more powerful weapons. Nobody on our Oscar is going to like these new truths. My own reaction is gut-level, instinctive. I feel revulsion. But if I shoot back my disgust, my grief and resentment at our own losses, my wish to defeat and even exterminate all of them—the total effect of my Skyrine training and esprit de corps—

The other user could just give up on us—let loose the ice and crush us.

Somehow, I filter and control my negative instincts. I feel that the other is doing likewise. She does not in any way enjoy addressing me, and her doubts are if anything stronger than mine. She and her warriors have come far, for many different reasons, to fight on Mars and on Titan. Nearly all of their warriors are female. Males form the upper ranks and rarely engage in combat.

But their doubts have changed many of them. The information from the archive, and the evidence of their returned dead, have driven them as well to betrayal and treason. Like us, they have skeptics who wish to resume the war. They need another and very different perspective. They need objective confirmation.

We hear Borden's voice explaining that Box has arrived and dispersed its seeds. The seeds are gobbling up whatever was left of the station, making new weapons—dozens of them.

"Reinforcements are here!" Jacobi says with relief.

"They're not here to help us," Joe says. "They're here to hunt us down and kill us all. And then they'll do their best to kill Titan. Believe it!"

Who's more powerful and more dangerous?

The enemy in front, the humans above?

DJ moans. His voice rises to nightmare screams. Then he goes quiet. The suit has done something to flatten his distress. He's out of the game.

But as long as I can keep my connection open and keep

exchanging information, I'll be useful. As long as their skeptics don't get the upper hand—a distinct possibility—

We'll live.

"They're holding fire," I say. "If the forces from Box get to us—"

"The hell with that!" Jacobi shouts. "This is cat-and-mouse. We got to break loose and head back to the station."

"I don't think so," I say. "They want to keep us alive. They need us."

"*Who* wants that?" Ishida asks, her voice dark and dangerous. "Who needs us? Who the *hell* are you talking to?"

"Antags," I say.

The reaction in the Oscar's cabin is electric. What should have been obvious all along has been cloaked in many layers of denial. Now doesn't seem the best time to give them the really acid news—about our being fighting cocks. Dupes. Naïve victims of an ancient con.

"You knew that!" Joe calls out to them. "It's what we expected—it's the reason for Division Four and everything else we've done. Why else would we come here?" He sounds angry. How long has he known? Even before Mars? Maybe he's one of the Wait Staff. Who the hell is Joe Sanchez? He's been in so many places at so many convenient times... throughout my life.

"Because we wanted to access the old knowledge!" Tak says. He's said very little throughout our journey in the Oscar. "To wipe out the enemy. Power, that's what we wanted."

Joe says, "Vinnie and DJ are our scouts. I go with what they recommend."

"DJ's out of it," Tak reminds him.

"Maybe, but Vinnie is reporting back. We either trust

him, or return to the surface and defend ourselves against the weapons dropped by Box. You still think they're here to rescue us?"

The others are silent on that.

"They're here to find us and kill us. I guarantee they won't show any mercy. If we start a fight down here, we also die. If we listen to Vinnie—maybe we live."

It's hard acquiring so much tolerance all at once. I'm not at all sure I wouldn't prefer to fight Antags again and die. Still, I keep sending—keep visualizing and trying to interpret the return feed. The other user's feed is turning nasty. I keep seeing battle in space and on Titan, on Mars—I keep seeing dead Antags, friends and lovers, commanders and soldiers.

And dead humans. Lots of dead humans.

She's testing me.

"We don't have time," I say. "They expect a solid answer."

"What do they want?" Jacobi asks, voice hoarse.

I ask, and receive a kind of picture: humans and Antags standing in a cabin. No armor. No weapons. Separated by mere meters. Can we just talk to each other?

Can we even breathe the same air?

"They want a face-to-face. On their terms, on their ships."

"How you going to arrange that?" Ishida asks. "They going to crack us open and scoop us out like lobsters?"

"New machines descending," Borden says across the cold fluid. "We need actionable. What's Venn doing?"

"He's *communicating*," Joe says sharply. "He's doing what you brought him here to do! We got problems down here."

"I say go back and surrender to our own kind," Jacobi says. "At least they're human."

Borden says, voice far away, "I'm in command."

"Fuck that!" Ishida says. "Turn around and go back."

I hear Kumar's voice from Borden's vessel: "That would be suicide. They are killing all who deny the Gurus."

What we're engaged in is a *fratricidal war.* And the Gurus put us up to it. How in hell can I convey this to Tak and Jacobi, to Ishikawa and Ishida? To Ulyanova? Ishida lost half her body to the war! Most who already suspect these bitter truths—Borden, Kumar, possibly Mushran—are on another ship, along with Litvinov.

The Antag vessels are still holding. We have maybe thirty minutes before Box's reinforcements arrive and all hell comes down on both of us.

Joe says, "It's on you, Vinnie. This is why you were born."

That does it. I want to shrink up inside my suit, dry up into a little nut. But the other user is still touching parts of my head. Still trying to find common ground. And providing scenarios, little road maps of how we can proceed. If we don't attack.

"They can take our machines inside theirs," I say. "They can get us back to the surface, away from Titan."

"You mean give up without a fight?" Jacobi asks, outraged.

"Take us where?" Ishida asks. "To their *planet*? Never go home again?" Those seem like optimistic appraisals, actually. Kumar, Mushran—Borden. They're all agreed. Makes me sick to think of who agrees with me.

"Guarantees?" Joe asks, though he knows better.

"None at all," I say. "But it's why I was born, like you said—right?"

"Yeah," Joe says, and communicates with Borden. The

shouting in our cabin is fierce. "Do it, Vinnie. Let it go!" Joe says. I tell the other, my Antagonist counterpart, to open up their ships and take us inside.

All of us.

We surrender.

Then our ballerina speaks up. She's having difficulty interpreting the rapid back-and-forth. "I get this straight," Ulyanova says. "They are enemy? I say, *kill* them. I say die trying!"

The next part is going to be very, very hard.